Afro-Latin@ Diasporas

Series Editors
Natasha Gordon-Chipembere
Heredia, Costa Rica

Miriam Jiménez Román
afrolatin@ forum
New York, USA

Edward Paulino
Department of History
John Jay College of Criminal Justice
New York, USA

The *Afro-Latin@ Diasporas* book series publishes scholarly and creative writing on the African diasporic experience in Latin America, the Caribbean, and the United States. The series includes books which address all aspects of Afro-Latin@ life and cultural expression throughout the hemisphere, with a strong focus on Afro-Latin@s in the United States. This series is the first-of-its-kind to combine such a broad range of topics, including religion, race, transnational identity, history, literature, music and the arts, social and cultural theory, biography, class and economic relations, gender, sexuality, sociology, politics, and migration.

More information about this series at
http://www.palgrave.com/gp/series/14759

Dorothy E. Mosby

Quince Duncan's Weathered Men and The Four Mirrors

Two Novels of Afro-Costa Rican Identity

palgrave
macmillan

Dorothy E. Mosby
Department of Spanish, Latina/o and Latin
  American Studies
Mount Holyoke College
South Hadley, MA, USA

Translated by Dorothy E. Mosby

Afro-Latin@ Diasporas
ISBN 978-3-319-97534-4   ISBN 978-3-319-97535-1   (eBook)
https://doi.org/10.1007/978-3-319-97535-1

Library of Congress Control Number: 2018951044

Translation from the Spanish language edition: *Hombres curtidos* by Quince Duncan, © Cuadernos de Arte Popular 1971, and *Los cuatro espejos* by Quince Duncan, © Editorial Costa Rica 1973. All Rights Reserved.

Series logo inspired by "Le Marron Inconnu" by Haitian sculptor Albert Mangones

Cover credit: Stuart Pearce/Alamy Stock Photo

This Palgrave Macmillan imprint is published by the registered company Springer Nature Switzerland AG
The registered company address is: Gewerbestrasse 11, 6330 Cham, Switzerland

A mis ancestras—
a las que siempre llevo en la punta de la lengua
y las ancestras cuyos nombres se desconocen,
pero vibran en mi sangre.

Acknowledgements

First and foremost, I would like to express my sincere gratitude to Dr. Quince Duncan for his patience and generosity. I am grateful for his permission to translate his work and the enormous trust and confidence placed in me. This translation emerged from a humble request at the end of 2011, and it is a joy to bring his work to a wider audience of readers.

I am indebted to Natasha Gordon-Chipembere, whose encouragement and belief in this translation helped make this dream a beautiful reality. I am grateful for her determination to make sure that don Quince's work reaches an English-speaking public.

A generous sabbatical leave from Mount Holyoke College during the Spring 2016 semester enabled me to complete first drafts of both novels. I also thank my colleague Roberto Márquez for reading an early and very rough draft of *Hombres curtidos*, and for his sage advice to a novice translator. Additionally, I want to acknowledge the work of Dr. Dellita Martin-Ogunsola who paved the way for me. As don Quince's first translator, she did a masterful job translating his short fiction into English and I am thankful.

As always, deep appreciation for my US and Costa Rican family, whose support has offered me more than I could ever express with words, especially my parents, Helen and James Mosby, Sheridan Wigginton, Franklin Perry, Dlia. McDonald, Gustavo Córdoba González, and Karla Araya Araya. Thank you to my faithful writing accountability buddies, Patricia and Madeline, whose words of reassurance and inspirational example kept me motivated through the vicissitudes of department chairing, teaching, advising, promotion, mid-career malaise, administrative work, and simply being human.

Finally, I would like to share my heartfelt gratitude for my spouse, Carol Knight-Mosby. Carol has been my Jamaican Creole native informant for almost twenty years and made sure the bills got paid during prolonged sojourns in Central America. In the words of Miss Lou, "Me darling love, me lickle dove,/Me dumpling, me gizada,/Me sweetie Sue, I goes fa you/Like how flies goes fa sugar."

Contents

Introduction

Reading Quince Duncan's first two published novels, *Weathered Men* and *The Four Mirrors*, almost fifty years after they were first published in Spanish, readers may be struck by the timeliness and currency of the issues raised by the Afro-Costa Rican author and intellectual. The context of Costa Rica in the late 1960s and early 1970s is one that still holds resonance and relevancy in the twenty-first century for not only Costa Rica as a nation, but for other parts of the Western Hemisphere and beyond. Two of the greatest challenges raised in Duncan's novels are the forces of migration and coming to terms with exclusionary notions of national identity. Readers in the United States will be familiar with debates over the intense political divide over immigration from Latin America, the Middle East and North Africa, and South Asia, as well as the fate of undocumented immigrants including the almost 800,000 young people called "Dreamers."[1] These debates have heightened the anxieties of a segment of the dominant white, Protestant population

---

[1]"DACA has shielded nearly 790,000 young unauthorized immigrants from deportation," Pew Research Center, http://www.pewresearch.org/fact-tank/2017/09/01/unauthorized-immigrants-covered-by-daca-face-uncertain-future/.

© The Author(s) 2018
D. E. Mosby, *Quince Duncan's Weathered Men and The Four Mirrors*,
Afro-Latin@ Diasporas, https://doi.org/10.1007/978-3-319-97535-1_1

1

in the United States who are witnessing their privileged status as the nation's majority vanish with each passing year. This disquiet has caused the powerful nation in the North to examine its history of immigration, its construction of national identity, and how Americanness includes some but excludes many. Costa Rica, not unlike the United States, is a nation constructed by a complex history of conquest, colonization, exploitation, and immigration.[2] After the Spanish conquest and subsequent extermination of many indigenous peoples, Costa Rica relied on the labor of oppressed Indians and enslaved Africans. As the country entered into the global market, it looked to the labor of peoples from elsewhere to build its economy: indentured Chinese immigrants, contract laborers from the British West Indies, invited waves of white Americans and Western Europeans, workers from Nicaragua, El Salvador, Colombia, Venezuela, Haiti, and the Dominican Republic who were seeking both peace and prosperity in a new land. Costa Rica has had to reckon and reconcile with the past as it was once imagined by the founding national elite with the lived historical experience of indigenous and Afro-descendant peoples. Quince Duncan's work has been quintessential in bringing attention to the exclusionary nature of national myths of identity and the challenge these narratives pose for a sense of belonging, particularly for the descendants of Afro-Caribbean immigrants who helped build the modern nation.

Before the tendency in Costa Rican intellectual circles in the late 1990s and early 2000s to interrogate the national myth, which identified the country's whiteness, Europeanness, and absence of a past history of chattel slavery as paramount to its exceptional economic progress and stable democratic institutions, Quince Duncan was among the vanguard of Costa Rican intellectuals who questioned the veracity of these notions and who engaged in conversations about the power of narratives of national identity. Beginning in the 1960s, Duncan asserted his claim to a Costa Rican national identity that also embraced blackness and West Indian cultural identity with his celebrated works

---

[2]"There's no such thing as a pure Costa Rican," Tico Times, http://www.ticotimes.net/Immigrationcr/.

of fiction, collections of essays, and recompilations of Afro-Caribbean folk tales. The two novels presented in translation in this volume, *Weathered Men* and *The Four Mirrors*, are the first novels published in Costa Rica—and perhaps even the first in Central America—written in Spanish by an author of West Indian heritage about the experience of Jamaican migration to the region and affirmation of Afro-Costa Rican identity. Together, both of these "novels of identity"[3] work to dismantle the myth that to be a *tico de pura cepa* (of pure Costa Rican stock) means being white, of European descent, Spanish-speaking, and Catholic with a nostalgic affinity for the country's peasant roots. These novels also bring to the forefront greater awareness of the contradictions and idiosyncrasies of exclusionary notions of national belonging when it comes to blackness, Costa Rican history, and democracy.

Duncan was born in San José, Costa Rica in 1940 to Eunice Duncan Moodie and Adolfo Robinson and grew up in Estrada, a small town along the railroad in the Caribbean province of Limón. During an interview I had with the author in 1997, Duncan jokingly stated that he was "born twice."[4] This notion of being "born again" is not in reference to some religious awakening, but rather in reference to the fact that although he was born to a Costa Rican-born mother, his birth certificate declared that he was Jamaican because the nation had yet to fully embrace the possibilities of citizenship for people of Afro-West Indian heritage. Later, when his mother became a naturalized citizen, he was then given a birth certificate that recognized him as Costa Rican.

Duncan spent his formative years with his Jamaican immigrant grandparents, James Duncan and Elvira Moodie, in a household and a community that valued literacy and education. When granting interviews or speaking with students, Duncan frequently talks about how *The Gleaner*, one of Jamaica's most revered periodicals, was a fixture in his household growing up and that his grandfather kept a personal library of classic books under lock and key. His early forays into

---

[3]Mosby, "Novels of identity: *Hombres curtidos* and *Los cuatro espejos*," *Quince Duncan: Writing Afro-Costa Rican and Caribbean Identity* (2014): 50–103.

[4]Personal interview with the author. For a more detailed explanation, see ibid., 5–6.

storytelling may have been influenced by Anancy stories, which are tales about the wily trickster spider derived from the traditions of the Ashanti peoples of West Africa. British slavers imported large numbers of Ashanti to Jamaica and the stories of how the tiny spider was able to use his quick wit to outmaneuver larger, more powerful creatures provided an essential survival tool for oppressed peoples. Duncan was also influenced by Miss Rob, one of his neighbors in Estrada who encouraged Duncan to read as a boy and retell the stories he had read. Many of those early influences as well as his own witness to Afro-Costa Rican history and culture in Limón are woven into Duncan's writing.

Duncan grew up during a significant juncture in Costa Rican history when the nation was slowly recognizing its black citizens and also struggling with the meaning of blackness. Although there have been peoples of African descent in Costa Rica since the colonial period, this population was already culturally assimilated and their identities, such as the Afro-descendant population of Guanacaste province, were resignified as *mestizo*, *cholo*, or indigenous.[5] A distinctive black culture did not emerge again until the arrival of thousands of free West Indian workers, primarily from Jamaica, in the late nineteenth and early twentieth centuries. Like Duncan, many contemporary Afro-Costa Ricans are the descendants of these West Indian workers who were called to the country beginning in 1872 to build the railroad that linked the coffee-rich Central Valley with the Caribbean port city of Puerto Limón. The Costa Rican government contracted North American railroad builder, Henry Meiggs and his nephews, Henry Meiggs Keith and Minor Cooper Keith. After unsuccessful efforts to recruit Costa Rican nationals and foreign labor from Italy, China, and the United States, Minor Keith actively sought out English-speaking labor in the West Indies. The majority of these workers were literate and skilled Jamaican men who clung to a dream of making enough money to return home and buy

---

[5]The Guanacaste province is located in the northwest of Costa Rica and borders Nicaragua. During the colonial period, this region used enslaved African labor primarily in cattle production. *Mestizo* means "racially-mixed," generally Spanish and indigenous. *Cholo* is sometimes used to describe people from rural areas with darker skin. It is typically seen as a pejorative term because it is also used to describe individuals or groups as "backward" or "uncultured".

property, support families, and supply school fees to ensure that their children had the opportunity to move into the professional class. The work of constructing the railway through 100 miles of dense rainforest was arduous and the men were subjected to dangerous working conditions, days of work without pay, and tropical diseases like malaria and yellow fever.

After nineteen years, the railroad was completed in 1890 at the cost of the lives of 4000 workers, including that of Henry Meiggs Keith. Eventually, Minor Keith determined that the transport of coffee and passengers between the Central Valley and Limón did not render the profits he expected. He ordered the mass planting of bananas along the rails and began to export the fruit in large quantities to the United States. In 1899, Keith merged his Tropical Trading and Transport Company with the Boston Fruit Company to form the United Fruit Company. That infamous brand became a defining example of the modern multinational corporation and as a monopoly wielded such wide-reaching power that it determined the path of Central American governments and economies for much of the twentieth century. The United Fruit Company encouraged the migration of more Afro-Caribbean workers to Costa Rica to provide labor for the increasing demands of the banana industry. Among the thousands of men and women from the West Indies who arrived in Puerto Limón were Marcus M. Garvey and Duncan's own grandparents.[6] In spite of the challenging conditions of the tropics, poor sanitation, inequitable pay, and suppression of workers' attempts to organize and advocate for themselves, the West Indians managed to recreate their home cultures in a new environment through "English" schools, Protestant churches, mutual aid societies, and cultural organizations. Their lives were not only different from the national population but also geographically isolated from it.

---

[6]Marcus M. Garvey (1887–1940) was an important Jamaican visionary. His sojourn in Costa Rica (1911–1912) was brief but impactful. His denouncement of working conditions in a self-published tabloid lead to the termination of his employment as a timekeeper for United Fruit and eventually his expulsion from Costa Rica. However, Garvey's experience in Costa Rica provided significant fodder for the founding of the Universal Negro Improvement Association (UNIA) in 1914. The organization amassed a following in the USA, England, Canada, Jamaica, Cuba, and Central America.

They maintained their communities without much need or desire to integrate with the Hispanic culture or customs and the white and mestizo Costa Rican nationals responded similarly to this black, "foreign element" within their borders. This history played a crucial role in Duncan's upbringing and contributed to his vision of Costa Rican society, as well as the direction of his literary production.

Weathered Men and *The Four Mirrors*, along with Duncan's five other novels, six collections of short stories, and numerous essays, have firmly cemented his place in Costa Rican literature and culture as a writer giving voice to the nation's misunderstood and misinterpreted history of Afro-Caribbean migration and settlement. Duncan is viewed as the primary translator of West Indian culture and history for the Spanish-speaking, white and mestizo-identified national population of Costa Rica. His work also connects Afro-Costa Ricans of West Indian heritage to the cultural landscape of the African Diaspora and engages the local history of Caribbean migration to Central America as part of the larger story of the dispersal of peoples of African descent in the Americas. Prior to Duncan, West Indian characters appeared in texts by previous generations of Costa Rican writers, such as Joaquín Gutiérrez and Carlos Luis Fallas; however, these earlier representations of Afro-Caribbean peoples in Costa Rican literature written in Spanish, largely reproduced and reinforced anti-black cultural stereotypes. The publication of *Weathered Men* introduced a human portrait of the lives and cultures of the black inhabitants of Limón that put them into relief, adding great depth and sensitivity to the portrayal of their history and struggle to be considered as equal citizens. The first generation of Afro-West Indian immigrants was weathered by adverse conditions but was not destroyed by them. Those who decided to remain in Costa Rica rather than return home to their islands of origin are not portrayed as troublesome foreign elements in Duncan's work, but rather as men and women weathered by hardships who persevered to make the Caribbean lowlands of Limón province a habitable place where they could provide for their families and hope for a prosperous future for their descendants.

For some readers familiar with the African American texts, such as Ralph Ellison's *Invisible Man*, may also see literary resonances in themes about citizenship, recognition, cultural resistance, and survival, and discrimination in *Weathered Men* and *The Four Mirrors*. Duncan's novels also connect to an Afro-Latin American literary tradition following in the footsteps of notable figures such as Nelson Estúpiñan Bass and Luz Argentina Chiriboga (Ecuador), Nicomedes and Virginia Santa Cruz (Perú), Manuel and Juan Zapata Olivella (Colombia), Virginia Brindis de Salas (Uruguay), and Nicolás Guillén (Cuba). Duncan's generation of Afro-Latin American writers includes Gerardo Maloney, Carlos Guillermo Wilson, and Melva Lowe de Goodin (Panama), Nancy Morejón (Cuba), Norberto James and Blas Jiménez (Dominican Republic), and Lucía Charún Illescas (Peru). This group of writers emerged after the Latin American literary "boom" that prominently featured writers like Carlos Fuentes, Mario Vargas Llosa, and Gabriel García Márquez who engaged with important issues of politics, imperialism, and identity, but also neglected to profoundly engage with the marginalized populations of the region, most notably indigenous and Afro-descendant peoples. The post-Boom Afro-Latin American writers address issues of blackness, identity, history, and the construction of the nation, while also calling out the erasure and invisibility of Afro-descendants, the historical impact of slavery and capitalism, neoliberal economic policies, and imperialism in their creative fiction.

In Quince Duncan's work, the concept of "Afro-realism" (*afrorealismo*) is important in telling the stories of Afro-descendant peoples. Afro-realism is a term he coined to describe how black writers incorporate an African-derived sensibility into creative work that highlights cultural resistance, the vindication of African symbolic memory and neo-African belief systems, and challenges the distortion of Afro-descendant voices by the dominant culture and affirms the concept of an ancestral community.[7] Duncan presents Afro-realism as a contrast to magic realism. According to author's framing, magic realism calls upon the fantastic as a stylistic element to advance the narrative, whereas Afro-realism is rooted in Afro-descendant cultures and purposefully incorporates aspects of neo-African belief systems such as

---

[7]Quince Duncan, "El afrorealismo: Una dimension nueva de la literatura latinoamericana," *Istmo* (January–June), http://istmo.denison.edu/n10/articulos/afrorealismo.html.

those that recognize the spiritual coexistence of the living, the dead, and the unborn. There are examples of this in both *Weathered Men* with the ritual ceremonies of a priestess that recount the Ashanti War and the powerful conversations between a dying woman and her deceased father-in-law in *The Four Mirrors*.

In addition to Afro-realism, Duncan's fiction also displays several intertextual connections. In both *Weathered Men* and *The Four Mirrors*, the author includes references to other texts, including Duncan's own writing. *The Four Mirrors* incorporates references to several stories from *Canción en la madrugada* (*Dawn Song*) and features many of the same characters we see in *Weathered Men*, as well as mentions some of the events that occurred in the novel. There are numerous citations of Jamaican folk songs, the Bible, the history of Jamaican migration to Costa Rica, including Marcus Garvey's Pan-Africanist vision, the African heritage of the Guanacaste region of the country during the colonial period, and the legal prohibition of Afro-West Indian labor from the Pacific coast United Fruit Company plantations. Both novels are self-referential, especially *Weathered Men* where the protagonist is also the author of the text we are reading, which is framed by his return to the Caribbean town where he grew up.

Weathered Men was originally published in 1971 as *Hombres curtidos* by a small press in San José, Costa Rica. It tells the story of a thirty-year-old man who returns to the home he left when he was sixteen. But this story is so much more than the tale of the "hero's return," it is a story about reconciliation with the past and redemption. The life of third-generation Afro-Costa Rican Clif Duke is our entry to learning more about the struggles and triumphs of the earlier generations of Afro-Caribbean immigrants who labored and eventually settled in Costa Rica. Central America has a complex social and political history; however, the history of black migration to the region from places like Jamaica, Barbados, and St. Kitts is rarely foregrounded. These patterns of Afro-Caribbean migration serve as a critical component to understanding the labor and economic history of the Americas, as well as the flow of black cultural capital as Afro-descendant peoples moved between the West Indies, Central and South America, Cuba, United States, and England.

In the prologue to the original 1971 edition of *Hombres curtidos*, Lia Coronado recognizes that this novel delves into the untold history of West Indian immigrants who came to Costa Rica. Many of these workers dreamed of returning home, but over time and after the birth of another generation, they made the difficult decision to remain in the host country. Over time, they also had to decide whether to conserve their ethnocultural heritage or assimilate the Spanish language and Costa Rican national culture. Coronado writes, "The weathered skin of the black people of the Atlantic region masks a drama that we Costa Ricans still do not know." She continues to observe in the prologue, "Quince Duncan is one of those young blacks who has courageously and enthusiastically stepped forward with the urgent task to make public in an intelligent and profound way, the history of this ethnic group that is soulful and proud of their heritage." While celebratory and congratulatory, Coronado's prologue still underscores a notion of the irreconcilability of blackness with Costa Rica's dominant culture where the unfolding narrative of Afro-Costa Rican history still remains to be seamlessly woven into the fabric of the nation. The notion of blacks as a foreign other is precisely one of the misperceptions the novel attempts to address by demonstrating the contributions of multiple generations of Afro-Costa Ricans.

Weathered Men also relates the story of three generations of the Duke family in Costa Rica, told primarily from the perspective of Clif Duke, a third-generation Afro-Costa Rican of West Indian descent. The generations face different challenges and choices. The first generation strives to make a way in the midst of inclement conditions of the Caribbean lowlands, as they struggle against floods and harsh work conditions. This generation must choose whether to persevere in Costa Rica in spite of their political and economic circumstances and the whims of a national government that does not welcome their blackness or to return to the island homes they left behind that are still subject to British colonial rule. The second generation, some born in Costa Rica and others brought as small children, have their own decisions to make as well. They have the choice to embrace the nostalgia of the islands of their parents, demand political autonomy from the Costa Rican state for the largely English-speaking province, or integrate into the national culture by learning Spanish and adopting some of the cultural practices of the Costa Rican nationals that their parents rejected. This challenge of the second generation is depicted in Chapter 6, "The Vine," through a conversation between Grace Duke and her boyfriend, Clovis about the decision their generation must make about their relationship with both Jamaica and Costa Rica.

Clif Duke represents the condition and hopes of the third generation of Afro-Costa Ricans. The third generation, which comes of age shortly after the 1948 Costa Rican civil war and the eventual extension of the rights of citizenship to Costa Rican-born blacks, has the difficult task of reconciling their ethnocultural difference with a nation that identifies with its Spanish heritage, Catholic roots, whiteness and the foundational myth of ethnic homogeneity. The protagonist of *Weathered Men* finds himself in this situation. Clif is in a challenging space of finding belonging in a nation that has finally recognized the citizenship of the Afro-West Indians who contributed to its economic development but also has difficulty accepting their blackness and cultural difference. As he tries to reconcile his Jamaican heritage and his national identity, Clif struggles to answer the question posed to him by his grandfather, "Are you Costa Rican? Are you really?" He attempts to find an answer by returning home to the small town of Estrada in the Caribbean province of Limón with his family in tow. After leaving the mainly Afro-descendant coastal region to move to San José, the nation's capital located in the mestizo-dominant Central Valley, as a sixteen-year-old adolescent, Clif Duke makes a return home to his origin as a thirty-year-old man with his wife and sons to write his Jamaican grandfather's history. While staking his claim to his rights as a Costa Rican citizen, Clif connects to Jake's memories of Jamaica while also documenting his grandfather's struggle to make a home in the new land for himself and his family. As part of this process of memorializing his grandfather, Jake, and searching for his identity, Clif remembers conversations he and Jake once had through flashbacks to his childhood.

Although *Weathered Men* is principally told from Clif's third-generation perspective, the narrative voices of his Jamaican born great-grandfather Jonas, his grandfather Jake (also called Jakel in the novel), and his mother Grace are woven in a Faulkneresque way, along with temporal shifts between past and present and stream of consciousness narration. Duncan's narrative style uses fragmented language and elaborate descriptions to reflect the characters' emotional or psychological state. As in some of Duncan's earlier short stories, the inclement weather and difficult geography appear almost as adversarial personages in the novel because of the stake they have in dramatically altering the fortunes of the first generation of West Indians who managed to conquer the land and make it home.

The Four Mirrors, published in 1973 as *Los cuatro espejos*, is Duncan's second novel and also is fundamentally a story of reconciliation, redemption, and home. However, if *Weathered Men* tells the story of three generations of an Afro-West Indian family in Costa Rica, then the focus of *The Four Mirrors* is much more personal and internal. It tells the story of an individual Afro-Costa Rican man and his determination to reconcile his double-consciousness, or twoness as a black man of Jamaican heritage with his struggle to understand how he disconnected from his West Indian roots and eventually finds belonging in the nation, as well as in his own skin. The African American intellectual and sociologist, W. E. B. DuBois observes in his landmark text, *The Souls of Black Folk*, that double-consciousness is, "this sense of always looking at one's self through the eyes of others, of measuring one's soul by the tape of the world that looks on in amused contempt and pity." DuBois continues to say, "One ever feels his twoness – an American, a Negro; two souls, two thoughts, two unreconciled strivings; two warring ideals in one dark body."[8] In the case of Charles McForbes, the Afro-Costa Rican protagonist of *The Four Mirrors*, his lifetime of looking at himself through the eyes of others leads to devastating consequences and sends him on a "heroic" journey to bring the past and the present together.

One morning, the protagonist McForbes wakes up next to his white wife. He launches into a state of confusion and restlessness after remembering words uttered during a lecture held the night before about the deficiencies of Afro-Costa Ricans and their culture. When he goes to the

---

[8]DuBois, *The souls of black folk* (New York: Pocket Books, [1903]/2005), 7.

mirror, McForbes discovers that he cannot see his face and realizes that he is either going blind or having a psychological breakdown. This quest to find the answer to his sudden "blindness" sends McForbes out of the middle-class comfort of his home in the capital and sends him into the streets of the city. As he wanders the streets seeking an explanation as to why he is unable to see his face in the mirror, we learn of McForbes' two lives. He was once a farmer and pastor in Limón who was married to his first wife, Lorena. After her death from a mysterious illness, he fashioned a new life for himself in San José as a man who suppressed his West Indian origins and whose marriage into a white Costa Rican family supported his meteoric social climb. His physical and psychological journey takes us from the bustle and coldness of the national capital to the slow pace and suffocating heat of the Caribbean lowlands of Limón. Ultimately, it is in Limón where the protagonist is finally able to face his past, his identity, and make peace with the events that led him to leave Limón and stifle a significant part of himself.

In *The Four Mirrors*, the author deepens his experimentation with narrative style. He uses flashbacks, stream of consciousness, sentence fragments, staccato phrases, repetition, and conjunctions placed at the start of sentences to convey McForbes' mental state as the reader accompanies him through the streets of San José and the rural footpaths of village life in Estrada. Duncan engages with intertextuality as he brings characters from *Weathered Men*, such as members the Duke family, Clovis Lince, and Howard Bowman into the narrative. He also references Clif Duke as a writer and playfully includes a scene of Charles McForbes reading selections from his 1970 collection of short stories, *Canción en la madrugada* (Dawn Song). McForbes offers a scathing critique of the work as something written for "romantic women and their compliant husbands." In *The Four Mirrors*, Duncan also relies on multiple narrative voices to present the perspectives of McForbes' two wives: Lorena Sam, the Afro-Costa Rican daughter of a Jamaican obeah man and Esther Centeno, the privileged daughter of a medical doctor who is an esteemed member of the Costa Rican elite. Lorena's slow and painful death is the thread that links McForbes with the Centeno family, as well as a moment of transition between his life in the province and his strivings in the capital.

It is a privilege to present the first English translation of Quince Duncan's "novels of Afro-Costa Rican identity," *Weathered Men* and *The Four Mirrors*. First and foremost, *Weathered Men* and *The Four Mirrors*, are works originally written in Spanish about West Indian English and Creole speakers. The project of translating *Weathered Men*, in particular, was indeed a challenging one largely because of the question of which language (English or English-based Creole) and register to use. It became a matter of not just the art of translating the nuances of the author's words and cultural references into another language, but how to faithfully transmit the emotions, thoughts, and experiences of characters who are West Indian English and Creole speakers from a text written in Spanish into a type of English widely accessible to a broad base of English language readers. The earlier drafts of the translation had the majority of the dialogue written in both Jamaican Creole and Standard English. Although I felt that the incorporation of Jamaican Creole into the text gave the first generation characters in the novel a particular cultural authenticity, some early feedback from readers indicated that those familiar with Jamaican Creole appreciated the earnestness and humor of the dialogue, for example, the banter between Jake and Walter about winning Leonor's affection. However, readers less familiar with the cadences and Jamaican Creole's phonetic spelling were challenged to catch the rhythm and meaning of the dialogue. In this translation of *Weathered Men*, I have attempted to use a type of language that follows some of the patterns of Creole English and some phrases in Jamaican Creole to indicate not only the cultural roots of the Afro-Costa Rican population but also to mark the uniqueness of the first generation. I wanted the language of the second generation, as exemplified in the exchange between Clovis and Grace, to reflect the Jamaican Standard English received from their formal education. Clovis and Grace would have attended schools organized by the various Protestant denominations (Methodist, Anglican, Baptist, Moravian, and Adventist) that followed a rigorous curriculum that adhered to the structure of the British colonial educational system. While they may have spoken Creole at home or in informal settings, some members of this generation would have been encouraged to adopt more British modes of respectability and customs that would facilitate their entry into the West Indian professional and colonial administrative class when they returned "home." Similarly, Clif would have received an education similar to his mother Grace, but perhaps also obligated to attend Spanish school by national authorities.

For *Weathered Men*, I made the difficult choice to forgo the majority of the Creole, while attempting to conserve some of its patterns in a more standard form of English and making it accessible to a wide range of English speakers and readers. In most of the text, I use Standard American English; however, when contextually appropriate I try to approximate the voices of the characters with different registers of speech and colloquial language. Similarly, in *The Four Mirrors*, I decided to follow a more standardized form of English with some attempts to conserve the patterns of Creole-based English during the flashbacks in Limón. The protagonist's social distancing from his Limonese roots and alienation from the Caribbean culture of his rural village generated this choice.

Additionally, for the sake of clarity, I have included in some footnotes in both translations. The footnotes in *The Four Mirrors* are more contextual whereas the notes in *Weathered Men* contain definitions for some words that are unique to the English-based Creole spoken in Limón, also called Limonese Creole, as well as some Costa Rican Spanish words that appear in the text that I chose not to translate (for example, *cholo* and *tepezcuintle*). These notes in translations are an effort to convey aspects of ethnolinguistic difference, while also making the language accessible for a wide readership.

In *The Four Mirrors*, I faced another interesting decision point in translating the word "cursi" into English. In contemporary Costa Rican Spanish, *cursi* means "corny," "cheesy," "poor taste," "passé," "banal," "boring," "trite," "pretentious," "obnoxious," and "worn out." Charles McForbes uses the word *cursi* in the original text as his signature word. *Cursi* appears so often in the text that the word almost becomes a character itself since the protagonist uses it frequently to describe himself and others. I settled on the word "cliché" because it seemed to fit the majority of the contexts in which the character says it and like *cursi* in Spanish, it has the same type of auditory quality that seemed to read well in the text.

For both *Weathered Men* and *The Four Mirrors*, I decided to use the "n-word" to convey strongly and powerfully the brutal and unforgiving anti-blackness the characters experience. During this process, I have been mindful that a translation is a work of creative writing in itself and through the act of translating these two novels, I have attempted to imagine the characters, the choices they make, the perspectives they hold, and how others view them. Through this process, I had to think about the role of power and how to depict this in translation. Spanish descriptors are challenging because *negro/a*, *negrito/a*, *moreno/a*, and *morenito/a* are all terms that are used to describe Afro-descendant people and dark skin. On the surface, these words do not carry the same cultural charge as the English word "nigger." They can express affection, especially in the diminutive form, but they can also be used disparagingly to cause harm or offense. Unlike other areas of the Spanish-speaking world that have large Afro-descendant populations like the Caribbean, there is no clear equivalent to the "n-word." However, it is important to note that all of these racial appellations, including *negro/a*, *negrito/a*, *moreno/a*, *morenito/a* are part of our historical legacy of slavery, but even more profoundly it is the legacy of over five centuries of a paradigm which has "inscribed blackness as negative difference."[9] The word "nigger" is harsh and it is ugly. The power dynamics at play are apparent not only when a white person addresses a black person with this word, but also when black people use it with one another. Even in jest the word carries with it a particular history of ownership, domination, and the power to name, define, and categorize.[10] So, in my translation, I have used the English word "nigger" when the context has called for it and being cognizant of the dynamics of race, color, and power in Costa Rican history. For example, in *Weathered Men*, when Jake Duke is denied his human dignity when he needs to use a restroom in a San José neighborhood, he knocks on door after door and is repeatedly denied, not because of his condition as a man, but rather because of his condition as a black man. The unwelcome, the

---

[9]Jerome Branche, *Colonialism and race in Luso-Hispanic literature* (2006), 2.
[10]Ibid.

power at work, the dehumanization that Jake experiences—he is treated as less than human and the utterances of *negro* and *negrito* are not out of affection, but rather out of the purpose of othering, diminishing his personhood, and displaying the privilege of whiteness.

Duncan has been a champion for the Afro-descendant, indigenous, and immigrant populations in Costa Rica and beyond. He has been recognized throughout Central America and Latin America for his expertise in social justice education and cultural activism. For this novice translator, this project has brought me great joy and I am honored to share these translations so that Quince Duncan's work may be able to access a wider readership beyond those who have been fortunate to read his work in Spanish. Any errors in the translation are mine.

Weathered Men

Contents

© The Author(s) 2018
D. E. Mosby, *Quince Duncan's Weathered Men and The Four Mirrors*,
Afro-Latin@ Diasporas, https://doi.org/10.1007/978-3-319-97535-1_2

Part I

Chapter One: The Return

"The act of lifting the suitcase, hoisting the child, and exiting the train is all one motion…"

My wife timidly follows behind me, trying in vain to hide the contours of her shapely legs. A futile effort. Her hands grip the handbag as if she's protecting a stash of precious jewels. I place the suitcases on the platform. I feel the inescapable emptiness of my pockets and that same feeling of emptiness creeps into my gut. With a wave of his hand, the conductor gives the signal to depart. The halting metal machine. I have returned. The train station is still here, intact, unchanged in fourteen years. On the other side of the tracks, the town hall, offices, and houses, all there unchanged except for the SNAA sign that has replaced the old water tank, which only means that water is now more expensive.[1] Nothing has changed. Not even a sign of paint or repairs. Everything is static. Things just are—decaying, lurching toward self-destruction, or simply resigned to deterioration. A tenuous state that in its own way traces the violent and contrasting future. My wife looks at the town in silence. You could see in her eyes that she's still uncertain of the reason for my return. No one, perhaps not even I, knows why. My friends in the capital will never forgive me for leaving the big city and the fast-paced life our generation's artistic elite is trying to create. The lectures on "ultra-literature," art, service to humanity, and all the things that define urban life.

"You're a writer. You've got real promise, so why you going to bury yourself out there in the bush?" But I am searching for my roots. I've got the revolver I bought in my suitcase after deciding that I'm in danger of becoming like so many other writers. My wife looks at me again

---

[1]SNAA—Servicio Nacional de Acueductos y Alcantarillado (National Service of Aqueducts and Drainage).

with a familiar question in her eyes. I know her doubts, the interruption to her everyday life, the never-ending arguments about fear, struggle, and splitting herself into two—one half drawn to middle-class comfort and routine and the other just as absurd as my own spirit with a view of the world just as unreal as my own. But, maybe that unrealness is the only real truth in this world.

"Let's go my love." She takes a step.

"Let's go," she responds. "Is it far?"

"Five minutes on foot…"

"Alright," she holds on tight to our eldest son, "Let's make the most of our time."

And she grips him tighter, propelled by a burning instinct that surges from within and materializes in her way of seeing things almost as an act of heroism as if it's necessary to protect the boy from me. But not really from me, more like that thing inside that sometimes seems to possess me. I shouldn't have brought them to all of this, but it's too late. We keep walking, over the wooden slats. People greet us along the way. Everything is the same. They've lived seventy plus years like this, without it ever occurring to them to cluster together to create a town center. All along the rocky and irregular path, people greet us. My wife's footprints and those of my son form indistinct shapes. The house emerges from between the fresh leaves of the cacao grove, and the sensation of returning overwhelms and startles me. I am home. The pent-up nostalgia of the years crescendos and frees itself. The memories are violent and strike relentlessly. Something indiscernible that explodes into a crossroads before my uncertain future. But I'm home, and that's important.

"This is the house."

"Oh, wow! The outside is lovely."

"Yes, of course, and big. Comfortable. Be careful on the steps."

Holding my neck, my youngest son is sound asleep. (*Suddenly an unexpected image assaults him: the child holding the old man's neck, asking him to explain the contents of the newspaper.*) We get closer to the door, with an incredible expression of guilt on our faces.

"Goodness, it's big. Turn on the light."

"The generator's out."

"For goodness sakes! And it had to happen now. Good Lord, what are we going to do?"

He used to run through the blossoming fields of the burning plain, sometimes barefoot, with his knees covered with mud and straw, soaking up the dense air, without a stove, without electricity, without a bath—except for the river, without a refrigerator... He had left fourteen years ago and he remembered that morning like it was yesterday. They had gotten up early, around three o'clock in the morning. His grandfather told him to get dressed and then called him to the table where he gave him a list of the household debts, specifically asking him to do what he could honor them. It was as if suddenly, at sixteen years old, he had been formally emancipated so that he could take on his inheritance: the blood, the culture, and even more importantly, the responsibility of lifting up the honor of the Duke name to the highest degree, following the century-old norms of village's inhabitants. Now, fourteen years after that solemn morning, he was once again in his hometown.

His wife would never understand. He kept that secret deep within—the trips to the river, the anguish of imminent death, the humid evenings, and the merciless solitude of the road. Alone, absent. Life had been eating away at him for a long time. Life was unmerciful, unrepentant, and unsympathetic. That was the afternoon when he got a hold of the pistol... It was not the first of those afternoons. Many times before, his mouth would turn red-hot, his steely eyes would burn in the sun. In this particular instance, his hands were ice, and if it weren't for the incessant hum of the river's current suggesting to him the possibility of trying again, his story would've been different.

"Clif, why are we here? Oh, I know – you're the heir."

Profound words that soak through to the depths of his being—the heir—as if he were the old man's son, instead of his grandson. When his mother was pregnant, his grandfather refused to oblige the guilty party to take responsibility for his actions, first because he considered it a situation that could be overcome, and second, because according to his own criteria, the initiative should come from the young man. Words that soak through to the depths within him. And another reason, the third reason, was the weight. But he kept the third reason to himself, reserving it for a night to share with a friend between drinks. He felt proud because the child would carry the Duke name and he began to pray that it would be a boy-child. So, he placed in young Clif's head his inheritance and welcomed the increasing glory to the family name so that in turn he could pass it on with greater glory to his children and continue in this way for generations to come, until perhaps among his lineage a pristine Ethiopian male would rise up to be the pride of his race and cover the Duke family name with splendor.

"Clif... your mother will come for you... I'm old and tired... but most of all I'm not well..."

It was just the two of them, yes, he remembers it, together at the table in the tense daybreak. Yes. And Clif placed himself at his grandfather's side because it was an overwhelming moment.

"You already know how to take care of a farm and you know how to earn your bread without thiefing. Always be good Clif, my son – a good son is his mother's joy." These were familiar words that he often heard at the table. While clutching his grandfather's neck, he glanced over his shoulders at the pages of The Gleaner. Grandfather would position his reading glasses at the end of his nose, his sharp grey chin and his opaque skin absorbing the light. Perhaps the owl would interrupt the interminable rattle of the toads. Then the boy clutched the old man's neck even tighter, repeating the saying he inherited from his grandmother, "pepper an' salt pon yu backside" the phrase that his great-grandmother first repeated to the point of exhaustion, and perhaps also his mother after that, as the old man pointed out with morbid satisfaction that no one would dare to take it seriously.

Who would have believed grandfather's words! That morning he looked rejuvenated.

"Clif, my boy, you know I only got 'Good Hope,' this plot of land to pass onto you. It's not worth a fortune, but it is yours. Don't be like the people who just stick out their hand without working a day in their lives and think that they deserve their inheritance. Know that you receive your talents from the Lord, the One we all serve."

No, no one was going to believe grandfather's words. Not even Clif. But he was standing. Perhaps he sensed the solemnity of the moment. Perhaps. But that morning would slip through their fingers.

Chapter Two: The Dance

Jake Duke looked to the sky. The sun glided through its daily dance above the tall palms of Montego Bay. The strong scent of banana invaded the boat. In the distance, the sea sank back into itself. The two crying women on the shore dissolved into the azure distance. His father's letter was in his pocket. He could recite it from memory. The lettering was typical of Jonas, full of unnecessary repetitions, poorly placed capital letters, and other errors.

"*DeaR SON: Its Likely dat dese lines Will reach Yu hans after me Death…*," he was assaulted by the multifaceted, blurry image of his father. The humidity of the morning covered his skin, the fresh smell of Kingston made his body shiver. He moved forward, enjoying the clear spectacle offered by the restless coming and going of buyers and sellers gathered near the market. Fifteen yards ahead, he could make out a well-dressed man, who changing course was coming toward them.

"Jake, straighten out you clothes."

"Sorry, what did you say sir?"

"Fix you clothes."

"Yes, Paw…," he quickly responded though he didn't like his father's tone.

"An' furthermore, take off you hat when that man comes near…"

"Jonas Duke…Pleasure to see you…"

"The pleasure is mine Mistah Edwin," he said smiling ear to ear.

"Is this your son, Rumina's boy?"

"Yessir. Jake, say hello to your great-uncle. Remember how we talked about him?"

Jake worriedly looked at him. It's not possible to remember something that never happened. He could swear the name wasn't even familiar. He was being asked to bear false witness and he would've preferred to not struggle with the consequences of making his father look bad. He nodded, but this gesture was not enough for Jonas's withering look, and he had to utter the words.

"Yes, Mistah Great-uncle,"—what was a 'great-uncle,'—"I am very glad to meet you and my mother will also be happy when she learns that I met you."

"What a well-mannered boy! So well-spoken. It's amazing! Take these…five shillings," as he reached into his pocket. "Here you are, my dear boy. You must take him out to get know the world."

Now, aboard the ship, among the stench of bananas, the letter from Jonas continued:

"Witout Wanting TO, I hav failed Yu. De Fevah to Blame…"

But it wasn't the fever that made him fail when he didn't know how to protect his son from the emotional shock he suffered when he found out in such an unpleasant way about the existence of his white great-uncle. He found out from Jonas that this great-uncle was the son of the same white man who fathered his grandmother and his great-aunt Marne. He hadn't heard Mistah Edwin's name before and he wouldn't hear it mentioned again after that day when an unmasked Jonas, sat down next to him and explained hatred and Mistah Edwin's unforgivable offense of having kept his black sisters' inheritance for himself, hardly giving them forty pounds sterling for the two of them. Already being a free woman, grandmother abandoned the old, big house, taking Marne who vowed to serve her older sister as long as they lived together. Forty pounds sterling, and now many years later, offering a generous gift of five humiliating schillings, as if that could erase from his conscience the sin he committed against his own blood.

"I am deducting the expenses for food and clothing," he said, "the attorney's fees and other expenses. Take into consideration I have given you a roof over your heads and food since the day my father, your owner, passed away. I found you employment with a Scottish gentleman and I have given you a letter a recommendation." With incredible cynicism, he added, "One has to be Christian to do so much for a pair of Negresses…"

He never mentioned that those "Negresses" were his half-sisters. Jake remembered with rage his father's false smile of enthusiasm and held back the urge to scream "hypocrite" at him a million times and "coward" many others. An ancient legend. Yesterday. After everything, a smile was the charity that all the descendants of slave owners needed in order to sleep peacefully on their bed of silenced and complicit disgrace.

The letter continued:

"I lef all Me Saving with a Neybor, mrs. Rosslyn Scoott. Shes a Trustworthy person. With wat lef, Yull be able to ern what Yu need TO Liv…"

From a distance, the sea appeared to sink back into itself again. The fragile figures on the shore were no longer discernible. The palm trees on the coast descended into the depths of the ocean. The ship advanced with an accelerated rhythm, setting off out to sea, opening behind it a widening infinite triangle. It wasn't necessary to read the letter; he knew it by heart. But, he took it out of his pocket one more time and opened it in his hands. His eyes began to run after reading the beginning of the letter. He stopped to observe the spelling errors as if in them he could see not only Jonas's hazy image, but also that of his generation.

"In Othah wurds," the letter went on, *"Yu cayn ern wat Yu need TO tek care of Yuself day to day. After dat. Jake truss GOD. yours truly, Jonas Duke. Come soon. Sen my regard TO Evryone fa me."*

Perhaps Jonas had left enough so that his son could have the freedom that he never had. Jake had sometimes thought that his father never tried to free himself, that the decree signed by Queen Victoria in London—or wherever it was—had been enough for him. Instead of the oppressive slavery of plantation owners, he settled for another type of slavery that was much more refined and by its nature, far more insidious.

"What a sad, sad face!" someone interrupted.

"Excuse me?"

"You look troubled."

"Yes, it pains me to leave Jamaica."

"You leave a sweetheart?"

"Not exactly. It's just that my mother and my grandmother depend on me."

"Well, ev'ryting have a remedy."

"So, what's mine? What is it?" He asked with some surprise. It was as if the stranger had been lying in wait for the opportunity to show him the package.

"Look," he took out some semi-dried leaves.

"What's that?" "

"Many people don't know it. Is ganja."

"Ganja! Good Laawd."

"Yes, for free men. For people have no prejudice."

"I don't see how that can help me."

"Try it."

"You smoke that?"

"I don't have no problems. I sell it. Want some?"

"No thanks. So, you don't smoke it?"

"The doctor don't take the medicine him prescribe."

"And according to you...well, that's their problem. You have customers?"

"If I have customers? This is my living. Try it..."

"No, no ganja man. I prefer the salt-air."

"It's better than dancing pocomania."[2]

"Perhaps, but..."

He would never have the courage to try it. Perhaps that was his inheritance.

Jonas never dared to sit in the front pew at church. He always sat in the back. Yes, as if he could rebel against his servile position in the next to the last pew.

"Paw, can we sit up front?"

"Up front?"

"Yessir, to get to enjoy the service more."

"Boy, you forget you born black?"

"It's just that..."

"Stay in you place. If you put you nose inna where it don't belong, them will cut it off."

"Maybe so," said Jake, "this herb could be better than pocomania, but I rather not try."

"Alright, look for me if you change your mind."

Jake Duke returned to the many-sided memory of his father. Coward, submissive, it was all true. But he knew very well that, above all else, Jonas loved him. And that, only that, saved Jake from hating

---

[2]Pocomania, also called Pukumania, is a Jamaican folk religion, characterized by rituals that include African-influenced dance and musical expressions, drumming, and spirit possession.

him. It was this undeniable love that compelled him to leave the safety of St. James and venture overseas, risking his life so that his only son could study mechanics.

He then thought about the curt letter from Mrs. Scott and suffered a violent spasm.

"I deeply regret to inform you of the death of Jonas, who passed away yesterday. He will be buried today with the honors that correspond to his merits. Please accept my condolences. Truly, Rosslyn Scott."

The letter seemed accusatory, faulting him for Jonas's death.

"My Sons ambicious; he want to be a mekanic. I'm goin for de panama Canal – oveh dere yu cayn ern in gold. Wit wat I save I cayn sen him to skool."

"I will claim my inheritance," Jake said to himself, "and become a mechanic. And I won't allow myself to languish."

The trafficker approached him again. Jake went in search of the urinal.

The second night aboard had a touch of the poetic. A black, profound silence marked the hour. The darkness still radiated a youthful glow and the most sentimental of the sailors strummed a guitar. His companions among the crew positioned themselves around him to listen to his powerful masculine voice and the interwoven notes. Someone tapped a bongo with soft strokes, encouraging him. Calming itself, the sea joined the sound of the African symphony. Timidly, the instrument made a muted hum. The anxious glances were all on the troubadour, thirsty ears waiting for the moment when they could hear the glory of their tribe flow from the singer's voice. They could hear the history they all know—the parts silenced by shame and distorted by the quills of Caucasia. Yes, this history was hidden in the blood, and because it was his, it was the only truth. Palpitating and necessarily musical.

The guitar became the word. The voice, a living note. The bongo kept the barely audible rhythm with the vigor of the past on the sacred shores of the Ashanti.

"Because in the land of the Ashanti
They say
The cannon-like furor broke on the breeze…
Smothering the clamor of the drums…

Outside in the sea, Her Majesty's ships cough up death with a satanic drive. The warriors flee from the coast, the invaders disembark."

Then, the night came. The priestess cried out to the God of Israel, the one David served, the sovereign and his direct line of descendants… "I am dark, but comely, O ye daughters of Jerusalem!" Incense and myrrh before the altar. Night of invocation among the legion of Ashanti. The priestess, cleansed her body and spirit, covering her beautiful contours with a blanket and raising her hands to the sky, while everyone, including the King, kneels before the altar… In the sublime moment of sacrifice, the blood once given on Golgotha according to the Apostle Philip, mixed with the blood of African soil for the atonement of sins…

At the end of the invocation, a great prayer arose in the midst the rhythm of the drums and the warrior dances so that the King and his subjects may be freed from the hands of the enemy. The priestess, now cleansed with blood and smoke, rose up in ecstasy. The sacred essence revered by the people, beyond all the lust, the flesh, certainly even the flesh. The troubadour took an unexpected pause to wipe away the sweat running down his face. The bongo kept up and intensified its tempo. One of the spectators stood up and began to dance and two others followed. The guitar rocked again, soothing the bongo. Subtle violence, subtle fire, subtle passion…

"When the sun came up, when the sun came up,
Let me tell you about the time when the sun came up…"

Thousands of warriors approach the handful of soldiers; their broken spears cover the sand and there is violence in the ferocious discharge of the cannon. In the unassailable assault of thousands of Africans, their blood is shed on the impotent shore…impotent blood.

The troubadour inhaled the ash and wind deeply. The guitar took on the character of an outburst, a possession. He found a frenzied tone when the bongo, which was silent until that moment, broke out into a cry. But the proud British legion could not advance one step. Stuck on the coast, despite their might, they managed to turn an entire village into a cadaver.

Then there was a truce and a challenge. They chose a black warrior and a white soldier to resolve the criminal conflict: black and white tangled in a savage battle. The black man shoulders the responsibility of saving his heritage; the white man carries the legendary pride of Her Imperial Majesty (the emissaries of the Admiral and the spokesmen for the Ashanti King had met to resort to this course of action). "If we win, you retreat once and for all with the right to carry away all that belongs to you. And on the contrary, if you win, we will submit to your dominion…"

The Africans witnessed the fight with naivety, abandoning their positions. In good faith, they waited for the result, convinced that whatever the outcome they would not need their weapons because the Admiral and the King had met…the British soldiers in the meantime took their positions.

"Fatherland…Fatherland… How much villainy I do in your name!"

"Ah, it is not worthy of a civilized people nor the honor, the sweat, nor the brutal hour! Such are primitive emotions."

The white man's flank was broken and he sunk into the sand. In Africa, the cry of victory emerged from the hero, followed by the clamor of the people and the drums that announced the good news to the continent…. Sad news. The cannons exploded. *"And I will not tell you of the miserable death of the Ashanti army because God left them in the hands of their enemies, for their many sins."* The African people wept. The sweat wailing. The intimate tears of a race weathered by the centuries. Mixture of legend and history, confusion of truths superimposed, tied, amalgamated now without remedy. Cries that slide from the brow and fall into the eyes.

Chapter Three: Yesterday

But, courage endures. He carried that same courage to Panama. When Jake Duke set foot on the Isthmus, his blood turned into ash. He greeted Mrs. Scott and it was hard for him to hide his discomfort. She responded to him coldly. Without a doubt, she was astonished that he was able to make the trip to claim his inheritance so immediately. What once belonged to Jonas, now belongs to him. Jake somberly presented his credentials—Jonas's letter and the unadorned letter from Mrs. Scott. Some doubt still lingered. So, he referred to his family tree, an important detail since the time of emancipation: "I am the son of Jonas, who was the son of Eustaquio Duke, a slave freed by Queen Victoria and direct descendant of an Ethiopian prince (who once free, wasn't ashamed to take his former owner's name as his own and in doing so subjected himself to the myths of a race that exploited him mercilessly)." There was not a single reference to his maternal line, as if unaware of Queen Nanny's history.

After they went through the formalities, satisfying the concerns of the executrix, he visited His Majesty's Consul, who was entrusted with the inheritance. The neighbors calculated that Jake scarcely received a third of the original sum, but this was impossible to prove because it never occurred to Jonas to specify the amount of the inheritance in his last letter to Jake.

Courage and the lost inheritance commanded Jake to Panama, and now he was determined to try his luck in Puerto Limón.

Costa Rica suddenly came into sight, rising out of the sea. He reached the dock and freely made his way toward land. Walter, his childhood friend who had been taken in and raised by Jake's grandmother, waited for him halfway. Jake and Walter grew up together in the Old Scotsman's house. The Scotsman was grandmother's lover for thirty years and he died without ever marrying her because he thought his clients would disapprove of their relationship. It wasn't a problem to have a black servant and sleep with her, especially if she had a fair complexion, but marriage was out of the question because that would have elevated a lowly beast to the status of a woman.

Walter greeted Jake, full of memories and questions. But what interested him the most was the fate of the old woman. The Scotsman died on the high seas on his way back from London, his entire fortune going down with him. He made an ill-fated decision and withdrew everything from the London banks to invest in Montego Bay. In the meantime, Jonas also moved away for some reason and died far away, leaving her again separated by the sea and unable to bury him. After Jonas, Walter left when he was 23-years old. He thought that he was old enough to leave home and free himself from his adoptive grandmother's influence. He immediately went off in search of adventures and freedom, according to his own account, and now Jake, who also left for unknown reasons…and as always, they all drift overseas.

She felt justified in her hatred of the sea.

"Poor woman, Walter. You know what she say to my mother? That she never understand why the men of our race love so little."

"She never understand that we love her so, so much."

"One thing for true, she would rather be dead than ignore it."

"But even so, she loved us bad, bad."

"It was her inheritance."

Sighing, Walter glanced at the sky. "Dammit," he said between his teeth, "it's her damned inheritance. But she also had white blood. Maybe that's why we could never understand her."

Probably. Her paternal great-uncle told the history of her white heritage, dramatizing it in a scene that he overheard while hiding behind the curtains. *The slave trafficker coughed with arrogance and while he sat at the table, he pretended to go through some papers. The plantation owner was visibly nervous; it was easy to perceive his state of mind. His wife leaned against the wall at the back of the room. She was as pale as the clouds of St. James on a sunny day.*

"No, I can't give you Nicky."

"I like that gal and that's that. I didn't force you to sign the contract."

"Give me a couple of months at least, and I promise you…"

"No, I have already given you two extensions."

"I can give you four strong Negroes," the owner insisted. When he died, everyone knew that Nicky was more than just a slave to him and his will indicated that the children of the slave were also those of the Master. It was

all in vain. The slave dealer refused to budge. They ripped the slave from her former home, snatched her away from her daughters. The little girls would never forget their mother's desperate cries as she threw herself her master's feet. He sold the pain inherited from his parents, guarding his secret. He restrained his instinct to conform to actions that would be viewed as socially appropriate. He lifted her up and whispered something in her ear (perhaps, I'm sorry, I'm at the mercy of this wicked man, I'll miss you terribly), turned his heels and quickly distanced himself, taking with him his wife and his children, including the two girls from Nicky.

"Yes," Jake said, "You're right. You get it right when you say it's part of her inheritance."

"You can bet on that."

"To love so many and fear losing them at any moment. Sharing out love in tiny pieces just in case one get lost or leave and never return. Then sparing loved ones the pain of loving us, and play at being tough. What a mess."

"Even so, she loved that old Scotsman and she couldn't hide it."

"That's because he was white and the source of all our sadness."

"Ah…," Walter let out a hopeless sigh, "Even though Queen Victoria set us free, we're still enslaved."

"You remember the old Scotsman's library?"

"From when?"

"Well your memory not too, too bad. You should remember what that author say about slavery – it's based on a story, that we're inferior."

"Uh huh, but that's not true."

"Even so, them and some black people believe it too."

"We black people have that put inna our head since the day we born." Jake sighed.

"You know something? I still have the mark from the whooping the Scotsman give us when he find us with his books."

"He give us a big lick and then he lock the library shut with a key."

"And then we take away the piece of plank from the back…" The ripple of their laughter merged with the Limonese sea and a gentle breeze adorned the terrible heat.

"Even so, the old man did love us."

"Uh huh, just like how somebody love a dog. You know, even though somebody can love another a whole lot, he'll always be a dog, like for instance, he never marry grandmother."

Walter was quiet. He lifted his eyes to let them roam the infinite marine surface. They walked in silence, then Walter said, "There's going to be a big set up tonight."

"Alright, I come just in time."

"Seems so."

"You get invited, right?"

"Cho, man! Of course, me best friend get married."

"Wonderful, you a guest of honor and I'm your brother!"

"Don't show off too, too much."

"And you know what really sweet me so? Is that this time we won't have to fool grandmother."

Their laughter receded into the cadence of the sea. They dragged their heavy boots through the muck in the streets, their rustic breeches splattered with mud, showing off their suspenders, embroidered shirts, and felt hats. They carried with them the clothing they would wear to the ceremony. Jake only spotted two buildings along the entire stretch of road— the British Consul and the Municipal Building. He noticed two children playing between a puddle and the small shack next to the church.

Jake and Walter stopped at a house to change clothes. The owner was a light-skinned gentleman of about forty years of age. The color of his skin bore witness to a night of a white orgy. Children conceived without love, but proud of their blood and the color of their skin along with the social importance they would inherit from British colonialism. A higher caste.

"Come on in…come on in…"

"I want you to meet Jake…The brother I tell you bout."

"Oh yes, yes. Welcome."

"Thank you, I hope we won't be strangers no more."

"Me too." They shook hands, "Gregory Swart, everybody call me Greg."

"They also call him Bullet," intervened Walter, "and this ole fool is Bugle."

"Nice to meet you."

"Bugle is blind," Walter continued, "He lose his sight building the railroad. That happen by Zent."

While they were getting dressed, another friend of Bugle's also arrived with the same idea of getting dressed before the ceremony.

"Salve is the orchestra leader," Jake heard someone say, "an' everybody friend."

"Yes, Bugle is as the *paña* say, a *cacique*."[3]

"Yes, an ole chief. Most of all if he have money, he will treat his friends good, good."

The conversation carried on for a while. The groom's father built the chapel just for the occasion and the space was completely full. The sermon was nearing its end when the men arrived. The women's black hands, covered by white gloves, were perfectly coordinated with the fans, dresses, and suits.

The bride was "imported" from Jamaica because there were too few women in the province, but she didn't come through any of the bridal agencies, rather she was brought directly from Spanish Town with the approval of Mr. Malcolm, the father of the groom. He wanted to avoid the same misfortune that happened to Gregory, who got his wife through one of those agencies. Bugle would later tell Jake that the woman Gregory brought over was skinny and ugly. It seemed to be the most logical thing for someone to do who couldn't get married any other way except to marry someone either by contract or proxy. He even added an example to illustrate her lack of education. One morning, Gregory's wife went to the butcher and asked for "two pound a ox fans an a quatah a tube." An expression of disbelief came over the butcher's face and spread to the others in the market. In the corridor, a woman who passed by the shops every day gossiping and talking about yesterday's news, raised her hands to her head to dramatize her astonishment and exclaimed:

---

[3]*Paña*—a pejorative term for the white and mestizos Costa Rican nationals. It is a derivative of *España*, or Spanish and means "Spanish people" and their customs; *cacique*—chief.

"Lord, me dying trial!"

"Excuse me, ma'am?" The butcher responded perplexed.

"Wat dont yu 'ave? Hif yu dont 'ave fans den sell me de trotters."

The patrons could not contain their laughter. Only Bugle stepped up to explain that the distressed woman wanted two pounds of oxtail and not "fans" and a quarter pound of tripe and not "tubes," and that if there were no oxtail, then sell her two pig's feet and not "trotters."

Jake could not contain his laughter and deserved the reproach of one of the wedding guests.

"And then what happen?"

"Greg end up bawling her out an' it seem after that them walked hand in hand together 'til the fever cut her down."

The high point of the wedding was a duet sung by the Walker sisters, Leonor and Crosby. Jake etched the lyrics into his memory perhaps because they were the first words he heard from Leonor's mouth.

Just like in olden days your strong word
Creating breeze, earth, and sea
Now your voice joins them
And it will live forever

Mr. Malcolm recognized Walter and bowed his head with reverence.

"He is a cheap ole man," Walter said to Jake, "but, besides that he is a good, good man. His friendship is big here – one of the four big men in town. The others, for true will be at the festivities."

Beneath a rain of fine rice, the newlyweds left the chapel under the palm archway that was quickly installed after Jake's arrival. There were many more men than women. Nevertheless, all the women were at the front of the church, waiting for their turn to be accompanied by one of the twelve attendants who were specially chosen for the occasion. Walter's voice announced that at last everyone should head over to the Malcolm house.

Walter turned to Jake to explain, "Everything is brought in from abroad… the bride and the wine and raisin for the cake. The governor will surely be there and the British Consul. Them two are also big men because of their position. Then Salve and Mistah Malcolm complete the picture."

A sudden drizzle forced the master of ceremonies to improvise for at least a half dozen of the bridesmaids. The sun, fading in the distance, was still shining despite the light sprinkle.

During the reception, Jake was introduced to the Walker siblings and he soon struck up a conversation with Leonor. He couldn't take his eyes off her. With her beautiful figure, her star-like eyes, and her bright white teeth. It was as if she were the very embodiment of the night and Jake was enchanted by the night. He was also introduced to Brother Bow, the wedding officiant, and then to the newlyweds. At the end of the reception, the master of ceremonies asked everyone to rise, and the bride and groom retired from the table to change clothes and return in time to dance the first quadrille. Leonor and Jake continued their conversation despite the evil glare one of the guests shot at them. Amid the envious glances of the other gentlemen, Leonor mentioned to Jake that the woman who stared at them so intensely was one of her relatives without specifying their relationship.

He had never seen a black woman before who smiled with such grace. Her gums peeked out from between her lips, a natural burning flame, enveloped by the intense radiance of her skin. She was an authentic African beauty. Authentic face and body, real. Her dress only served to enhance her beauty: cream-colored with lace roses that descended until they covered her high heels. A pink braid hung from her waist and gathered at the hem of her dress, falling to the back and onto one side. A hat with a lace veil completed the ensemble, together with a classic fan and a brilliant jewel that dangled from her gloved wrist. The other women, feeling a little less than ignored, showed their bitterness. They were far from dazzling and their looks of resentment only served to highlight Leonor Walker's great beauty. She knew she was beautiful and for that reason, Jake intimated he was not searching for ephemeral physical beauty that changes with the same quickness as the "heart of a woman"[4] flower changes color, but instead he was seeking the purity of spirit and inner beauty.

---

[4]"Heart of a Woman (corazón de mujer) is the common name of a flower that grows in the Caribbean lowlands of Costa Rica.

Later the bride and groom returned and danced the quadrille. Without exactly knowing how he would be able to do it, Jake convinced Leonor to sing and they walked toward the orchestra. Salve was stunned.

"Sing? Sing here? Mek-I-tell-you something Jake. You don't know these people, this is a dance! If I play church music here, they bound to ..." And then with surprising fearlessness, she said, "Play 'My Kind of Love.'" For a moment, Jake believed that King Sax was paralyzed. His eyes simply looked at Leonor as if she were speaking another language. Then, his eyes widened and his mouth articulated an unpronounceable exclamation and Jake anticipating this reaction, triumphantly suggested, "Wha'appen King Sax, you don't know it?"

King Sax turned toward his orchestra yelling, "You hear that? Him don't believe we!"

Displaying extraordinary skill, he introduced the instrument between his lips and formed a few tentative notes. Then without stopping, he faced Jake with exaggerated gestures to let him see his devious smile.

"Hear me now, sweet boy! What Salve and his boys don't know, we make up!" The musicians began to laugh uproariously, and the people, delighted and proud of Salve, joined his laughter. Salve turned quickly toward his orchestra to give them the first note and then, spinning on his heels, again faced the public. Jake thought that he was going to make a fool of himself, but seconds later, from someplace beyond the brass instrument, beyond his throat's vibrations, from the very depths of his lungs and perhaps beyond, emerged the melody with all of its magic. Thanks to Salve's instrument, the anxious wait turned to agony, which then felt like an eternity. From the eternity of his spirit, Salve was in the present moment, living life's full measure through the music. Then finally, he remembered Leonor, and he made space so that she could enter his kingdom and share its enchantment.

Leonor performed with the music:

I offer you, my great affection
But I cannot give you devotion;
And always free, I have to be

And the orchestra in unison broke the feminine intonation, introducing a fascinating contrast to the harmony:

Rest your head against me and listen
And come if you want my affection

Salve, or maybe it wasn't him or just another instrument that reached high notes. Those notes, inaccessible for the human throat, were also unreachable, beyond reality. And suddenly, Salve again, cruel, amazing…and Leonor's voice joining the chorus, and the song, now lost in the thunderous jubilation of the guests.

After the clamorous shouts, Leonor's clear voice rose above the orchestra. Salve's saxophone twirled around the melody, adorning it with almost unbearable intensity. Instinctively, the guests began to dance.

Carry me ackee go a Linstead Market
Not a quattie worth sell
Oh Lawd, wat a nite, not a bite
Everybody come feel up, feel up
Not a quattie worth sell
Fe wey dem mumma no bring
All di pickney dem a linga, linga
Oh Lawd, wat a nite, not a bite
Ow di pickney fi feed
Not a quattie worth sell
Oh Lawd, wat a nite, not a bite
Not a quattie worth sell[5]

---

[5]"Linstead Market"—a popular Jamaican folksong about a woman who goes to the market to sell her ackee (a staple fruit in the Jamaican diet). Customers look at her produce, but no one buys and she fears her children will go hungry.

The bongo kept marking the beat, while Salve wiped away the sweat that poured down his face. The other instruments were barely distinguishable and it was clear that they were there to support the saxophone's lament and the terrible cadence of the bongo—tiquitiquititá-ta-ta.

The ovation was over. Salve seemed intoxicated, effusively stretching out his hand to Leonor, Jake, Walter, Gregory, and each one of the orchestra members…and he commingled with some of his admirers and continued shaking hands. Finally, he walked up to Leonor:

"Young lady, I knew you had an enchanting voice, but to tell you the truth, I never imagined that you would dare sing with the orchestra… Congratulations."

"Thank you, Salve."

"And thanks to Jake…," he said winking an eye.

Walter took advantage of the great joy of the moment to ask Jake, how he managed to convert a Puritan into a calypso singer in just one night.

"In two hours," Jake corrected him. The festivities continued. Jake had played his first hand and the triumph was his.

Jake approached Leonor as best he could, respecting social rules, giving her time so that she could catch the rhythm. With her hand on his shoulder, they joined the caress of each other's presence to the fiendish beat of Salve's music. They focused on one another, completely forgetting about the others. And the others thought they were depraved.

"Where can I see you Leonor? I mean, I want to see you alone – I want to tell you some very important things…"

The expression on the girl's face changed swiftly. She vacillated, fighting to overcome her own prejudices. Jake expected that reaction.

Even before she could begin to hold back her smile, he suspected that she would give in. She would never admit that, though it was evident. He pressed her hand lightly and intensely looked into her eyes. Smiling, he murmured with a Don Juan air, "There's no rush Leonor. I won't rush you, but let me know your decision."

The next set was another quadrille. Jake refused to participate so that others could dance with her and give space for the idea to blossom. He feigned a modest resignation that sidetracked his rivals, who during the entire evening had feared a heartbreaking outcome. Heartbreaking for them. Now, looking at Jake, they consoled themselves with the presumption of his failure, which also made things easier for them to remove her from the golden cloud where she rested.

In the end, Leonor, Crosby, and one of their relatives signaled that it was time to leave. Jake did not move from his place and limited himself to only glancing occasionally at her, waiting with self-assured faith. Leonor gave in and walked across the room to say goodbye.

"There's a full moon," she said in a hush, and then she said aloud, "IT WAS A PLEASURE MEETING YOU. AND…" In a soft voice, she said, "Meet me at the beach behind the consulate." She said aloud, "I HOPE TO HAVE THE HONOR TO SEE YOU AGAIN," and then softly, "Walt will tell you where it is."

"I'm not going yet," he responded.

"I AM HAPPY TO HEAR THAT…don't tell Walter the reason why." She left.

An hour later, Jake noticed the moon began rising and quickly called Walter over to explain.

"It makes sense that she wouldn't want me to know and it also makes sense that you would let me know. You've never kept nothing from me. The only thing that don't quite make sense in all this is that we all have tried and failed, but you a total stranger come here so and get her to sing calypso, dance close with her, and now this! Whoa! Laawd, I feel proud. Our flair for conquering woman is quite alright, man. But, I ask myself, where did I go wrong?"

Both Jake and Leonor kept their date. She was dressed up in a simple dark colored dress.

"Jake, that you?"

"I'm asking myself that same question," he responded, sealing the conquest. "I've always been free, I'm in love."

Their hands met in the darkness.

"In love with you."

The moon obeyed the law of the universe. In the sand, near the stirring sea mist, her body, a point of magic, all magic. Night arrives and covers all. Living its moment, choosing not to let it pass by. There's an intense calm that follows every storm, exhaustion that soon follows a long voyage…and the sweat flowing down the forehead and lungs begging for oxygen.

Chapter Four: Knowing

Jake's great feat that night earned him a place in the group. A week later they all went hunting, Jake, Walter, Gregory, also known as Bullet, and another friend named Sidney who was their guide.

"You sure you know the way?" Bullet asked after an hour of walking.

"Shame pon you man."

Gregory looked at him intensely, scrutinizing him in search for the truth. Sidney held his glance. He did not hesitate, not even once and gestured with a certain violence that Gregory couldn't ignore.

"What's gone on with you Bullet? Wha'appen with you?"

"Hear me now," said Gregory, "I hope you know where you're going. What I mean is you gonna have to deal with me."

"What get into you? Shame pon you Bullet."

Spying a creature in the forest, Jake breaks the tension between Bullet and Sidney by asking, "They eat that?"

"Yeah man, the meat taste good, good."

"What you call it?"

"Tepezcuintle."[6]

"It sound like Indian food."

"Yeah."

They found themselves suddenly in the clearing of the forest where a shack stood in the center. They paused dead in their tracks and gazed upon a little boy hiding among the thickets. He looked at them with such intensity that it was almost as though he stopped breathing, then he desperately fled back toward the shack.

"Lawd, Jesus…Jesus," Sidney shouted, "Hold the dogs, Bullet."

"Boy, if the dogs get way from us, won't be nothing left of our little friend."

---

[6]Tepezcuintle—Also called a "paca" or "agouti," it is a large rodent found in the tropical lowlands of Central America. During the first half of the twentieth century, it was considered a prized protein source of peasant farmers. The paca is primarily nocturnal and prefers to burrow near rivers.

"Gregory, mind what you do, if they get way from you, we in a big mess."

"A mess? I bet me ass it would be more than a big mess."

"And what you think I would do with your ass?"

Distracted with controlling the furious canines, they didn't notice the old man who came to investigate the commotion. They only heard his piercing scream and the sound of footsteps hurriedly running away, as well as the names of all the saints and the seven curses of the devil.

"Eh! He get fraid?"

"Fraid? Boy, the poor man run for his life."

"Now he's going to tell them that he meet up with some cannibals."

They stood there looking at the man running to his shack. His wife and child were waiting by the door and he pushed them inside, without skipping a beat, he closed the door behind him.

"Well, let's go on our way."

"Wait a little bit. Let's let the dogs go."

They released the dogs and almost immediately they disappeared into the dense vegetation frantically pursuing their prey. After a short while, they saw a beautiful girl, who was barely a few steps in front of them. She was washing clothes along the brook. She wore a thin blouse with a deep neckline that partially exposed her breasts. Her multicolored skirt was tied in a point showing bare feet that were deformed by calluses. A black veil hung from the tree next to her and the men presumed that she used it to cover her shoulders. Perhaps it was because she was too busy with her chores or maybe the sound of the brook drowned out the dogs barking in the distance, but she didn't know the men were there until they met just a few steps away. She turned pale and in a panic, she dropped the clothes and fled, while shouting words in a language they couldn't understand.

"Eh, eh, what is going on with these people, cho?"

"That's the way these folks are, man."

"You want to say them backwards?"

"Eh! Haven't you noticed that them *pañas*? You should come to my house one day so Bugle can tell you a story about what he see. This is nothing. What do you think we're here for? Because Massa Keith[7] love us so much?"

The dogs barked with renewed force and the men leapt behind the brush to find them. As the men approached, the dogs strategically divided themselves, slipping behind the dense vegetation. It would have been easy to kill the tepezcuintle at that moment, but six peasants emerged from the thickets, threateningly gripping their cutlasses. Their eyes were inflamed, redder than the kerchiefs tied around their necks. Their mouths were contorted and foreheads tense. Gregory didn't shoot like he should have. He foolishly advanced toward them with an idiotic expression on his face and before anyone could react, he succumbed to the sharp edge of the machetes. Walter was the first to shoot, then Sidney and finally Jake.

The tepezcuintle left its hiding place and stopped long enough to have been killed with a single shot, and then he was quickly lost in the underbrush, pursued by the dogs. Behind him fled the four other peasants. Sidney blundered in discharging his weapon and couldn't even wound any of them. They hurriedly attended to Gregory who was on the brink of death. Nearby one of the peasants was lying there dead and another was gravely wounded.

"Let's go!" shouted Sidney.

"We can't leave them two there like that."

"Listen, Jake, save your pity and make we get out of here before none of us live to tell the tale."

Gregory died on the way.

---

[7]*Massa Keith*—Reference to Minor C. Keith, the US businessman who managed the contract with the Costa Rican government to build a railroad from the Central Valley to Puerto Limón. The project heavily depended on West Indian labor.

Chapter Five: The Legacy

Now, the memories were inevitable. The three remained motionless in the breeze's murky warmth, inhaling tomorrow, grudgingly tolerating the damp mud. Clif and Miss Ann, exposed to the almost cruel, mature calm of the old man—a stoic, noble, and altruistic cruelty, but cruel nevertheless. It's that certain knack humans possess that allows them to admit the truth without any sort of pretext. It's an inner strength that displaces the sweetness of the idyllic center of it all and moves toward something that is both symphony and silence.

"What you say, man?"

"Ann, my time has come."

"But for God's sake, Jake…you have barely seventy years…How could you think such a thing? For true you been a little sick, but…"

"Ann, Ann, understand me. I spent my life asking God to let me know the number of my days. Now you understand what I've been trying to tell you? Mark my words—I'm not coming back to Mangonía, at least not in this life."[8]

Who would've believed grandfather's words? Who would've been so naïve to accept such a ridiculous notion?

The tin of cacao that balanced on Miss Ann's head suddenly fell, struck by grandfather's resolute declaration. The white cacao speckled across the black mud. The cushion she used to soften the friction of the metal against her scalp also fell, but neither she nor Clif believed his words. No one picked up the load. Grandfather couldn't. Miss Ann wouldn't have stooped for something so insignificant because her friend Jake spoke of death and Clif was left standing there completely dumbfounded.

"Jake, Jake…a plea…a song…a prayer…"

There was something unreachable in the tone of her voice, something that perhaps transcended the moment in which Clif found himself. Who would've believed him? There was more. Something about the church and

---

[8]Mangonía—a reference to a fictional place found in one of Duncan's earlier pieces of short fiction.

something about the principles of the Lodge. A stillborn scream was trapped in Miss Ann's throat, a red ant crawled out of her hair and walked quickly across her glossy black forehead. She caught it, smashing it into bits.

"Ann, by God, death is as natural as being born. We go from one type of existence to another. That's all and you know it's true."

They both shared the same belief and maybe because of that same belief neither Miss Ann nor Clif believed that grandfather would die. Before the night always marches the day. Who was going to believe him?

"It's alright Ann." He smiled, imagine that, he smiled. An old man facing his death and he smiled. Who was going to believe him?

"Ann, don't give up the faith."

Trying to contain his tears, Clif resumed his stride in pursuit of his grandfather, on the same rocky road that he would cross years later with his own family. They went across footbridges, passed by the school and the mansion of a prominent landowner, and they stopped at the train station. And in spite of not believing grandfather's words, Clif cried silently, enough so that his view of the façade of the municipal building was bleary with salty tears. And there, they waited for the train's arrival, at the same hour the neighbors would wait for its arrival fourteen years later.

Nothing about my grandfather's story justifies my return. Nothing. Or, maybe it does? If it's a question of selling the farm, there's no need to come back and carry my entire family with me. And if it's about working the land, I never paid attention to that and fourteen years in the city is not going to help me bring in a harvest. The truth is simply that I have returned… I remember everything, the thousands of stories worthy of remembering. I think about them, I think about how the old man would come alive when he told them. I think about how he would make sure that I understood the truth—his truth and everything that it implied.

A month after I had left, I saw him again. I carefully observed his noble figure stretched out on the bed, his lips wearing the expression of speech as if he wanted to dictate just one more sublime sentence about the long history of poverty and anguish. Instead, he murmured incomprehensible sentences. Far removed from everything, he couldn't even recognize the voice of Grace, his beloved only daughter. His temples, silvered by the passage of time, appeared to announce the end of his story.

Without a doubt, he wasn't there. What I saw in the bed was only a defeated body. I could attest to this, I had seen him gradually disappearing over the last few months. Now, here at least, was the moment of truth. From the most unexplored places inside me, exploded a desperate denial of all the facts that lay before me. And finding strength, perhaps from my own exasperation, I made a heroic attempt to come back—from wherever I was—and return to my reality.

"Grandpa, grandpa…It's me, Clif. Don't you recognize me?"

You could say that time stood still. My mother hid her eyes while the most intense silence spread across the entire room. The hearts of all of those who were gathered in the room braided themselves together in a fervent prayer…Then, time went back to normal and the old man's eyes lit up as if he had returned from some place beyond this world. A weak smile illuminated his face, appreciable only to those like me who had known him for many years. I had no doubt, he was here, that he was present.

"Grandfather…It's me, Clif."

I could feel the sensation of relief that spread throughout the room when a smile burst out on his face and rejuvenated, he said with a vigor that was difficult to match: "Hello! Hello!"

For me, I could not contain my joy and the tears began to flow because those words were not just an affirmation of his presence, but also his affection—the way we engaged in our conversations. I took his hands and I kept them between mine, trembling with emotion.

"Grandfather…I am glad to see you…to see you again…"

"Well, well…"

With those words, it completed the formula of our greeting and as the echo of his voice faded into the most remote corner of the room, something ripped inside of him when he realized by some unexplained force, that those words were a good-bye. I stepped away from the bed as quickly as I could. The tears that I held back to the point of exhaustion, now overflowed…now unstoppable. I heard my name in the tender voice of my mother.

"Mum," I said to her, "he's no longer fighting. Do you see it? He's no longer fighting. He doesn't want to live. He is tired of it all…"

I held myself up with one hand against the cold wall of the hospital. I closed my eyes. I closed them tightly as if that were enough to allow me to stop time so that the present would never occur, so that the future wouldn't happen. Suddenly that afternoon I realized the gravity of everything the old man told me the morning I left the village.

"Clif, you well know that the land belonged to a family that never worked it. But remember that if I didn't have the title that give it to me, I would not be able to pass down to you the right to make use of it. That's what a title is for. It is true, son, the land belongs to no one. It belongs to everyone – it all belongs to God, no matter how you look at it. Those with titles are just stewards to use it for the benefit of everybody. I leave it for you on the condition that you work for it. We bring nothing to this world, Clif, and we can't take nothing with us, except you know what? The little bit of experience that we gather."

Those words have a different meaning now. It was no longer the ceremonial speech of an old frustrated mechanic, but rather a statement of faith. This is what grandfather had tried to do in his life, to serve as an example for me. I rested my other hand on the wall. My feet protested the mistreatment caused by the tight leather of my shoes, my knees refused to support my weight, and my body, abandoned by the air, succumbed to the intense, visceral heat. My mouth was dry and cracked my throat; I tried to say something to explain my condition. My head became an inferno; my eyes clouded by tears turned into salt.

Already insurmountable, my ideas fell one by one. The truth was that the old man was dying, his lukewarm fingers sadly confirmed that fact, and the denial of that reality, in spite of massive protest, dug deeper than consciousness itself, taking on gigantic proportions, and eventually exploded alongside the old man's bed.

What led to his death? Who's responsible?

My mother called me, begging me to come back, to come back to my senses. I opened my eyes to look at myself in hers, only to realize that in spite of everything, those eyes remained with me and I felt the warmth of her hand against my kinky hair. Despite the pain, there was a sweet and musical timbre in her weeping. The cold corridor presented a stark contrast—the tile floor, the concrete steps, the indifferent nurses who passed by. One thing after another, succession without time, living and vibrating, inevitably exposing our innate need to live and to carry out the unnamed responsibilities that our grandparents entrusted to us, to perpetuate the name and our race for our children, our children's children, and our children's children's children, children's children's children's children, and our….

"I'm alright, Mum…"

Grace exhaled with an expression of relief.

"I'm alright," I stressed, "Don't you worry."

"Boy, what a fright you give me."

"Yes, but I'm alright."

"He recognized you, right?"

"Of course, didn't you hear how he was talking to me?"

"Yes, you always use those words when you two talk."

I smiled with sadness. It was true.

We finally left for the cold street and we boarded a taxi. She leaned in to give me a kiss on the lips and we continued in silence. The tears fell on her dress, my hair pressed against her black cheek. His hands were lifeless, like stone. Filtering through the window, the wind caressed our ears without ceasing. Now, I remembered everything, the entire past that died that afternoon, the remnants of a culture descended into the grave along with the dead, generously ceding six feet of earth for each one. We stayed at Crosby Walker's house, a damp, adobe brick house, older than our host. She came out to receive us, stretching the worn lines of her face. We responded with a smile.

"How's Jake?"

"What can I tell you, Crosby? So, so."

The taxi pulled away, avoiding potholes in the battered street. A bit of muddy water splashed on an older woman walking by, which was reason enough for her to curse the driver's mother.

"Come in, come in…"

Night fell as she closed the door behind her.

Chapter Six: The Vine

That night, after our return from the hospital, Crosby, my mother, and I sat in silence. We knew that my grandfather was dying, but no one dared to admit it. Without a clear reason why, at that moment my mother began to speak of her regret for not getting married and started to tell us a story about an outing she had with Clovis, an old boyfriend.

"Grace," he said to her as they sat side-by-side and listened to the enchanting rumble of the sea. "I've been thinking about us and I've been thinking very seriously. You come from a respectable family. I know them quite well and I can swear by you, knowing the type of person that you are."

She stared at the ground. A footprint interrupted the symmetrical pattern of the sand. Opalescent shells rested in each furrow and in the distance, there was a grove of tiny coconut palms, atrophied in the battle of life. Their friends were playing ball behind them. Clovis continued, "In any case, I can say that from the very start we've gotten along quite well and you can't deny that there's a connection between us."

Grace Duke lifted her gaze to set her eyes on the water. The sea rushed against the shore with furious and immense waves. The end of a log bobbed between the chalky mist and seemed to carry the stories of a thousand tragedies caused by the formidable Atlantic. And she thought about what Clovis had just said.

"So, I've been thinking about all of this," Clovis said, "and the fact that I've made something out of my life…I've got a farm and it provides enough for two and eventually for three people to live comfortably, and it will even provide enough for four."

The sky lowered into the infinite horizon before them. The shadows of the palm trees along the coast faded and a majestic fan-shaped cloud floated beneath the intense blue sky and was reflected on the water.

"Clovis, what are you talking about?"

"What I'm trying to tell you is that, well, everything I've told you and we've shared some experiences together and we've got enough reasons to take those good things and secure our possibilities for the future…sorry, I'm not being clear…We should join our destinies."

"What?"

"Join our destinies as man and wife."

"Wait a minute Clovis…let me wrap my mind around this. If I understand correctly, you're asking me to marry you?…"

"Yes, Grace, I'm asking you to be my wife."

Another vehicle quickly passed by, making the same noise as the previous one. Grace watched as it moved toward the port and noticed the sign, "Buy Cacao Ltd." It was a weighty moment. The decisive hour. Standing in front of her was his curious, but mature silhouette. In her mind, she traced the outline of another that would persistently fade: *Clifton, Clif's father, his hands stroking the bongo. His voice was romantic and passionate and the totality of life vibrated through his handsome and elegant chest. She was his girlfriend, his only love. It became dark. Solitude approached until it blended their breath—skin against skin, lustrous sweat against sweat, and all the while feverishly whispering, I love you, I love you, you are my love, I will never forget you…He trembled.*

Just like she was trembling now. It was the kind of jolt typical of someone encountering death. She had to get herself together. The old man was dying. And what happened to the self-control, strength, and courage inherited from her father, the same pure courage and fire that emerged when she looked intently at Clovis that afternoon, as though she were disarming him with her gaze, and she thought and thought a definitive "NO." Cold, calculating, the aspiring suitor anticipated her excuse. "I know you already have a son. That's not a problem. I will take care of him."

"Clif wouldn't be a problem," she responded with a sense of pride, "the boy is glued to his grandparents and they adore him. But, I don't know. I have to think about it."

Grace stood up. Their friends had finished their game and were on their way home. The couple set out behind them.

"You don't have to tell me now, it's alright. Think about it for however long you need. It's better to be sure."

"He must think we're negotiating," she said to herself. He said all of this to her without any sense of affection, without any urgency for an immediate response: "Think about it for as long as you need." My Lord, how could anyone be so indifferent. Does he think I'm dying to be with him?

Some words came to her, maybe an ancestral voice or perhaps it was her own intuition that surged through her veins and echoed in her ears. They were the same words Jake and Walter used to say and passed down to Clif, the heir. Words that resulted from observation, practical wisdom, and instinct: "I don't know why the men of our race love so little."

In contrast to those words, the sacred and powerful black face that she loved so much emerged, hardened by the sun. His hands grasped the fence, his feet firmly placed atop an enormous rock. In the pasture, two cows tranquilly grazed the fruit of the land, guavas, herbs, and bits of sugar cane.

"My Lord, why won't I ever understand it?"

"Clifton, please understand."

"All I know is that we're going to have a child and you have to make your own decisions."

"It's just that I'd like to wait a little bit."

"Wait for what? I'm just a musician, but I can do some carpentry, some masonry, and I know quite a bit about machines. I can earn a living. I can support you and my son. Why can't we get married?"

"Oh, Clifton! What am I supposed to do? I'm not in a position to make demands, they love me."

"I love you too Grace, I love you."

She also loved him, she always loved him. But now she has to face the unexpected marriage proposal offered by a man who until this very day had been just a friend, and she never even remotely thought about the possibility of marrying Clovis. She still clung to the memory of Clifton and how death snatched him away. Her mood changed as she walked beside Clovis, a state of deep conflict. As they walked, a boy of around twelve-years old bounded out of his house and rushed to greet the passersby.

"I hope the lady and the gentleman have enjoyed their evening," he said, "and my parents wish you the same."

"Thank you, young man, you are very polite!"

Looking at him with pride, Clovis exclaimed, "It's such a pleasure to find such a respectful boy these days! Children today are so disrespectful, especially with those perverse ideas folks go around preaching. Ideas like we blacks should adopt Spanish ways."

"Are they wrong?"

"We're black, don't forget that. We have to keep our language, no matter what."

"Our language? What is our language, Clovis?"

"Well, English, of course!"

"I'm not as convinced as you about that."

"We're from Jamaica, right?"

"I was born here, Clovis!"

"You're missing the point. I was born in Jamaica and brought here when I was a boy, even so, I feel more Jamaican than you, but for me, that's not the most important part. What's really important is our race, our blood that connects us to Jamaica as her children. It's just like the Jews, who are spread all over the globe, they find unity in their race, religion, and customs."

"Clovis, hasn't it occurred to you that according to your own philosophy, we're actually African and that African 'nationality' is the only thing we can claim through our blood?"

"No, that didn't occur to me because, sorry to say, it's foolishness. We're not African, as far as our nationality is concerned, but we are by race. And we're also Jamaican with an even greater claim to that status by our birthright. Any claim we make on Africa can be easily dismissed, and all of these appeals for a nationality will eventually be handed off to the third generation. They'll be the ones who will either restore the past or create something new, following the progress of History. We've lost the right to call ourselves Africans. Slavery is over, the birthright of our race and our customs have been left behind, while at the same time our parents assumed the right to inherit the islands of the Caribbean and use the language of the race of people who conquered us. Thinking about these three generations that begin with ours, we must take another step—demand our right to self-government."

For a moment Grace forgot about the matter at hand. She thought over where she had erred in her thinking. She put her ideas before her emotions.

"So, according to you," she said with an undertone of anger, "our language, that body of violently imposed Anglo Saxon influences…"

The old man also put his ideas before his emotions and for that reason—if Clif was right—was now dying. But the truth is that nobody would ever forget, "In the land of the Ashanti, the lull of the soft breeze was broken by the fury of a thousand cannons"? Who would forget how the sand was blanketed by broken spears and how African blood spilled across the impotent shore? One would have to be ignorant, or perhaps it wasn't a problem of ignorance or even knowledge, but rather of understanding the monstrous scale of the blood they spilled, the horrible punishments inflicted on their forefathers, now all of that was lifted on high by their sons. No.

"History can be tragic, Clovis, and the expectation that we should deny our history again and again for the benefit of those who exploited us in the past and who continue to exploit us today. Well, good. Let's suppose that you're right and that I'm wrong. What would you say about people who go around preaching those ideas and telling folks that this is the 'true doctrine?'"

"What?"

"The vine, Clovis, you can't forget the vine. You've ignored that important detail. We can't bear fruit because we're no longer connected to the vine. It's been cut and we're separated and little by little we're losing our West Indian culture. Our generation, which I call the second generation, has been cut off from the vine. Our generation, and I repeat, can't bear fruit."

"We've borne fruit," Clovis replied.

"Borne fruit? Apart from sowing, reaping, and sowing again, what have we done? We have to recognize that the first generation, my father's generation, did the most difficult part because they conquered the land, and we have to admit that our generation has done relatively little in comparison to the hard work they did," Grace rebutted.

"We've kept our culture, our religion, and our language, and to be fair, we have to accept that's already quite enough."

"That all depends on your perspective. My father once told me a story about a group of women who were on their way to market to sell bammy[9] and the baskets two of the women were carrying burst open. One of them stopped and looked for a needle and twine to sew her basket so that she wouldn't lose a single piece of bammy. But, the other woman instead tied up her basket with her headscarf and started running as fast as she could. Several pieces of bammy fell on the way, but when she reached the market her customers were there waiting and it didn't take long to sell what she had left. On the other hand, Clovis, the one who stopped to fix her basket was the last to reach and when she did, the height of the market day was already done. The only good thing was that she kept all of her bammies. Do you understand my point? This is happening to us. We stopped to mend our baskets because we wanted to keep what we had, and in the process we have denied ourselves the opportunity to take possession of what the first generation fought hard for us to have, given to us not as a birthright, but through their labor and their blood."

"So where does this leave us?"

With her eyes lit with passion, Grace turned to her boyfriend to explain her argument, "What I mean to say is that it's not some kind of inheritance based on birthright, but rather through hard work and the blood that was shed in the process. But, we continue to be pig-headed, clinging to our own stupidity and the result is obvious—laziness, vice, and lack of interest in local civic affairs."

"I wouldn't make such broad statements."

New energy overtook them, separating rather than uniting them. Grace recalled her indignation, his words, and his tone of voice, "You can accuse me of exaggerating and I know there are exceptions, but the only thing our generation cares about with any seriousness is Joe Louis. We admire him because he represents something we have never been and never will be. We believe that we share the hero's glory, but instead, we magnify it—all the while, condemning our own isolation."

---

[9]Bammy—Jamaican flatbread made from cassava (yucca) flour. Traditionally it is eaten with a meal, sometimes soaked with coconut milk, milk, or water and fried before serving.

"Each one of us has courage, Grace." But she wasn't talking about that kind of courage and he knew it. Grace understood his attempt to evade what was at the heart of the matter because he didn't have any more to offer. Their differences were obvious, especially their way of thinking. He, the heir, forcing himself to hold on to tradition, but she was an heir as well. But, would she be willing to give up her heritage if it were necessary for the good of her son?

"So, Grace, you're saying that we should give up our heritage?"

"No, it's not that. What I'm saying is that we shouldn't pass on the same traditions to the next generation. We need to tear down our culture's foundation because it's rotted for the lack of life-renewing sap. We've settled for mediocrity and it has created the stagnation we find ourselves in now. It's brought about so many problems—economic, community, and social problems…"

"Social? Social problems?"

"Unemployment…"

"These social problems, Grace, we created by our own indecision."

"Yes, very well stated. Indecision, the result of …"

"Wrong ideas like yours," Clovis interrupted, "What I know for certain is that before, no one went hungry. Why?"

"Among other things, because of the good prices paid for cacao…"

Clovis interrupted Grace again, "Well, how I see things nowadays, not even good prices could solve the region's economic problems. Before, when we used to think of ourselves as Jamaican, we put in more effort when we worked the land. We never went without our daily bread. We didn't eat rice every day like now. We ate yam, yampi, dasheen and coco, breadfruit, ackee, arrowroot, and bush tea, home-made chocolate.[10] Each house extracted its own coconut oil and made yucca flour with our own hands too. When the price for cacao went up, we lived like kings. And you'd say the complete opposite when the price went down. Isn't that true? We never went hungry Grace. But then we

---

[10]These are foods found in the traditional Jamaican diet. Yam, yampi, and dasheen (taro) are tubers; coco is the meat of the coconut; breadfruit is a starchy fruit, usually roasted, boiled, or fried; ackee is a fruit, typically eaten for breakfast with prepared salted codfish; arrowroot is a starch derived from a rhizome used to make medicinal foods; bush tea is an herbal tea made from a variety of local plants and roots, typically has a medicinal purpose.

started to copy the *paña* and lose touch with those customs that were so good for us and now we eat rice and flavorless beans, sweet pepper, cauliflower and other such things and bread every day for breakfast and lunch and tortillas every so often and coffee the whole blessed day. They can be tasty, but when we eat them it only benefits the rich landowners far away in the Central Valley and we get poorer. Understand? They don't eat yam and they don't want to. And we're so stupid that we don't recognize the nutrition in our traditional diet and we run like fools to consume their products. And then, if you say this to any black person in Limón and they would respond, 'It's true.' You know? And they would continue complaining without lifting a finger to help correct the damage. Your brothers have become lazy. The majority have already lost the culture that was passed down to them and it's their own fault because they've assimilated too much of the local culture—the culture of the *cholo*,[11] condemned to live in ignorance without ever learning one single iota. Not even in the two-thirds of a century we have been living been living side-by-side, have they learned to live in houses with actual floors, they continue to live in their primitive shacks without any floor except the earth. And now, whites and blacks go to the Chinaman to buy marmalades made in San José, while wasting the thousands of guavas that lie rotting in their pastures, even looked down on by the beasts that see them as something very common, their everyday food."

"All of that is well and good, if we are going to talk about customs, I've told you my ideas, Clovis, I-D-E-A-S. Besides, I'm not talking about the *cholos*, but the people who live in the Central Valley who possess a much more refined culture that has gone beyond ours in many ways…apart from the ridiculous way they dance…"

"Have they really gone beyond us Grace? In the art of cooking, in the way we dress…"

"I repeat, Clovis, I'm referring to I-D-E-A-S."

"They just threw stones at a Protestant church in the Central Valley."

"That's understandable. They inherit that from earlier generations. My father tells me it all goes back to the Spanish Inquisition…"

---

[11]*Cholo*—a pejorative term associated with the marginalized culture and customs of Costa Rican peasants.

"That's not our way, Grace. We're not descendants of Spain, but rather Jamaica." His tone of voice was almost threatening. Clovis seemed capable of striking her to try to get his ideas to sink in with blows.

"You carry on with your Jamaica. It should be put in a museum. As far as our nationality is concerned, it's dead."

"Good heavens! What blasphemy!" The veins of his neck expanded and he stood up. Their friends had turned to look at the couple, suspecting that they had just quarreled. Clovis smiled towards them, concealing his annoyance.

The refreshing marine breeze caressed her curly hair, as it also stirred the palm trees. Grace inhaled deeply, consoling herself with the gift of the unpredictable nature of the lowlands. Two women opened their lunch baskets and started to eat. The young boy, following his father's direction, passed by announcing that he had enough fresh coconut water for everyone who wanted some refreshment. Grace inhaled the breeze again, filling her lungs with its refreshing air. She thought about Jake's friend, Largo…*Largo took his fourth trip to Jamaica, staying there for three months. He traveled the entire country, observing all the changes that had happened, and when he returned, he told stories with never-ending detail, the relative miracle of the New Jamaica. And even though he was impressed and proud of his native land, he didn't want to stay there. He emphasized that, except for the fact that all the Jamaicans still hung their clothes on the patio and on the rooftops, the cities and villages that he knew during his youth were practically unrecognizable.*

"It is no longer our little home island," he had told them, *"It's made progress and it has a future. You know what my brothers? I don't think I could live there now. I wouldn't be able to make a way."*

"The vine, Clovis, don't forget the vine. The shoots are separated from the vine and their only hope is grafting one of the pieces…," she said in a soft voice, almost without wanting to, as if it mattered that she was depriving herself of her only serious suitor. The others never spoke of marriage and that wasn't unusual since she already had a child. "Keep the good, take in the best. Those are our watchwords. We're men and women weathered by pain, by suffering, by loving our neighbor and the soil. Because we've needed to love ourselves. Our baskets have burst open and we must start running."

"That sounds like one of your fantasies from one of those women's magazine. You've got to be kidding Grace! My good friend, I want you to hear me, the black man has a future in this country."

"He can't have one if he doesn't speak the Spanish language and he won't be able to understand anyone else. A graft, Clovis, that is exactly what we need. New sap, a little bit of new sap and you'll see how much fruit we produce."

"No matter how much you tell me, it's not like that."

"Think about the advantage Clovis, imagine having two ways of seeing, one in front and the other behind. Wouldn't that be such a great advantage? So, that could be us, if we had two cultures, joined together, and united in such a way that it would allow us to see the world in perspective."

"I wouldn't raise up my son that way—it's much too dangerous. Our culture could disappear."

Yes, a meeting of ideas and with that, her heritage stood out. She was a Duke. The old man was dying. They heard a knock at the door. "My Lord," she thought, "the telegram."

She couldn't remember when Jake, Uncle Walter, and two other men climbed Mount Chirripó in search of a tiger that had ravaged the region. They were resting on an island when the river began to rise. The logical thing was to leave as soon as possible, but while they were getting ready, the river rose at an astonishing rate. It took on a khaki color, characteristic of the rivers in the lowlands, which indicated it had rained in some other part where the river had passed through.

Jake and Walter leapt into the river without thinking about the possible consequences, and as luck would have it, they reached the bank with no problem. The other two men, thanks to their physical weakness, were imprisoned on the island for no less than twenty-two days during a major storm and they would've perished if some of the Indians of the region had not helped them. So, finding herself suddenly facing Clovis's anxious face, talking about marriage and dangerous ideas, she reacted.

"Nevertheless, I still believe that the youth will end up nowhere, Clovis if they follow those ideas. And the sad truth is that many think as you do."

Grace suppressed the urge to call him an idiot, pig-headed, stubborn, mediocre, and many other things.

She continued, "We're just merely shadows Clovis, we have nothing to lose. Shadows moved by the light, moved by our resolve. There's nothing stable in us, nothing solid. We stay in the same place, clutching onto the land without ever looking to the sky. Don't you see, Clovis? That would be our first problem – the education of our children."

"Well…"

"I need to think about it Clovis."

"Yes, I understand, think about it for however long you need to. I won't rush you."

Now, sitting in Crosby's house without even having a bite to eat, she shuddered upon hearing the knock on the door. Was the old man dying or was he already dead?

Part II

Chapter Seven: Incoherence

So, while his daughter and the grandson were caught up in their own inner philosophical and emotional struggles, the old man hovered between life and death. Everything, everything present, everything completely real. The shimmering images of the past in the lowlands and the here and now, all present, superimposed one over the other; trees that fall in all directions, the machete and the ax, the strong arms of farmers, opening the virgin rainforest, giving into the civilizing impulse. It was as if a ribbon had passed before his eyes, faithfully replicating his entire history from another dimension. Would he be able to understand now the courage of his brothers back then—the positive, the negative, the absurd? The incessant and meaningless discussions of Largo and Pete McForbes.

"We almos' done!" Largo shouted.

"We just need one more day."

"An' one day is one day."

"Largo, Stop talk like you a idiot, one day is always one day."

"Not all the time. Sometime one day turn to two."

"Stop talk foolishness."

"To fools, everything seem like foolishness."

That's how it always was with Largo and Pete. They had an abundance of energy to use only when they saw fit. From work to jokes, their shallow discussions lacked common sense. Now, he no longer had that assurance. On the contrary, with each passing moment, his thoughts were less solid, less cohesive. The images flowed in never-ending succession and he was there, living it all over again, and perhaps for the last time.

Suddenly, he heard Gretel's voice. "Jake, Jake…" And it was morning, and his wife's voice, "Good morning Jake." And in the afternoon, in the silence of the farm, he heard his wife's voice with God's accent, "Jake, Jake…" And at night, as the shadows hung over the town as they had for thousands of years, he heard her voice, warm, soft, "Jake, Jake," a sublime state of delirium, a distinct dimension that when drawn in perspective, collected yesterday with all of its strength—Gretel's figure crossing the bridge over San José creek, moving rhythmically, dancing the ballet of her race. Her feet barely rested on the wooden planks, as if she were afraid to trust them beneath the weight of her body, her eyes fixed on the path… With sophisticated elegance, he supported his body with the stalk of sugarcane he was carrying and allowed her to come toward him… toward life. He loved her intensely and he now wanted her to be by his side, to share these last moments with him. Although, perhaps she was already there just like that day in church, radiant with pride, a white veil covering her eyes, calmly responding, "I, Gretel, take this man to be my lawfully wedded husband…"

"Jake, Jake…"

He needed her now. He had shared everything with her—the joy of every achievement, the pain of each failure. He now calls up all the memories of yesterday, the tragedies and the intense pain like the when they celebrated their tenth wedding anniversary and prosperity seemed to smile broadly upon them. It was October and the rainy season had not yet begun, but there was an unexpected flood.

"Jake, Jake, there go the others, over there so."

"I'm going Gret," he said and he quickly joined the others to help the elderly and the single women in town.

"Wha'appen Jake?"

"Everything's gone, the water's come in the house and reached my ankles."

"Yes, and your house in a low, low area."

"Well, that's part of the reason," Pete intervened, "But remember the prophet Jeremiah…"

"Look, Pete," Largo interrupted as usual, "leave the prophets alone."

"But the prophet…"

"We don't need no sermon now, it's time to get to work. Pete go see if that lady over there need something. I'll go over to this other house. You, brother, go see about the old man and Jake, you go to Miss Ann's house. Alright?"

"Alright Largo, but you know what…"

"Please, I beg you, gentlemen, no quarreling now," Jake pleaded.

The flow of his tears, now dry forever. His life force was waning, the light was fading, and blood started collecting in the soles of his feet. But, now he needed to think about that humid morning at Miss Ann's house, trying to get her to smile.

"How you doing Ann? How the flood treat you?"

"Alright. That's to say I kill one piece a snake I find the living room and I put out a fox with a broom, but sides that, everything alright."

"Good Lord, Ann," he sighed moving his head.

"You a laugh after me?"

"No, I'm laughing with you Ann, with you."

"With me you say? This a one funny thing, eh?"

"You laugh at life."

"I laugh with you."

"So, make we put we tears into one," they said in unison, "and make we laugh together."

Your life's full of bramble
My world is full of pain;
So, make we put we tears into one, and make we laugh together

"Lord, Ann! This is no time to laugh, right?" In spite of it all, they always had the courage to laugh and dance in the midst of any adversity they faced. But now, Jake found himself lacking that type of courage because at that moment he had the nerve to say to Ann what everybody already knew.

"We've lost our bread and butter."

"Yes, yes," she sighed, "that don't even begin to tell the story."

They remained silent. Together their hearts beat the anguished rhythm of their tragedy, which expanded into the cold morning and undercut their stubborn perseverance.

"You want something from town?"

"Just some kerosene," she responded sadly. Jake thought she was going to cry.

"You sure? Alright. It treated you pretty bad?"

"I'm ruined, with capital letter."

Again, they were silent. Their hearts constricted by the overwhelming sorrow, words couldn't express their feelings.

"I think I'm going to leave Jake."

"Leave! Why does everyone want to leave?" The question seemed like logical one until now. But now that it had been openly asked, sounded cruel to him.

"Jake, you think what happen to us was a small thing?"

"We're not cowards, Ann. We're people weathered by difficulties. We have to face this trial and overcome it."

"This is something that hardly happen. Think bout it, Jake. A flood in broad daylight. Just imagine what that mean. Three day of sunshine, the all of a sudden …. bluuff! Everything under water…livestock drown, all the harvest gone, things in storage, even the things in the house, gone. Flood take them all. And the pickney, Lawd Jesus![12] I think bout them just open all the time to all manner of danger. Whatever which day, when we least expect it…. bluuff!"

"But Ann, we've played this hand for too long to just pick up and leave now. We've struggled against all these trials and tribulations for all these years, we've made this a place we can live. We've gone too far to abandon it, let alone for us to just go without even putting up a fight."

"Jake!" Largo called from the railroad tracks, "What you doing to Miss Ann?"

"See you later Ann, we'll talk later."

"Yes, come when you ready and we talk. Tell everybody at your place hello for me."

Then came the plea. The Chinese shop owner had charged twenty or thirty percent more than usual and the villagers were powerless. The local political chief was indifferent to everything that happened because according to him the Chinaman followed all the sacrosanct capitalist laws of supply and demand. The brutality of capitalism was far from being upended, yet there remained prayers to the God of Consolation and the collective pain shared in love. Unquestioning

---

[12]Pickney—Jamaican and Limonese Creole English word for "child" or "children." May be a derivation of the Spanish word, *pequeño*, which means "small" or "little one."

blind faith, the Promise made once and forever, and God, the same God of the Promise, powerless. Powerless? God powerless? And the reward of eternal life. Powerless? Or, perhaps, ensnared by his own laws; liberty versus justice; and evil, relative to all good, relative to all virtues, even evil, is it a necessary good? There were innumerable sufferings present along the road; the cadavers of almost all the townspeople's livestock, wild and domestic animals, all of them joined and buried in a common pit, enriching the earth along with sweat, rain, and blistered fingers. Mr. John's stiff fingers served up cold meals and there came more graves and more burials and more pain and more ruin. But the nighttime was a bundle of delight. Cinnamon water, heated on an improvised stove tasted like glory. Also, the pleasant taste of fat pieces of dasheen, cooked in coconut cream, a delicious homemade rundown.[13]

He wanted to say, "Ah, my blessed Gret. I need you now." And now, the hunger…the terrible hunger. Death, gradually coming closer, short breaths, blood betraying the hands and the feet terribly swollen, the cramping…

"Miss, Miss," cried a masculine voice.

"Yes, what is it?"

"That man is gasping for air."

"Which one?"

"The black man."

"Just a moment, I'm coming."

"But Miss, he's suffocating."

His chest uncontrollably raised and lowered, its usual rhythm, absent. An intense pain traversed his body, and then, he felt nothing. It was as if he were free from his mortal flesh. From a distance, he heard voices, barely audible voices. He heard them for what seemed like a fraction of a second and later he stopped hearing them. Even though time had seemed so brief, he was perfectly aware of what was happening.

---

[13]Rundown, also called rundung or *rondón*, is a Jamaican stew typically with fish or seafood with coconut milk, tubers, aromatic vegetables, and seasonings.

"Miss, this poor black man is suffocating."

"I'm coming, can't you see I'm busy?"

Jake noticed what kept her so busy. She was looking for the last word to complete her crossword puzzle. The complaints of the other patients forced her to respond. The nurse walked to Jake's bed with a look of disgust. She stopped in front of the dying man trying to overcome her annoyance. Her skin turned pale and she called a coworker for help. Someone said that they should call the doctor in case of emergency…

"Gret, Gret, where are you? Your hair has been silvered by the passage of the years, your face has become, weathered by the innumerable hardships, your trembling hands, serving me mint tea and white bread without butter."

"Grace eat yet?"

"No, poor thing. She said she wanted to wait for you, but she fell asleep."

"You're not going to wake her up?"

"No, she wouldn't want me to."

He took a sip of the tea and smiled with satisfaction. He let a few moments pass by and then, building up courage threw out the big question:

"Gret…do you want to leave?"

"Leave?'

"Yes, head back to Jamaica."

"Have you grown weary of me?"

"No woman, stop the foolishness. What have you done for me to grow weary of you? I'm trying to tell you is that the flood has left us in ruins. We have enough to leave and go back home I have the farm that my grandmother left me. It wouldn't be difficult to…"

"Jake, I don't want to leave. But if you want, we'll do what you say. You know me."

"It's not that, woman. I want you to be happy."

"Oh, in that case, leave me here."

"But the plans we made in our youth were always that we'd go back someday."

"And what about your sweat Jake? The blood you spilled so many times. The many wounds I cured with so much devotion. My God, you put your whole life into this land…"

"Any moment the government could take it away and that's it."

"No, Jake, you know very well that's not going to happen."

"They can do it if they want to."

"And why would they want to? Nobody could put up with this land besides us. If they could have done it, we would have gone back to Jamaica a long time ago."

"Gretel, think about Grace…"

"She's studying Spanish. She already knows enough, so she won't be left dragging behind."

"And our bones, Gret?"

"Let them be part of our offering! Maybe with all our sacrifice and effort it's cost us, we've earned the right to the land for our children."

"Gretel… Gretel," he said with solemnity, *"Blessed are all those years from the moment I met you!"*

He recognized nature's songs, toads and crickets, voices multiplying with the progression of time, voices of human history. The images all flow, flow in prolonged succession, the metamorphosis of time. And it couldn't be explained how it all had been so foolish, since he didn't have enough courage to abandon the land, having loved her to the extreme point of forsaking the relative security that they would have attained for their golden years by just returning to his never forgotten St. James. And all of it was because of his heart—his ungrateful heart that finally learned to love. That moment triggered memories of his childhood. The multifaceted figure of his father Jonas rocking him in the swing built by his incessant boyhood pleas and the image of himself as a child, happily kicking his feet. He wanted to transform that moment with his father into an eternity. Gleefully, Jake went up and down in the swing, wanting to forget the assignment that was imposed upon him when he was ten years old, to stay with his grandmother after the death of the Scotsman. After all, she had Walter. Once before, Jake attempted to return to the protection of his parents' home. He moved away and they set him up again in his old room. They couldn't hide their delight. But after a few days, he went to visit his grandmother and found her depressed, perilously depressed, as if she had given up on life. Later he spoke about it with Walter.

"You leaving is the reason she's that way, even though she would never admit it."

"But Walter, you're there."

"I'm fed up."

"With her?"

"No man, never of her! I'm sick and tired of my boredom and loneliness. I don't know why you're so happy."

He didn't say it, but he had his father. Jonas with all his cowardice, Jonas with all his hypocrisy with the white folks, Jake had him and his intense love.

Not finding another solution, he returned to his grandmother's house. A week later, the old woman was as alive as ever. Once again, he faced a dilemma—the struggle between loyalty to the old woman and his brother who both needed him and the daily affection of his parents. Each of them had adopted an entirely passive attitude, leaving the decision up to him.

Jonas sang one of his favorite melodies:

Pass de ball and de ball gawn roun'
Jigga Nanny show me how de ball gawn roun'[14]

Then he was in the hospital again, not in his mind, but in reality. The very essence of his being was moving in time without the limits of space—everything lived, everything real, everything present. They adjusted the apparatus on his nose and now breathing was less difficult. He felt something hot on his chest, but he couldn't tell what it was. He couldn't even move his head to glance at the nurse that the other patient had to beg earlier to attend to him—he would've enjoyed seeing her. Near the window, three physicians consulted one another with noticeable interest, looking his way every so often.

"Doctor," said a trembling voice, "he's back to himself."

---

[14]From the Jamaican folk song "Ball gawn roun'" sung to accompany a children's circle game where children pass the ball from one to another behind their backs and one child who is "Jigga Nanny" has to find the person holding the ball. For more detail on this folk song, see Jim Morse, *Folk songs of the Caribbean* (Bantam Books, 1958) and Tom Murray, ed. *Folk songs of Jamaica* (Oxford, 1952).

The doctors drew near. Among them was a female physician and Jake thought she was much too young to be involved in medicine. They began to examine him. It was clear that they did a thorough exam and Jake was pleased with that, although he thought in the end that it was all pointless, but then again, he wouldn't want it any other way. The male doctors entertained themselves by looking at the young female doctor, which seemed to him ridiculous given their ages and the setting, but an innocent glance at the young woman with olive skin, large eyes like those of his daughter, slender hands, serene and benevolent smile, made a favorable impression on him. Something inside him seemed to say that he knew her somehow, in some intangible way. After the exam, one of the physicians approached him and said in perfect English, "How do you feel old man?"

"More or less."

"How do you feel old man?" He repeated the question as if he had not heard the reply, "Better?"

"More or less."

"That's strange," said one of the nurses, "his eyes light up when you speak, but he's not responding."

"Of course, I hear you!" Jake shouted, "I hear you and I'm speaking!"

But everything remained the same.

"What's wrong with you?!" Jake shouted again, "Can't you hear me!"

The expressions on their faces changed slightly. He had a feeling that a new series of exams and tests were about to come and he tightly closed his eyes. "Go on with your problems," he heard himself saying, "I won't be here."

For the last time, he thought about Clif, the grandson that he sent out into the world to embrace his native land. The same land that had never decided whether it wanted black people or not. Once when he visited San José, the same city where he was now dying, and that curiously seemed uneasy. He remembered his steps through the capital city's streets and his urge to attend to a physiological need. He knocked on a door. "There's no toilet here." He knocked on another door. "I can't let you use it nigger, you'll frighten the children." In the last house, before the door had even shut, he managed to see a white robe.

He kept walking. The urge was even greater and he broke out in a cold sweat. Finally, he regained his nerve. His eyes were in great pain and half his body threatened to explode. He knocked on another door. "No, no, I'm very sorry." Two boys who were playing in the patio fled behind the house. "Hey, darkie … go to the police barracks. You know where it is? I'll give you the address." But his animal condition took over. Reason was severed or suspended, the brotherly body of all things, and on brothers weigh relentless laws. Then he saw an empty lot… As he was leaving, the police and neighborhood residents were waiting for him. Now nothing stood in the way of his arrival at the barracks. The officer had studied in Europe and knew English. Playing with his moustache, he said to Jake, "I understand your situation perfectly, but you must understand mine. Outside there's a bunch of simple people who believe that blacks are dirty. We have to find some way to fix this." He stands up and approaches a painting hanging on the wall. "Do you know him?" he asks. "It's the President!"

"I've seen his photo."

"We have to find some way to take care of this for you. I don't want to put you in jail." He bangs his fist against the wall and abruptly returns to his desk. "I've got it!" he says, "I've got a solution! Pay the fine that you would've had to pay anyway, then I will order them to give you a shovel and you'll go bury it. From there continue on to the train station and the matter is settled."

Fine or a bribe. Jake complied with the three parts of his humiliating sentence. And still years later at the hour of his death, he had no qualms about asking his grandson to integrate into this culture, all the while knowing how difficult it is to change a narcissistic society. He thought about Clif for the last time and closed his eyes.

Chapter Eight: The Question

The funeral cortege peacefully entered the burial ground. Family, friends, and other members of the procession lined up slowly, shielding themselves from the sun with umbrellas and parasols. As the coffin was placed into the grave, the Anglican minister gestured the end of the ceremony. A hymn burst forth from the silence.

One of the mourners, crying inconsolably with their belated regret, laid across the casket. Then the minister reached the end of his message—a voice that speaks from heaven, a hand that writes on the earth: Blessed are those who die in the Lord that they may rest from their labor. The town of Estrada was quiet for a moment. The world was quiet for a moment. Time was suspended—Grace's face and Walter's face and Gretel's face and … alright, alright. Clif squeezed the telegram between his hands, looking at his mother's stoic resignation. He subtlety opened it to reread it, the words written by some anonymous hand, and then he saw his grandfather's words:

"Are you Costa Rican? Are you really? That is the question you must answer, Clif that is the question you must answer now."

The boy repeated between his teeth, "Alright, alright, alright…"

Chapter Nine: Brutus

I remember one time my wife asked me how did my grandfather die, and I dryly responded, he didn't die, they killed him. Maybe that's the reason I've come back here, the real motive for my return. That also explains the pistol I have in my possession. But those reasons will never justify, no matter how many times I return, the fact that I've brought my family here. No.

Three hundred eighty days before grandfather's dying moments, the sun was hot enough to dry our bones with unyielding fury. The humidity was suffocating. Four respectable gentlemen of the town walked along the plank-covered footpath. Jake Duke, the church steward, Pete McForbes, the lead usher, Howard Bowman, an honorable official of the lodge, and Clovis Lince, a young and prominent local farmer. They were summoned to a solemn meeting by a venerable church Mother, a sister in faith and in the struggle.

"Welcome brothers, come in."

"How's the old lady doing today? You looking good."

"Your eyes deceive you, my dear friend. How is it that men can be so dim-witted? Have a seat, help yourselves, gentlemen."

"Don't worry yourself over us, we'll just follow along. You feeling better?"

"No, not at all, I don't have any other choice. No, there isn't always a cure, there are such things as incurable illnesses." There was a tense silence in which no one dared to respond. She had spoken with such conviction, with an assertiveness that they had never heard before. She then said:

"Gentlemen, I have called you here because I will be leaving you pretty soon. My life is getting shorter, brothers."

"But if you…"

"Please brother, I'm the one who called this meeting. The reason is this, I have no heirs. I want you to take charge of my possessions and the money I have in the bank. I intend to leave it in the names of the four of you so that you may serve as my trustees. I will leave a portion for the school, another portion so that you can prepare a nice grave for me and for the other burial expenses, and, if there is anything left over you may divide it amongst yourselves as payment for your selflessness. Gentlemen, are we in agreement?"

"Sister, you don't have to ask that. We're here to help one another."

Jake Duke was designated the president of the committee. Looking back at that moment as a child, I thought that he never should've accepted, but I also asked myself how would he have known what was about to occur. The elderly woman was loved by all and died at her appointed time. She had a beautiful death surrounded by songs of faith and hope. A smile covered her face and her last words spoke of indescribable wonders. They faithfully followed her wishes, but then, one night, one of the four men murmured between drinks and among friends that Jake had pocketed a portion of the dead woman's money. That was the fatal blow. He had been able to withstand the severity of the land, the fluctuations of the cacao market, and his own failures, but he always kept his good name. He never took anything that didn't belong to him, and he believed, as he would declare without beating around the bush that a man owns nothing but his destiny, that he's only a steward of the land and its fruits. The tragedy of waking up one morning and discovering that at seventy-something years old that your good name had been dragged through the mud, though not completely ruined, but disgraced nonetheless by one of his best friends. It was too much for his heart to bear. Howard Bowman became Judas, forgiven for his guilt, but not free from his responsibilities to restore the integrity of the name he besmirched and to reinstate the loss that Jake's bereaved relatives were going to suffer. Because even though death is inevitable, no one doubted that the old man, tired of this world, would hasten her arrival.

And I knew other things that grandfather ignored. One Sunday morning the committee, organized by the old woman, met with the church ushers without Jake to discuss ways to end the ugly rumor that had spread throughout the town. Someone accidentally left the door open, which allowed me to overhear part of their conversation.

"I say this, gentlemen, our brother, who is here with us today, insists that Jake took some of the money. We should believe his word."

"That's not right," Pete protested, "you can't condemn a man without letting him defend himself. Let's call Jake."

"He's told us that he has nothing to explain."

"That's true. But if we ask him on behalf of the church for a report…"

"We have to be tough with this type of thing because it can damage the reputation of the church."

"Jake committed an error, we have to…Brother, do me the favor and close that door…"

The old man never found out about that other part, at least not from my mouth because I thought he already knew, or maybe it would've been more than he could bear. Suddenly, they all forgot about the twenty years of service to the Community Council, fifty years of friendship and struggle, and a name that he kept immaculate for so many years. With more than enough evidence to prove his integrity, Jake was now defamed in such a devastating way. That's why I say, in reality, my grandfather didn't die, they killed him. When someone lives for his sense of honor, it's his reputation that keeps him going…when his interest in the world depends so much on the miracle of having created a name for himself and his family, you work yourself into the ground to make the unreliable source that shaped public opinion disappear. That source was Howard Bowman. Maybe no one knew that it was a question of jealousy. They all saw him as a grandfather and lifted him up out of disgrace, liberating him from the dark myths surrounding him. He was presented before the eyes of the village, which covered him with his very own corona, and that was enough for him to first gain the people's absolution and later, respectability. The role of Judas belonged to Bowman. He played it with frightening coldness, striking his friend in the place where it would hurt the most, "Even you, Brutus." Even him.

My wife glanced at me with a faint hue of suspicion drawn across her face. I accuse Howard Bowman of murder, with the complicity of others in town. Their blindness allowed false information to spread, which brought on the old man's death. They never understood that the only lasting glory is that which comes from righteousness. Treading on the backs of others may only soothe a temporary desire, or it may lead to a road that follows the ancient law of reparation and righteousness. Maybe that's the dilemma. Now, we're home. I have my pistol. I have pen and paper. My family will not experience hardship—except for the usual events of rural life. And, above all, I will rely on the sworn resolve of the river banks. And I return with the unstoppable assurance of all of the Jakes, Walters, Bullets, and Bugles… Grandfather's resounding words remain present, the ones he pronounced with such solemnity the morning I left Estrada.

"Clif, you're black. That doesn't make you superior or inferior to others; it simply makes you the heir to thousands of years of persecution, and because of that you will experience things that you may not understand. And although we black folks aren't one people—the Europeans aren't either—there's something particular that makes us out of many peoples, one. Something particular Clif. It's something that goes much deeper than skin. We are weathered men Clif, that's the matter at hand. Weathered by pain and suffering. Weathered peoples are…they're more profound. But Clif, before you are black, you're a man. Beware of hate."

Chapter Ten: In the Beginning

I am standing in front of the window. Life goes on, the same as always. Maybe it's been that way since the beginning—the torrential rains create swamps and the verdant green of the lowlands, the mosquitoes' sting, the faint groans of a monkey, the beasts loaded down with enormous sacks of cacao returning to the farms, plodding through the thick mud, while their backs are covered with calloused skin, the battle-hardened farmers walk behind the animals, declaring in silence their eternal message that everything will go back to being as it was, back to the glory of bygone days, while I, and all the young people, watch them lose ground in the struggle against adversity, without the help of the government promised long ago, and the now worthless hope of better prices and better harvests. I watched and thought about all of this from the window. The timeless echo of grandfather's voice came back from the forgotten grave, like a blood-red light emanating from yesterday and tomorrow. I, Clif Duke, descendant of Jamaicans, but that doesn't make me Jamaican. It's not through some sense of pity nor through the charity of some benefactor, but as a right, earned, not by me or those of my generation, but rather by the elders who came before us, the second generation together with the first. Because there's nothing shameful about our arrival to this country. We came freely, not to be exploited, but to work the land, the hostile land—empire of the Reventazón River and of Mount Chirripó, virgin and savage, free and violent, only inhabited by a few mestizos or Indians with a very primitive culture. They allowed the land to control them and were not masters of it, as humans should be. Because when God created the world, he instructed humans to be stewards of the land and to have command over the natural world. The vast lowlands were beyond the physical strength of the inhabitants of the Central Valley, and if it had been up to them, this region would have remained uncivilized. Only the black people could withstand this place. The presence of a people weathered by pain and whose bodies were tried by fire, resistant to the inclemency of Mother Nature, and capable of the intense work necessary to dominate the lowlands and in the process, rescue a piece of it for themselves.

"But why grandfather, why? Why does the sun shine? Why does the land bring the harvest? Why does the rain fall on both the good and the bad?... And didn't the blacks die?"

Grandfather let out a sigh when I asked him that. It was the core of his argument. Blood gives rights. To him, the sacrifice black people made was worth more than any dollar amount one could possibly pay. The land needed them and she beckoned them to come. He seemed immersed in the past, almost absent when he began to tell his story. And he said:

"One afternoon just like a million other afternoons, the men had finished their work for the day and returned home, walking lazy-like along the path. A few small hand-powered rail cars were waiting about five hundred yards or so to take them back to camp. After they reached the vehicles, they drove them toward camp. On the two sides of the railway, the immense green jungle rose up like walls. They never noticed that the bridge had collapsed ahead of them until the first car let loose from the rails and sank to the bottom of the river. The men in the next car had just enough time to jump from the vehicle before it met the same fate, but the eight of them in the first car, all went down with it. Bugle was the only one to survive, but he was blinded by the blow he took to his head."

"The blacks didn't die?"

He was transfigured, elevated to the sublime. His eyes glimmered and the light forcefully radiated. And he spoke of the freshness of the morning, of the gentle wind, and of the vigorous torment of men...

"They chopped the forest in that area with particular force. They had been working for four weeks without pay because the government didn't have the money to pay them. But, one morning news reached that the paymaster was coming later that day and their energy returned. One of the foremen walked up to the British engineer to tell him of the danger one of his men faced. It looked like a tall tree was about to fall down because the cord holding it up was about to break. But the engineer gave a distant glance and said with surprising coldness, 'The cord will hold up, go on.' And he mentioned in passing about how proud he was of the crew this morning, but to him, they were things that he could easily replace if one failed, he would simply get another just like the first. All this to say, there was one frightened worker standing under the tree."

"The blacks didn't die?"

I sometimes wondered if the things my grandfather said in his stories really happened. In truth, they were profound, wise, and vibrant. The way he would bring to life the cruel and merciless force of the fever that wasted men's bodies, of the rigid hands that while pointing to the horizon, framed lips that were petrified in their vain final words. The world gradually falls away, little by little illusions become like ashes, along with the deathbed, trampled on by those who watch over his agony. In a distant, very distant village, a mother waits, a bride waits, and children hold onto the hope of returning to the everyday presence of their father at breakfast. They will wait for him forever. Their savings taken by someone and minute by minute his lips become drier. The word gets stuck in his teeth and not even a prayer, mumbled at the last minute, could come out, not even the last plea for water could save him from the inevitable, and black hands with white palms closed his eyes for eternity. It had to be this way—the anguish, the pain, the widows, the orphans.

"In spite of all of this," I told him, overwhelmed, "they kept on fighting, grandfather, like they were going to receive some great reward and they had no idea what would happen. They were dazed by the hostility of the zone and isolated from the West Indies, just like my mother says very well, 'They conquered the land, but they lost their culture and today have none.'"

"They were not intellectuals," he responded to me, "the well-educated stayed in Jamaica. They had no need to leave. The common laborers and farmers came; those of us with some schooling, almost came here by accident. And of course, we had more learning than the *cholo*, but by no means the best example of West Indian culture."

"And grandfather, this is according to what value system? Apart from polished floors and…"

"Polished floors, if you want to talk about that. The *cholos* did have dirt floors. But we had our way of dressing, we prepared a better and greater variety of food, and we had Christian customs like saying grace before each meal, reading the Bible, and prayer. All of this is the opposite of their way of shouting over the table during meals, reciting prayers, and the belief that you get salvation by paying for masses and the like."

"But you're not counting the people in the Central Valley."

"What about them? Not able to handle the climate because of their culture…"

"Because of their culture?"

"Yes, because of their culture and some other things. Our culture teaches us about 'bush medicine,' how to use certain herbs to protect us against almost all manner a disease, or at least help us survive."

"And in spite of all the bad experiences you faced, you came here to honor your work contract and then stayed to farm the land. You stayed here, but we don't have a country."

"Don't have a country! It wasn't the well-educated men who came here—you have to keep that in mind—so, because of that it took them longer to get use to this place, besides they planned to return home as big men and that created a certain mentality. But you can't deny the value of the blood that was spilled, and the bones, and the sweat, and even the tears nourished the land just like the manure spread over the fields. Besides, the law or decree or whatever you call it that you showed me once before was something they approved. They signed the contract with their total consent and then the government added later that we couldn't live outside of our designated zone."[15]

"And that, for what?"

"Fear. The young people always break down the barriers of prejudice and end up really loving each other when they're allowed to be free, especially when they grow up together. Think about it, we were much more athletic than they were and black women with their skills as homemakers and their legendary good looks posed a threat to the high and mighty 'Spanish purity' that they always like to show off about, as if Spain were…Anyway, it's fear son. The accusations about the threat of black labor was just the official excuse because we plainly showed them that we worked hard in this part of the country and we went beyond

---

[15]This is a reference to the agreement reached in 1934 between the Costa Rican government and the United Fruit Company that prohibited Afro-West Indian workers in Limón from seeking work in the company's banana plantations on the Pacific coast. This was seen as a measure to protect national labor interests.

what the peasants in the highlands could do. Some of us turned land-owners. All of us put our muscle into our parcels of land. We civilized this region, and in turn, made it easier for that so-called pure race that couldn't withstand malaria or mosquito bites."

"But, what about my friends…"

"This land also belongs to you. It's is not mine, just like it never belonged to the Spanish people, and even so, their descendants fully claim ownership, not so they can fence it off with barbed wire, but so that it can be shared just like the light of the sun. We conquered the land and we must hand it down to our grandchildren to be continuously passed from one generation to the next…"

"But…"

"The land once belonged to the Indians and they lost it in a one-sided struggle. It was taken by violent force and the claim of ownership was passed down to the descendants of the conquerors who under the authority of their own laws, discriminated against those who once held the land. As you well know, if the law is to be just, it must be impartial so that it can help us make our claim to the land that we wrested from its primitive state so that we may be able to pass it on to our descendants. You will take possession of it, knowing that it came from our sacrifice and labor, and that if some blood was spilled, that blood was ours. Take it in the same spirit as the sun, so that all may justly share it."

I filled my lungs and thought to myself, "My grandfather is racist." That struggle was inside me, reaching the very depths of my being. Yes or no. It was "no." Something trembled, vibrated, imperceptibly pursuing me. All at once, I felt rage, pain, pride. All at the same time.

"But grandfather," I tried desperately to defend my own myths—the ones I had learned in the classroom—against my grandfather's.

"You were…they paid you…"

"They paid us for what?"

"To build the railroad."

My grandfather took a long pause, forcing me to think about the reach of my own words. He slowly added, emphasizing the first two words he uttered:

"After Keith thought it was a good idea to plant bananas, we all started to plant them and it was good business. And I say it again, all with the approval of the government and the Costa Rican people. From the past several decades up to now, we have farmed this land, and it's not that we didn't think about going back home, but it was God's plan for us to work the land for our children and grandchildren."

"But Mummy says that many hid their pickney so that they wouldn't go to Spanish school."

"Many did, but not all. You must understand that we had to hold onto our West Indian culture if we were going back home. Language was the key that would open the door to eventual integration and what we knew of this country's culture was not very attractive, especially looking at how the *cholos* lived. Our attitude shouldn't be thought of as racist or as hatred, but it was simply a precaution. What would have happened to our pickney in Jamaica with Latin culture? They wouldn't have been able to adapt and settle back into life in Jamaica."

I stood there thinking while grandfather played with his wiry beard. The old man stared at me with a look of compassion.

"You never noticed how everything here is temporary? You can see it just by paying attention to our houses and our customs."

I knew what he was saying was true, I had inherited it. The Spanish teacher fought almost daily against that tendency of my generation.

"So Clif, you're Costa Rican. Jamaica is the land of your forebears and you should love it as such."

"The land of my forebears…so, am I Costa Rican?"

Part III

Chapter Eleven: The Conquest

When they got back to the village, they traveled alongside the river as it peacefully flowed in company with the advancing train. Yet it was still wild and every so often, the tranquil flow of the river was interrupted by retaining walls that shielded the tracks from the overflowing water.

Clif lifted his gaze to look at the other side of the river basin. The afternoon created harmonious shades of blue and white. His wife's warm hand held his, her soft, curly hair sought comfort in his chest while his older son slept in the other seat. While in his own placid dream, the afternoon gave way to enchantment.

"How beautiful, Clif, how beautiful!"

Below, white foam welcomed the passing of the train and the machine returned the greeting with puffs of black smoke. Above, the clouds danced in the breeze with the agility of ballerinas, the Ballet of the Universe. Clif looked again at his wife to take in the tranquility of her eyes.

"Yes," he said, "it's very beautiful."

"Of course, there are other beautiful landscapes…"

"But, this one's ours."

"Yes, Clif…it's ours."

The locomotive shrieked as it passed through the virgin jungle. Clif went back to looking out of the window and on the other side, he first spied the road he had traveled across many times, now flanked by telephone lines. He then made out the slopes of the mountains in the distance. The enormous basin of Deep Gorge, heavy with blue mist, submerged between both banks.

"Clif…tell me what was your life like during your first years in San José."

"Ahh, why should I remember that?"

"I'd like to know."

"There's not much to tell."

His first timid steps through the streets of the city remained buried by the passage of time. Voices on the corners were chanting, "Big lipped, smelly nigger," and between pinches wishing each other, "good luck for me and not for you," with the double sin of superstition and egotism.[16] The never-ending streets were conquered day by day with trepidation. Even blacks themselves crossed to the opposite side of the street to avoid encountering one another in the desperate struggle to pass unnoticed. "Mommy, it looks like it's going to rain," followed by the contagious and resonant laughter that infected faces like a germ, as well as the "Heló may fren," loaded with double meaning and cruelty.

A mother teaches her children the same ignorance that she had learned from her mother, "Blacks don't comb their hair; blacks don't bathe." And the poor little black girl who grew up among nuns who never combed her hair and never had her hair combed by someone else, was frightened to see the black women of Limón combing their hair. As if that weren't enough, the chorus of children and the much worse chorus of adults, shouting "Black SOB" without cause, without motive.

The troubadour at the festival in Plaza Víquez sang:
"Ay, ay, ay what a funny story
As you will see
Here come the niggers
With the monkeys from Bataan"
And so, laughter erupts among those in attendance and the stares, thousands of eyes focus on him, and the sweat, and the angst, and the pain of rejection—being there, knowing that he's part of a society that didn't accept him, and yet he couldn't run away. He thought about the never-ending walks through the city's neighborhoods, looking for a room, the glee of the people, young and old, congregating in hallways, curious to see him.

"Laugh, laugh, laugh nigger, laugh!"
"Sing, sing, sing nigger, sing!"
"Dance, dance, dance monkey, dance!"

---

[16]Pinches—Reference to the mid-twentieth-century folk practice in Costa Rica of pinching something or someone new in hopes of receiving good luck. Blacks traveling from Limón to San José and other areas of the Central Valley were sometimes subjected to the pinches of strangers as they made their way around cities and towns.

The face of a horrible old woman diplomatically responding, "We already rented it," and the sign that was there before he inquired, was there again, and remained there for a week, and later, much later they took it down.

"Ah," Clif sighed, "there's not much to tell."

There wasn't much to tell. The shop manager harassed him—go buy this, leave that, do this other thing—and in the meantime his goal to learn a profession evaporated. Finally, one day he reached his limit and resigned to take a different job. He had to go on with the weight of destiny on his shoulders.

"That was a good job," his wife observed, "why didn't you stay there?"

"Why didn't I stay there? My love, do I have to tell you everything?" She sighed, pleased after hearing the magic word that humanity has believed in throughout the centuries, even in the midst of the worst moments.

"Yes, love," she responded softly, "I want to know everything."

He bore the chains of his own limitations, weighed down by his past errors that demanded an adequate solution, but were imprisoned by his powerlessness. He went up the stairs that led to the manager's office. He had a premonition about the cost of his integrity, but the truth was a cluster of venom had lodged inside him and he had to release it. Even though he was aware of his powerlessness, he decided that the least he could do was try. So, he carried his broken limitations on his skin as if they were dreadful antibodies that infiltrated his pores and seeped into his veins. Sweat ran freely down his forehead, stinging his eyes. An intense headache came over him and his temples burned like embers.

"I will never forget the manager's viciousness when I condemned the wrongdoings I witnessed. I have no hard feelings, but that man represents a social cancer that we must root out."

He's not sure how he managed to walk down those stairs, dragging the weight of his powerlessness—the weight of being a black adolescent male—and he went out into the cold street. She will have to imagine the pharmacist's face reddened with anger. The tone of his voice, the hate in his eyes.

"So what," his shameless cynicism, "Didn't it cross your mind that perhaps all of the hospitals in the country don't do things the same way?"

"I don't know nothing about that and I don't care," spoke the boy's bravery, "what I'm asking myself is, how many children died after injecting distilled water instead of the medicine that was prescribed? Besides being thieves, you're murderers."

"Cowardly nigger, watch your words or else I'm going to throw you out."

"There's no need to do that Rafa Ofebre, I'll leave on my own."

"You're going to pay for this."

"You can't come after us all. It's just not right."

At the time, he didn't think about his children, nor did he think about his mother. He thought only about social justice. The manager asked them both for their resignations.

"But your co-workers," she said with uncontainable indignation. She only believed it because Clif told her. If it had come from any other source, she wouldn't have believed it was true.

"Those who weren't involved in the scheme were looking out for themselves and their livelihoods."

And after that, he looked for work, and looked, and looked. For every job, there were forty applicants. One day above all the rest, he really counted on the certainty of getting himself a job. A good friend had recommended him and Don Tancredo said, "Come back tomorrow." Thinking about the importance of that meeting, he walked to Central Park, avoiding the northeast corner so he wouldn't have to deal with one of the shoeshine boys in the syndicate. He hoped one of the unaffiliated kids would pass by on the eastern side of the park. The plan worked and within a few minutes a young boy, barely six years old came by to offer his services.

"Should I clean you up, darkie?"

"No, I already took a bath, but if you want, you can shine my shoes."

"Pssss!"

"How much?"

"Well…a quarter!"

"Alright, shine them up for me."

The clock on the cathedral never had the correct time and showed a quarter past the hour. Without knowing why, he thought about the news broadcasts that were always wrong two out of every three occasions when giving the time, but especially during the moments of greatest haste, and sometimes they don't even bother to correct it. Time was one of the great problems of this country, for good or bad, no one had learned the value of being punctual. But he would be. The boy struck the box, and as expected, Clif lowered one foot and raised the other one. The old pendulum of the Cathedral clock, far from his thoughts, continued its monotonous mania. Three minutes had gone by.

"Hurry up…I have to go."

"Yeah, I'm finishing…"

He stopped at an open window and ordered two packets of chewing gum and a box of mints. He picked up his change, ignoring the friendly smile of the girl who waited on him, and he carefully placed the coins in his jacket pocket. Those were his last twenty-five cents—and he kept on walking.

There had been better times. In days of sun and rain, in spite of all of it all—the annoyances, the heartache—he knew there were better times. He walked down the main street. He was forced to stop on the corner by a passing cart. One minute later, he was in front of the Northern Hotel and he armed himself with courage. He walked through the glass door that opened with the least amount of resistance and entered the elegant foyer. Without hesitating, he confidently stepped up to the reception desk.

"Don Tancredo will speak with you in a moment. Have a seat."

Two elderly women passed by, studying him. They whispered a few words and both smiled.

"Mr. Duke?"

"Yes, Sir. At your service."

"Thank you. Please, have a seat. How is it going?"

"Quite well, I would say quite well."

"Guillermo was here and he came to see if I could give you a job."

"And?"

"Unfortunately, we can't do anything for you."

"But…"

"I explained it to him. I should've let you know from the start."

"Let me know?"

"Yes, the hotel regulations…"

There was a certain tone of guilt in his voice. The glass door opened once again and an unidentified man entered the lobby. Don Tancredo rose to his feet. He was visibly worried, bothered by the crude reality that faced him. Stronger than his will, more sovereign than the laws of the country, the imposition of foreign interests and customs wounded him in the most precious corner of his national identity. But Don Tancredo swallowed his impotence in order to keep his salary in dollars. He swallowed fear and with it, he behaved with cowardice and weakness. And with that, he also honored the hotel's regulations.

"Duke, I..."

The street became cold, it lost the romantic hue that I had painted it with. A bus passed by, puffing out a trail of smoke that vanished in the wind, while it zigzagged down the hill. "Chinese and whites," I thought many times, "in my own country, Chinese and whites, and never 'citizens of the black race." Nothing was left for me, understand? The promises of the revolution had been forgotten and the blood of the fallen was betrayed in the most despicable way. And we, being naïve, were deceived once again."

His wife kissed him on the cheek, struggling to hold back tears. She imagined him standing on the corner, looking at the exterior of one of those elegant buildings in the city center, seeing in them the imprint of human pain, similar to her own anguish. Because God gave man hands to create, someone made his daily bread through the intricate corrugated ironwork. He was still just an adolescent. They would cut off the lights, disconnect the water. He would have to abandon his studies while he continued looking for work from one neighborhood to the next in his worn-out shoes. Every once in a while, a friend would give him a few pesos. But no one knew of any stable work. And when one of his friends mentioned that the Party would help finance a small business, but the other stipulations made him realize that the Party wasn't operating from pure philanthropy. Finally, after much struggle, Guillermo managed to include him on the list of advisors for a campaign that was starting up. He then had renewed hope: the triumph of the party in the elections.

"Ah! If only you had been with me during those months and if you could have seen my work, you would understand me better. I gave myself totally and completely."

"No there's not much to tell, we lost the elections that time."

Just like that, he valiantly conquered the city. He reduced her to his liking, sometimes with pain, always with struggle. He tried to change her, humanize her, make her more compatible with old Jake's hallucinatory and idealistic dreams, but the city carried out an alternate plan, dehumanizing him, repudiating him for the grave sin of being black.

In the end, Clif triumphed. Not the adolescent Clif who reverently listened to his grandfather's words that morning long ago, but the adult Clif who had just dreamed about Jake in his final moments of life. But, was he really Costa Rican? It was not the automatic and mechanical question of having been born in a specific country, but it was a matter of being included or not in the nation. The reality of his marginal situation. What were those essential components that made someone Costa Rican or not? What were the obstacles? And what power gave him the right to claim his place?

During that morning of impure tepidness, he resisted his grandfather.

"Grandfather, and so what do you think of Garvey? He said the black man should return to Africa."

"People have many opinions. Garvey thought we should return to Africa, others believe that we already have the right to live on the land that we made fruitful and share the wealth that we helped to create with our children and grandchildren. Well, that's according to us, because according to them we would just show up on ships uninvited. I want you to just think about it a little, son. They conquered us, raped our women, and exploited all the enormous wealth in our country. They enslaved us physically and they terrorized us ideologically to the point of making many of us believe that we were an inferior race, and then, when they couldn't do any more to us, we decide to take a seat on some ship to go back to our land! What land, Clif? We don't even know where in Africa we come from and to go back there we'd be foreigners in any part of Africa. There's something in common for all of us, but a black Cuban is more Cuban than African, and more Latino in his way of thinking than an Ethiopian. Do you think that the Africans would let us come back all of a sudden and allow us to impose our ideology on them? And now that they are freeing themselves from the chains of empire, do you think they would just stand idly by and accept the authority of Western blacks who don't even know what tribe or nation their ancestors came from?"

He stopped, raised his hand to his head and stayed there a while looking into emptiness. His eyes revealed a certain intuitive wisdom, something he couldn't have gotten from the Scotsman's old books.

"Clif," he said, "this hour marks the awakening of the race. The time has come for us to free ourselves from race. The moment has come for us to free ourselves from this millenary bondage—the world over, blacks will suddenly rise up and they won't be able to keep us down."

"Well, Grandfather, tell me one thing, in spite of the countless floods, infestations, tragedies and all of the things you have told me, the ones that Mummy told me about, and the ones that I've seen, we stayed here."

"You really think after so much sacrifice that we could just pick up and leave and go home? It was impossible for us to leave this land because we grew to love it. That's the truth why we didn't leave. If we had, the bones of the dead would have risen up, Clif, to tell us about their sacrifice."

"Grandfather, I'm thinking that… well you're right, grandmother Gretel died, and her sacrifice should be respected. The bones of the dead would rise up in protest if we were to leave."

"Well Clif, is now my turn to ask questions and I'm only going to ask three: Are you Costa Rican? Are you really? You understand what I'm saying? Having the right is not enough, there's something more. That's the problem you must figure out, Clif. That's your problem to figure out now."

Chapter Twelve: Something Important

Everything about my grandfather's life justifies my return. Everything. In spite of my wife's obvious and natural incomprehension, as well as my own indecision. Or maybe it's the reverse? Howard Bowman approaches the house.

I have him in front of me, standing before those eyes that I once saw cry. He's here. I sense him, I feel him, I perceive him. "You're the heir Clif, the true source of the family's hope and glory." I now need the courage that he once had, the courage that took him to Panama, and the lost inheritance that summoned him to this land. The limitless courage that he possessed for so many years that gave him the strength to bury his wife and keep on living. But, it was that same courage that acquiesced to Howard Bowman's criminal actions. I needed to return, to reconcile with the mud, the scrape of metal against his skull, the tin of cacao, grandfather's lessons. I don't know if it's even necessary to reply to my wife's question, to gather up the memoryless flow that circulates fleetingly in the air of May, of April, of March, until it returns to the age of six when I discovered with surprise that it was true that I did grow and my grandmother laughed at me. But above all, I would have to forget the gun because I can't bring myself to use it in His presence. Soft hands suddenly caressed my neck.

"My love," the voice begs, "why have we come back?"

Howard Bowman's feet vibrate against the steps, they tremble as if they want to be free of the intolerable weight.

"Clif, I have the right to know."

Yes. She has the right. Howard Bowman knocks on the door. My wife suddenly becomes pale. I draw near to kiss her, to assure her that I'm here.

"I came to write my grandfather's story."

"Here?" Her eyes dilate with astonishment, her mouth sharpens. She rises up and stands to face me. Bowman knocks again.

"So, you mean to say that we've come…that we've come to this… this…place, just so you could write a book that at best no one will care about and will collect dust on the self—I mean shelf—and my children and I have come here to put up with life in this damned bush…"

She takes a pause to possibly to think about what she was saying. She sat with her mouth open and looking. Bowman knocks again.

"Let him knock," I murmur, "we've already gone to bed."

"Just for this."

"Well,…it's important…"

"Important! And you say it so easily, just like that. Well, but if the book doesn't sell. If it doesn't turn out to be a bestseller, you know what I am going to do?"

"No…what?"

"By God in heaven, I'm taking my things and my children and I'm leaving."

Bowman has grown tired of knocking and leaves. I get up and I go to the typewriter, I put the paper in the machine and I set off to write without a care as if I had lived the story I'm starting to write, I begin the narration. She comes out to see what I'm doing and reads the first words:

"The act of lifting the suitcase, hoisting the child, and exiting the train is all one motion…"

The Four Mirrors

Contents

© The Author(s) 2018
D. E. Mosby, *Quince Duncan's Weathered Men and The Four Mirrors*,
Afro-Latin@ Diasporas, https://doi.org/10.1007/978-3-319-97535-1_3

Part I

I

A strange feeling crept over me, as though I were outside my own body. It was a mix of unfamiliar sensations and exhaustion. As this feeling crested inside me, it took me back to the floodplain of my youth and the wide riverbed, twisting like a snake, winding without clear boundaries. It was just like the sensation that had mercilessly seized control of me.

I stretched out my hands. Far from my body, I saw my own hand, still and defenseless. In spite of my efforts, it didn't respond to my will. It felt like death. In a way, it was a threat against the rest of my body. Total inertia hung above me like a ghost and the worst part was my inability to rationalize what was happening to me because, from any way you looked at it, the whole situation was absurd.

Instead of fading away, the feeling intensified. Now nebulous, now too real. My head languished outside of my body, possible symptoms of a traitorous dementia that took advantage of my sleep and overpowered me. Whatever remained of my sanity—I thought to myself—would end up in confusion. Cell by cell, the equation was disassembled until it triumphantly displayed the remains of a being that once had tried to be a man and then ended up in the insane asylum, just like all the others who had tried. Although, unlike many of the others, there are some who reach the point of being human and die before the final frustration that comes without warning when you discover to be a man is not to be an angel. The heroes, the ones whose defects justify our brutality until it turns them saints, on top of it all.

But to me, it seemed to have signaled another type of death. Perhaps the most degrading of all because it was a passive and useless death. I tried to look back—I wanted to go back a little bit in space and time, a few feet or an hour. Perhaps that was enough to get back to normal. It was a question of putting my head back inside of itself and to get my feet to move at the same time, and getting my cold, indifferent hands back to life. But in my ridiculous position, on my back like someone

who was conquered, only served to frustrate me and fuel my desperation. I felt incapable of breaking the chains, limited by plans that were
not of my own design. Men shouldn't have limitations because such
limitations are another subtle way of denying their humanity.

I'd like to be transcendent, relegate my own being to the past. But
my philosophy wasn't just some sort of stupidity and a hallucinatory
relief before the clear evidence of death. Perhaps a truce of the subcon-
scious will hold back the passage of time for a little while. A subtle way
of clinging to life.

Nevertheless, while I tried to rationalize my situation, I pushed aside
the concrete and I took up another less painful enterprise which was
drifting into thoughts that were far from my current situation. Simple
abstractions. And precisely in that effort, I try to recover control over my
nerves. And then I realized that I was dreaming, which gave me an enormous sense of relief. Because by moving outside of the realm of the real,
things took on a sense of normalcy, the same dimension, almost comic.
It was a pleasant feeling. I suddenly felt alive and I could slowly abandon
the dream. In any case, it was the easiest thing to do and with that, I
acted just as I had learned in the capital—let things work themselves out.

Over in the Caribbean lowlands, I also saw this same attitude and
they all considered it normal—the violent flow of the river over the
floodplain, across the capricious depth of the earth.

I woke up hours later and extending my tired hand; I stroked my
wife's body with particular urgency. She was there, her warm body outstretched in my bed. My fingers ran across her delicate skin, looking to
gather the loose ends of my existence and tether them to her like a sailor
tethers his ship to the pier. I felt her body shift, responding almost auto-
matically to my urgency without interrupting the tranquility of her sleep.

"Don't mess up my hair," she said without pausing her snores. I kissed
her. I too was captive to the automatism that enveloped her. I sank
into her like one who carves a new road, my heart palpitating happily,
without distress, affirming life. She continued, half consumed by sleep.
"Don't mess up my hair, my love," while she firmly pulled me against
her shoulders, I was seeking new energy along the length of her back and
settling into her body as it lay in the bed and then after settling into her,
my own abstraction became a firm reality. This woman, her body and

her being so open to me, her voice, a "don't mess up my hair, my love," and the constant light shining on her body and a weak word swallowed by sleep.

As dawn was breaking, I dreamed, without remembering many of the details to be able to explain it, but I was clinging to the edge of a cliff, one that I had seen before in another dream. Suspended and gasping for air, I felt my hands failing me and that my life was coming to an end. In an instant, I was thrown across the rocks, my head split open, my guts exposed to the sun. I woke up sweating and shaken. It was just simply too much for one night. I got up hurriedly, but I put on my shirt and my other clothes with as little effort as possible as if I had all the time in the world. I reached the bathroom in a state of crisis and closed my eyes. Then, without haste, I watched as my slow-moving spasms folded into one another, as if my body had disconnected from itself at the urging of the necessary physiological need that had just occurred.

So, I looked at myself in the mirror. A man with disheveled hair, dressed in blue pajamas, appeared before my eyes. Something was missing from the image in front of me.

"My God," I screamed, but the sound was violently swallowed up by terror. There is something mysterious in terror. I have seen people stand mute before danger and others who fall into the most absurd impotence. I imagined the world as a planet trapped between two poles—frenzy on one side and stillness on the other—and the tension between them either gives us hope or frustration.

Then it occurred to me that I was going blind and I called out to God. That's one of those things that happens to us, we remember God only in certain moments. In any case, I rubbed my hands across my face with such violence that I injured myself in the process. I rubbed my eyelids, over and over again, trying in vain to make the image appear. An inexplicable blackness shrouded my face during the night. "My God, I'm going blind in the most brilliant moment of my life." Then, I remembered the dream, imagining that since that moment my eyes had not returned to their proper place.

My life has had its ups and downs. Failures, sacrifices, journeys, and homecomings, all in all, too many to count. What I knew for sure at that moment is that there was no way that I would be left blind. Since that moment my decisions were totally irrational.

The feelings of listlessness started the night before when Esther and I triumphantly entered the National Theatre to attend the lecture on racial minorities in Costa Rica. My wife had a distinguished air with her classical elegance, large eyes, and the slight trace of German features. She came from an illustrious family, not wealthy but descended from one of those prominent families with a rich past. That perhaps sounds a bit cliché, but that's the way Lucas Centeno says it. Lucas Centeno Vidaurre is a distinguished physician and I forgot to point out that he's also my father-in-law.

But I was telling you about our triumphant entrance into the National Theatre. My wife was elegantly dressed. She's got a lot of style. That's one of the things that I like about her. I like a woman who knows how to dress well. It makes it worthwhile to look at her. I've always said that if a woman doesn't know how to dress well and she's not willing to listen to advice, well she may as well just walk around naked and save herself the ridicule. It's true. Some women just drag on the first thing they get their hands on and go out into the street. Not Esther. She's different. Not too sexy, but it's precisely her expertise in the art of dressing that makes her very attractive. Well, it's not just that. She's intelligent and nice. Please forgive me for being cliché because saying that a woman is nice is a bit cliché. Everyone says that, am I right? Anyway, if everyone says it, then it's cliché. You'll see that I'm cliché, but at least I don't like it. Now, what was I talking about? Oh, the way Esther was really dressed that night—her heels and dress perfectly matched her blue eyes. Delicate fingers, lightly blushed cheeks, and her beautiful light brown hair pulled back with a pink headband. We walked deliberately, fitting with our social role. People expected that from us. You don't run into problems when you do what is expected of you. If anything, you attract the sympathy of all those who stand to reap the benefits of your behavior. Clearly, we go back to the same thing and all of that stuff about behavior is a bit cliché. But, you'll forgive me. Esther and I sat front and center so that no interested party would go without seeing us. People liked to look at us for some reason. I lowered the seats for us to sit and smiling, I folded my wife's overcoat. It was a grand moment, yes, it was. We had organized the event and the theater was full. They were all personally invited and they came. Our popularity was at its peak.

What's more, we had just left our new car in the parking lot. It was a luxury vehicle, including all of the extras like air conditioning, AM/FM stereo, and cassette player. It's true, we didn't need any of that and perhaps you're asking yourselves why do you need air conditioning when the climate averages 72 degrees Fahrenheit. Well, if you believe that you buy things purely for their utility, then you're the only ones who think that way. People don't buy things because they're useful, they buy them because they want to show off. Shoot! You have to be honest every once in a while, am I right? No need to get defensive, no one's accusing you. We had our car to show off to whoever and we had the money to buy it and that's why we bought it and it shouldn't bother you or anyone else. Besides, we have a gardener. A real first-class jackass named Marcel. You know what a jackass is? It's a cliché type who encompasses all of the characteristics of a particular role, but who is so stupid and clumsy that they can't get anything done with any sort of efficiency. Marcel was a first-class jackass. And it's true, his name was Marcel. Imagine what it's like to walk around with a name like that and be a chauffeur-gardener. It was as if from the time of his birth, his parents had a feeling about what his social status would be, or maybe they defined his destiny. It's a corny name. But anyway, he didn't choose it, so it's okay. Holy shit, we don't get to choose anything in this world.

When the speaker saw us enter, he stood us and took a deferential bow. That's so cliché. What a jackass! Then, the lecture started. His words were so odious, but they held the auditorium spellbound. They were completely seductive.

"The alienation and marginalization, as well as the tremendous degree to which black and indigenous peoples are victims of exploitation in our country, is not exactly a shining example of democracy. Their situation is disheartening." What disheartening situation? I had heard similar words before somewhere. Verbal diarrhea, that's what it was, because I've been to parties and I've danced with black women and white women and I've seen white men dancing with black women. These weren't downtrodden people, they were educated people. Above all, it was one of the parties that I attended. I mean, I'm going to say that because it occurred to me while I was listening to the talk. There was a gathering at the Yellow

House,[1] some dinner in honor of some old guy. There was a black woman there with fiery eyes. Her hair was relaxed, her lips were painted red—not a bright red, but a soft red—her eyebrows were shaped, her eyelids were green, and her cleavage drove the most impassioned admirers absolutely mad. No one there was offended by her presence and if they were, no one dared show it. Quite the contrary, all attention was on her fiery eyes. Once again I'm being cliché, right? Just look here, all eyes were on her. We're not talking poetry here. What I'm trying to say is that this black woman was beautiful in spite of her color. All night long the son of the Minister of the Interior and I competed for her attention. She was beautiful, smoking hot. Her breasts were well shaped, her waist … black women when they're young tend to have an incredible waist. And, she was a good conversationalist. We could talk just about anything, but the Minister's son brought up a terrific topic, an analysis of one of the opposition party's delegates. We had a great time! That delegate was a bit tipsy and I declared that he was certifiably piss-drunk. So, that's when Yvonne intervened. That was the black woman's name, Yvonne. She stated that a delegate couldn't be drunk because he was a delegate. At first, we thought she was defending the Minister's son, but later we found out differently. She intended to attack both of our positions. She said, "Luckily for him if he were a worker or a farmer, we could call him drunk. But, because he's a delegate, we can't say that he's drunk. We have to say, 'He's had a few too many.'" Turning to the Minister's son, she said, "Go, ask him and you'll see" and when all was said and done, he came out looking worse than me.

Well then, nobody displayed any displeasure at her presence. Just the opposite, it was more like people were dying of envy and some probably wished that there could have been more black women there with us.

Anyway, the speaker was talking. How should I say this? … He was talking pure nonsense. Do you know what a windbag is? It's a person who just moves their mouth just so people don't think they're mute. At that moment, a feeling of lethargy began to rise from my feet and I had to stop listening. I think that I thought about Esther at that moment, and

---

[1]The Yellow House (La Casa Amarilla), a Neo-barroque style building in San José that houses the Ministry of the Exterior.

if I'm right, I leaned over to kiss her. I mean, I kissed her on the cheek, right there in the theater, in the middle of the lecture. After all, it was a beautiful thing to be Esther's husband. I'm not going to make any claim that she did me any great favor by marrying me, no, it's not that. But, what I can tell you is that I gained quite a bit from being married to her. At least that's what I thought that night. Just imagine, it was a moment to be grateful. I was a Mr. Nobody, a simple man from the country, and she was a Centeno. Some guys are just lucky, right? To marry a Centeno, hardly possible. And not only marry her, but marry for love. That was it, love. And so Lucas and Pérez and Magdalena, and I don't know who else, were infuriated. That's it, so let them be mad, let them explode with anger.

Let's take Magdalena. I made her no promises and besides, she made me suffer! If something nice happened and she liked it a lot, she had no right to complain. Her attitude made no sense. It's as if someone hands us a glass of water when we're thirsty. You're grateful, but you don't marry the person because of that.

Now, after getting out of bed, my head was in terrible pain and I couldn't see my face in the mirror. Thirst voraciously chapped my lips and my breathing became more shallow. Moments of sadness sprung from my eyes, already weary from the cascade of silent tears. Damn. It was an intense sadness.

As I opened the door to the street, I thought about Esther's problem. I'm talking about that thing with her hair. Damn, compared to me her problem is nothing. Here I am going blind and there she is with her "don't mess up my hair, my love." I don't know why I thought about that and I confess that it was a nuisance to remember it. But, I had no reason to hold anything against Esther. Her dedication to me had been total, unconditional.

The sky held the promise of early rain. The fresh morning breeze filled my lungs, imparting a feeling of physiological well-being that let me know if the situation didn't get resolved, at least I would go on living. I'm going to explain a bit about that to you because I think I'm once again becoming cliché. This thing about physiological well-being… what I want to say is that one feels good. Should I have mentioned that right from the start? It's hard to talk like regular folks when you've been around academics for the past six years.

So what I decided to do was to go see the eye doctor because I really hadn't ruled out the possibility that I was going blind. It's funny, I didn't even remember the car. I started to walk to the bus stop, just like in those moments in the past now buried by abundance. I passed by my friend, Professor Luxe's house. He just joined the middle class a few months ago. He pulled it off and was now among his people. He wanted it and then he became it because you have to want it in order to be it. The people who have a lot are the ones who come from good families. And even though neither you nor I would dare to say it, but what is inferred here is that those who don't have it are from bad families.

Luxe and I were neighbors once in another neighborhood. We both belonged to Puma's gang. Puma was a scoundrel and a traitor, by the way, but Luxe was a good friend. Like me, he was one of the victims of the gang's savagery, but he more than I because he was raped during his initiation and then punished for coming to my defense. But Luxe rose up from his ragged clothing and graduated from the university with honors. That's why we had so much fun with him the night he showed up at our house. He was so proud to tell us about his accomplishment. His great accomplishment because we all aspire to that, to be among those who have also done well. And the rest is pure bullshit.

When he told me how much his house cost, I couldn't believe him. In truth, it was big, pretty, and well-built, but I couldn't believe it when he told me the price. It was indeed another great accomplishment and I thanked him because I knew we were the only ones that he would share this with.

"No way," I said to him, "Your house is huge!"

"Yes, you heard it right, that's what it cost me."

"It's worth four times that amount."

"Yes," he said and Esmulín, our mutual friend from the old neighborhood, a builder, went inside.

Luxe didn't tell me how he did it, but a few days later I found a drunken Esmulín in the corner bar. He was completely beside himself and I think he perked up when he saw me. Dammit, whatever problem he had was really killing him. After talking to me for a while, he started to cry. "Those scoundrels, they played an evil trick on me."

A short time later, the builder's eyes were swollen, his hands trembling, and his skin was inflamed. "I even bought food and a gas stove. My brother loaned me his place at Jacó Beach and that's why I told my wife, 'You've been busting your butt, let's go and get some rest for the week. Let's enjoy this little set up we got.'"

"Did you want to screw him over?"

"Me? But, God as my witness, I was doing everything legally. They picked me up for being truthful."

Another rum. Maybe the liquor helped him say what he didn't want to share with anyone. Some injuries are just too great to be forgiven, too deep to be shared. That's the truth. From there, every so often, he'd say "another rum."

Like I said, some injuries are too great to be forgiven, at least if you want to give up your dignity because sometimes that's what forgiveness means, giving up your dignity.

"I got screwed trying to reach the deadline in the contract. I did everything for him with extraordinary affection and care. You know where we come from, you know Luxe. It's so messed up. I feel so good when I see one of us make it out and does well. I feel almost as if it were me and that's why I put my all into it. I didn't fail in nothing I did. Nothing. Look at that house, you can see it's worth something. What a stupid fuck I am! It's worth a thousand times more than you could even imagine. We finished three days ahead of schedule, but see I wound up in debt."

"You wound up in debt?"

"I owe the Professor 2,000 pesos."

"2,000 pesos. But, how?

"According to the contract, I finished two months late."

"But Esmulín, how did that happen if you built the house in four months?"

"Three months and twenty-seven days. Messed up paperwork. Another rum?"

It took a lot for me to stop thinking about Esmulín and his situation. In reality, it really wasn't something to cry over, but it was enough to want to kill Luxe.

I walked for about two kilometers before I decided to take the bus. While my mind was engrossed by the Professor, I passed bus stop after bus stop. Engrossed? That was a bit cliché. I meant to say that I spent the time caught up in the Professor's little world. Out of every five, four had built their homes using their own cunning. Or at least, thanks to the help of some banker friend. Even so, it didn't do us any good that they nationalized the banks because the service you get depends on having a good friend in place there. Well, that's one of those things that perhaps wasn't clear. I mean, the money. It takes a lot to call things by their name, but every so often you have to be frank.

But the best thing of all was everyone's attitude at Luxe's get-together. Luxe would say with pride, "we've got this little place." And while his friends' astonished eyes would be adorned with a mix of jealousy and admiration, he would add, "it is very humble, but at least we have it." Then he would step back a little bit so that someone could discreetly ask him the price. Most of all, he wanted them to ask him the price. "About 100,000 little pesos." "Of course finished it's worth double that." And then he would wait, plainly and simply, for the group's astonished spokesperson to divulge all of the details to the rest.

From that moment his relations with the group would vary substantially. One older woman commented between sips of coffee, "who knows how he did it," because in that group almost everyone had to "do something" in order to reach his goal. And that same thing could be said of just about anything because the ends justified the means, in spite of the contrary opinion of everyone else.

Shoot, I admit that saying these things can be a bit unpleasant. But look, suppose that you all have a house and you've had to run a con game to get it. Then you're going think that I'm attacking you. But, it's not that. The problem isn't the con that you've had to run, the problem for me is that it's so unfair that you've had to do that in the first place. You get me? In other words, you haven't done wrong because otherwise, we'd have to think that we're all guilty. The issue is that running a con shouldn't be necessary and this is where I come in.

Before taking the bus, I walked by the front of the Castillo Sewing Factory. As always, the girls were waiting for him to open the building. In the early hours of the morning—I'm already becoming cliché again.

What happened is that I've got the mania of a poet. I mean to say that the sun was barely shedding its light. No, it's not that. It was an early light, that sounds better. It's much more precise. The girls were flaunting their hot pants, close-fitting blouses, and boots in the early light and all of this to the delight of old man Castillo.

Castillo was a Cuban exile who fled in a boat, risking his life, after Castro's government shut down his nightclub. It was a miracle that he wasn't captured either by the revolution's marines or the sharks. Once he got to Miami, he had funds available from the money he used to deposit in US banks. But he had a cousin in Costa Rica who advised him to start a common market business.

The Cuban was also part of the Professor's circle. Sometimes Castillo and Esther would discuss international politics. It's not that my wife would go for the Cuban Revolution, but she did say that without Batista and the corruption of the ruling class the revolution wouldn't have been possible. But Castillo denied such claims. It wasn't because of corrupt people, nor is it true that Cuba was full of brothels, nor the claim that Cubans were the most illiterate in the hemisphere, nor that rural women sold themselves in Havana to the delight of wealthy foreigners who all the way from New York could book a room complete with a woman. All of that, according to Castillo, was made up by the communists. In spite of those differences, the two of them got along very well. I mean they got along well in the sense that they mutually appreciated one another. But one day, Esther heard that the Cuban exile didn't pay his workers minimum wage, except those who got their position by spending a night of passion with him. She asked him and since then Castillo hasn't been back to the house.

Damn, she didn't have to ask him and I thought Esther was much too harsh. Damn, didn't I tell you it didn't make sense to think about those two jackasses in such a distressful moment? I was going blind, do you all know what that is like? A man in the prime of his youth and the height of success all of a sudden begins to keep to himself. But I imagine that it was a way of escaping my reality. I walked down the hill to the entrance of the city and I crossed the boulevard. Workers on a construction site asked me for a light for his cigarette in English.

That's another thing that happens to us, that we all have a gringo complex. True, I know that perhaps you all are studying English, but one thing has nothing to do with the other because English is one thing and Spanish is quite another. But, tell me if this isn't true that we have made a mixed-up mess that is neither one thing nor the other because you know what the guy told me, "Muchos thank yous." Now, if we're going to be honest here, who wants to say that?

It started to drizzle. I decided to take another bus. At first, I had intended to walk, but look I've gotten wet enough times in my life much less to get wet after buying a car. I encountered a woman on the bus who was blocking the aisle. The driver went to great lengths to get her to move toward the back, but she totally ignored his insistent pleas.

"Old lady," said one of the passengers who got on after me and was practically hanging out of the door, "it's because she's already inside, what does she care about the rest of us?"

The woman moved a couple of steps. The other passengers attentively watched the incident unfold, especially anxious for the outcome. Their little world was made up of such things. A superficial and severe world where the biggest dream you could have was a trip to Miami. A world that dreams of a new car and an eighteen cubic foot refrigerator. And a telephone. Maybe a stove with some prestigious brand name and a big oven. And if the neighbors were to buy something too, well then also an electric toothbrush.

The driver was indignant.

"Move to the back, darkie," he said to a black guy who like the others was waiting for the woman to move.

"But where do you want me to go?" The black man's response was sharp and defiant, "What! Are you afraid of her?"

"I told you to move back."

"Come, move me. Of course, it's easy to say 'darkie,' isn't it?"

The lady walked to the back of the bus in the midst of the enthusiastic laughter of the other passengers.

"What a pain, darkie!" someone said, "the driver really got to her with you."

"Yeah, he wanted me to push her."

It didn't sit well with me when he said that. There was no need to repeat that, but I had already said it. Everyone on the bus knew what happened. That's the way annoying people are, but the other guy I didn't like one bit, the one who spoke to the black guy, when he asked if he was Panamanian.

"No, why?"

"You speak Spanish so well!"

"I'm from Limón," he said with a smile.

I wouldn't have smiled. That guy made one of those great logical deductions: because all Limonese are of West Indian heritage, therefore, they speak bad Spanish. The words from last night's lecture reverberated in my ears and that made me very angry. "If a Latino person uses the wrong gender form for a word, the audience would understand that it was an error of little consequence. If a black person commits the same grammatical error, it will provoke the ironic smile of the public."

Damn, I would have liked to punch the guy who said that. I just hurled myself head-on into my problem again. Struggling I finally reached the eye doctor's house. A bag with the morning's bread and two liters of milk at the door, let me know that Dr. Pineres was still sleeping. My insistence, notwithstanding, managed to get the indignant doctor to see me.

"What do you want? ...," as he roughly rubbed his eyes, "Hey, it's you buddy! Come in, come in. What's going on?"

"I'm going blind, Agustín. Blind!"

"What do you mean blind?"

"Blind! You have to find out what's wrong with me right now."

"Is it that bad? Give me a minute."

At my core what I wanted to hear was an absurd question. "Your face, what happened to your face?" But not even the girls at the factory nor the passengers on the bus noticed anything strange and neither did the doctor.

Pineres' house was elegant. I should've paid more attention in order to borrow some ideas to decorate my own living room. Esther and I like to show off our things with style. Not extravagantly, but with just enough elegance to make life pleasurable. Besides, those lean days are behind us already.

Medical device after medical device, one test after another, I can't remember being this well taken care of before. Afterward, breakfast in the company of Pineres' beautiful wife. The maid who served us was the exact opposite of the lady of the house who had a svelte figure, long blond hair, green eyes, and smooth lips. The maid was thick, but not fat, with short black hair, thick lips, and dark skin.

Pineres waited until we were seated at the table to give his diagnosis. I would have given him a piece of my mind for that. Why did he find it necessary to humiliate me in front of his wife? No reason, whatsoever! But like an idiot, he believes that if somebody comes to look for him at home, well he should be able to put up with anything. Some people are so hateful, you know?

"You can see perfectly fine," he said, "I don't know what's going on with you."

"But, it's that I…," I got up from the table and ran to the bathroom. Well, this isn't the time to correct trite remarks. I ran, that's what I did. I want to say, well, I mean to say literally. There in the bathroom, I confirmed that I wasn't dreaming about the mirror earlier, I couldn't see my face. My eyes, yes, and when I opened my mouth, I could see my teeth. But not my face.

"No," I said going back, "I didn't dream this Agustín. I can't see my face."

Pineres' wife changed color, turning bright red. She's known me for years and could sense the seriousness of it all. It was clear that her thoughts were mirrored in her gestures. She was worried and I don't blame her. Frankly, I don't blame her. "First he wakes us up asking for an urgent exam. So, my husband does it and gives him a diagnosis. He gets up and runs to the bathroom. Then, he comes back and tells us he's not dreaming and that he can't see his face. My God, this guy is saying such nonsense!…"

Pineres dialed a series of numbers on the phone. "Díaz? Listen, this is Agustín. Sorry to call you so early…No, I didn't get thrown out of bed, I have a friend who's in a jam. It's urgent. Buddy, no…No, what I'm telling you is that he can't see his face. Yes, that's it. He can't see his face. He woke up like that. He's here at my house. You want him to stop by your house? Ok, give him some time to get there and then call me."

"Díaz is a good psychoanalyst," said Pineres' wife in a low voice, "He's a good doctor and he'll help you. You need help."

My feet soon crushed against the pavement of this aristocratic neighborhood. The two doctors lived close to one another and so I decided to walk to Dr. Díaz's house. I liked the solemnity of the neighborhood. The fresh silence of the gardens, the mastery of its gardeners; the happy eyes of children who carried with them a fortuitous enthusiasm that was contagious and gave off the illusion of an absurd world of innocence. The elderly women showed off their white legs in the morning light and the housekeepers were visible in the doorways, with their cheap clothing, aprons, brooms, and their dissimilar legs. One of them stopped her work to look at me with total lack of shyness. Iron bars and fences and garage doors, everything out of the reach of greedy hands, from those who because they don't have anything embrace the idea of snatching it all from the ones who were born lucky and because of that rightfully possess all the goods in the world.

Before, I would never have walked here. Because there are streets hammered into my memory that don't have the same soft fragrance as these. Filthy streets abundant with filthy children. Streets with dogs licking their tails also gnawed away by the filth. Streets with stones, eggshells left from trash collection. El Agrandado's corner store, the Treinta fruit stand, Laura Montero's vegetable stand; mangoes, annona fruit in the windows; carts pulled by malnourished horses moving a tangled up mess of a bed from some random part of the neighborhood to another random part of the neighborhood. Or on a regular afternoon, all of the furniture tossed into the streets by the authorities. Or an old woman doubled over by defeat, her varicose veins burning in the heaviness of her skin. And a patrol car, with the lieutenant's vulture-like eyes casting suspicion on everyone. Water that looks and smells like misery, emerging from the streets with fragments of several days worth of human castoffs. The scarlet lips, pale color, the housewives mismatched clothing—broom, hair pulled back, plastic house shoes, hardened calluses—performing their morning routines. Streets that make the longing for the forest, the plains, the mountains, the air of the sea seem brutal.

A lovely blonde curved her lips when she saw me. The tight-fitting knit blouse she wore was perhaps just a sign of a beautiful woman. Her coquettish gestures, her playful eyes, her trembling hands that were like a paper flower in the breeze.

We exchanged smiles. Her face became bright red. It was noticeable that she was moved by my gesture and perhaps she will never know how to explain to herself the deep impulse that it gave her for a brief moment, the vital sensation of a woman. I walked by smiling, totally forgetting the "problem" and that I needed the "help" of Díaz.

And so I continued walking through these sober streets, admiring what I saw. The bright paint, the conservative colors on the walls, the buildings of cement block and carved wood; the laughter of children with a hint of afternoon tea; more and more garages and cars and cars and garages; a green roof leaning precariously in front of the walkway to a house; a row of recently planted small trees; electric organ and guitar music; a chain of open gates; morning glories decorating the railings.

There are streets that we irreversibly carry with us. They go down toward any old place, any old foul smelling place, to any old gutter. Both sides of the street adorned with open doors. Children's laughter too. And curses. Children with a hint of old age and drought.

"Dude, goddammit…dude, you're a dumbass."

The voices of diligent fathers, heads of their households, with tools in their hands and shouting, "Come here you little shit, I'll show you what happens when you go around messing with folks who are dying of hunger."

A bus full of uniformed children quickly passed by the corner. The echo of their voices spread out across the neighborhood. Without warning, a sudden stop and a voice. I slowly turned around only to be looking at the doctor.

"Doctor, I was heading toward your house."

"You went right past it. I came out and saw you walk by. You were quite distracted."

Díaz's car was roomy. He belonged to a "nouveau riche" family and because of that, he felt the urgent need to show off his new status. We stopped at a corner to allow a young woman to cross the street. Good-looking, almost naked, barely dressed in psychedelic colors.

"Look at that bon-bon," Díaz said. "And what's going on, my friend?"

"I can't see…," I said clumsily.

"What?"

"I looked at myself in the mirror this morning and I can't see my face."

Right at that moment, I wanted to take back my words. They were too solemn and because of that, they seemed absurd. Too conventional to be believed. In any case, how do you say to a psychoanalyst that you're crazy? Doctor, I'm crazy? Those words were also too conventional to be believed.

The doctor suddenly stopped the vehicle again. A black woman in a miniskirt crossed the street holding the hand of a white child. Her legs were thick and shapely, her breasts brazen and full.

"What a shameless nigger!" Díaz said. "Did you see that? They dress any kind of way, as if they're still in Limón. Only in Limón do people walk in the street like that."

The feeling of heaviness punched me in the back of my neck. The words of last night's lecture returned to my memory, "They are treated differently." And Esther's body, and the theater, and the dream from the night before and the mirror…The car turned down Third Avenue and headed west. The kiosk, the long line of busses with advertisements plastered on their sides; the smell of burnt exhaust; a man crossed the street without paying attention to his surroundings. "Did you see that?" the sudden halt, the friction of the rubber against the pavement. The sound of the machine accelerating once again, the American Embassy, El Carmen—an old stone house with a church inside, "It takes some work to get a parking space at this time. Almost seems unreal. It's crazy that the government doesn't do something about it. This government doesn't care about professionals. I mean, where does it think we're going to park our cars?" A quick and unexpected maneuver, the sound of hubcaps scraping against the curb. "Opa!" The engine turning off.

"Your situation could take several weeks, but don't be alarmed. We'll see."

The street had a dry heat. While I followed the doctor up the stairs, I found myself looking at the footprints left by someone who had gone up these same steps before us.

It was a simple doctor's office, contrary to what I expected. A table that also served as a desk, a few chairs, and a lot of pens and paper.

"Take these sheets into that room," he said, "and fill them out. I'll be right back." I watched him point to the small, adjoining room and I began walking to the place he signaled.

After an hour, I desperately left the psychoanalyst's office and started walking with my hands in my pockets and no set direction. I passed the Central Bank building and the park. I stopped on the corner and walked past the Metropolitan Cathedral. Millions of steps impressed year after year into the pavement, swept clean by the rain, polished by the relentless shine of the glorious July sun. The Modern Theater, where one night I had to define myself before all the possibilities offered by time. I remembered Esther's fiery eyes and the slanted eyes of Dora París. Images without color, spontaneous and imprecise; the popsicles that they sell in front; a line of cars on the corner where once upon a time I didn't apply the brakes in time.

No, not whole the stick, just take a little bite.

I came back because I felt lost, without a sense of time. The Modern Theater, and a half block later, what was that? The Civil Service or the Elections Tribunal?

Something was there, in the San José of my adolescence

Dora París, a million memories. She showed off her pink cheeks, her dark eyes, her passionate lips like melon.

Central Park, the Cathedral; the uneasy and unsteady steps, the suffocating heat burning my eyes; a seat under the morning glory between two old men, each one reading a different daily paper; a stupid voice insisting that the number 90 will be the winning number in Sunday's lottery drawing, without a doubt; the colorful language of the shoeshine boys.

"Look-a-here leg, you hogged it all."

"You suck pig-nose. You just got snookered."

The slang of the street captivated my attention for a long and useless minute. The man on my right distracted me as he flipped his paper over.

The memories of Dora París kept coming. The gathering of mothers, happy and full of ladies who would still come to the school that year and the years that followed, without knowing if their children did their work, but convinced that they would at least earn a better living after they graduated.

It was almost as if it were magic.

Because they weren't there to learn. In reality, I thought, no one is interested in knowledge. At least that's true of Costa Rica. Everyone studied to get a job. That's it, to get a job and improve their economic position.

"Will you dance with me, Dora?"

"No, my dear."

"Why not?"

"It's that...you know why? My mother is here and she's an evangelical. To her dancing is evil."

"Dancing is...but, does your mother even read the Bible?"

"Every day."

"The Israelites danced when they left Egypt."

"Personally, I don't have anything against dancing," she said, "It's my mother."

The shoeshine boys who filled the periodic gaps in my attention were in competition with the memories of yesterday. Then, I looked at the legs of a beautiful woman who was walking across the park. My hunger had opened up some space. An emptiness numbed my feet. Suddenly it occurred to me to analyze the often overlooked presence of toenails.

On another morning we went for a stroll along the river. I had been practicing the formal declaration of love that I would present that morning. With radiant enthusiasm, she waited for me alongside the bus, as if she had sensed the approach of a decisive moment for the two of us. She didn't contain her joy and I was happy to see her as well.

A woman attracted the attention of the shoeshine boys. She was pregnant, but perhaps it was her lack of aesthetics or her unconventional perception of herself that made her go out into the street with such a baggy dress. It was so loose that she could fit the outline of her future child and her own girth, but it didn't hide her beautiful legs that fractured the light as she walked by, decorating the edges of the sidewalk that determined her path.

Moment after moment, the memories of Dora Paris kept coming. The profound heat of the sun gleaming on the river, while the bus climbed, climbed, climbed; a bridge floating in the subtle wind and the water, bobbing between the infinite meandering of the countryside. We stopped and I confidently leaped off the bus. Then the driver started off without warning and I had to follow behind the moving bus. The laughter of our friends, the sharp words between the bus driver and I, and Doris' charmed eyes.

Without wanting to, I began to follow the pregnant woman. My eyes followed the elegant and sensual play of her legs, hands in her pockets, inclined head, legs without control. We crossed the street, we stopped a moment on the opposite sidewalk; we continued heading north, we went into a store; we stopped in front of the display case, "Sir, I will come to you in just one moment," the sound of change and Jewish dialect, "Now sir, how may I help you? … Sir…Sir…"

We went out into the street, we crossed moving toward some place that smelled like onions, garlic, plantain sap, saliva, and manure. We went into a diner—the outline not even curved, tough skin, young woman.

The engagement between Dora Paris and I was impossible. First, the inopportune interjection of a friend who mentioned Esther. Dora's despairing eyes sank into the river. And I would've screamed that it wasn't true, but a stupid paralysis stopped me.

Later I managed to get her to have a drink with me.

"One sip isn't going to do anything to you. Just try it."

"But, it's a sin."

"Sin? But, Christ drank wine."

"It was fermented grape juice."

"Fermented grape juice!" we started laughing.

"No, I meant to say unfermented."

"Unfermented! Dora, for Christsake, unfermented grape juice doesn't get you drunk."

"I didn't say that it doesn't get you drunk."

"You haven't read very well, Doris."

"Then we danced to a song. I couldn't understand my terrible luck to be close to a girl, loving her with the depth that I loved Dora Paris.!"

"Sir, may I get you anything?" The waiter had a look of worry.

"Yes," after a few moments of silence, "bring me a cas fruit drink.[2]"

"Anything to eat?"

"No."

---

[2]Cas, a fruit in the guava family with a tart flavor that is commonly served as a beverage in Costa Rica.

The legs left the diner, but I stayed there, pinned to my seat. I think the pregnant lady noticed that I was following her. Where was I? Not only did I lose track of time, but I also lost track of where I was. When I finally left the diner, I stopped on the corner to see a metal chain with human beings grafted in. Links. Chain of movements and the sounds of tires. I went back in the direction of the diner and crossed the street again.

"Pssst, pssst, the Big One," said one of the lottery vendors who gathered on the corner.

"What?"

"The Big One."

"If you know if it's the 'Big One,' why don't you buy it yourself?"

"I don't have any money."

"Get out of here…"

I lifted my gaze from the ground to look at the vendor. Some women were unloading watermelons from a truck with Nicaraguan plates. One of them had a face like a watermelon and the other, sweated profusely as she used her skirt as a face cloth.

"If you could do me the favor and move back a little more." The desperate maneuvering of a driver who was trying to take his vehicle out from between two others. Mirrors, mirrors. First, he tried to move the front of the car, then, he moved back.

Go, go, go. With the vehicle at a stop, the driver turned the wheel. Will he break free? He will, he will. Two cars waited to let him go by. A growing crowd of spectators gathered in the street and on the sidewalks. A transit officer intervened to add to the increasing wave of shouts. Transit officers have a way of doing that, I thought. You can be sure that whenever there's a traffic jam, it's because there's one nearby. They almost always stop right beneath a stoplight. Can you imagine that!

"Mirrors, mirrors," cried a boy's insistent voice. "Mirror, buddy?"

I decided to buy one. It was a sudden impulse. Buy one, as if that could resolve or confirm the existence of an enigma.

"Mirror, buddy?"

"How much? … Here."

My face? Trembling I leaned against the wall. My face?

Taking advantage of the fact that everyone was focused on the maneuverings of the cargo truck, I slowly brought the mirror close to my face. I could tell that I had a face…a face…

A mixture of joy, terror, and shock flashed through my consciousness.

"There was a black face!"

I broke the mirror. The boy approached with a look of concern.

"Hey, buddy! What happened?"

"Gimme another."

"What?"

"Gimme another."

The boy doubted my sanity and, just in case, he quickly ran down the street. Maybe he wasn't convinced that the mirror's destruction was due to an accident. Perhaps he doubted and with good reason. Getting away was a sensible and smart thing to do. It was a logical conclusion—a guy who breaks a mirror he just bought is crazy. He's crazy because he did it on purpose. It would have been absurd to condemn the boy for his instinct of self-preservation. He got away from danger and that's it.

One of the cars that waited to pass through the stalled traffic started honking. A little while later the sound of car horns scandalously flooded the street.

"Do I have a black face?" That became my obsession. It consumed me. Then again, I thought maybe it was an unconscious suggestion from the speaker at the theater from the night before because it's not possible to change one's skin color. Or maybe it was possible? I've heard some people had managed to temporarily modify their skin color, but those were experiments with chemical products. I didn't undergo any process that would result in my sudden, absurd mutation.

I cautiously brought the mirror to my face. (During some unremarkable time in an unremarkable place, someone was hanging from the edge of a cliff. Hands grasping the bridge, voice breaking in prayer—Lord, have mercy on me, a sinner; hand tense; because I am a worm, not a man. The endless wait for death and vertigo growing from within my veins. I am a worm and not a man, a worm and not a man, a worm and not a man…)

The coolness of the breeze held me back and I screamed. I screamed just before the stones split my brain into pieces. I suppose I really did scream.

"Darkie, what's going on with you?"

"Maniacs and retards, I suppose," I opened my eyes to look at the amused faces of a dozen curiosity-seekers. They looked at me with delight, but also with fear. Because, of course, what I offered them wasn't a common sight—a man standing and screaming at a mirror. Sweat ran down my black face.

"What happened to you, darkie?"

"This 'cat's meow' knocked over the pile of stones," someone said from the crowd just a moment before the first blow.

"Darkie, are you crazy?"

The victim fell to the ground with a bloody face.

"Black son-of-a-bitch," the assaulted man began to shout, but a well-aimed kick got him to shut up.

"Hit 'em hard! That's it, Cassius! Wallop 'em!"

The milk vendor shouted, "That prick's already down."

I heard a whistle and furiously started running. I heard voices behind me demanding, "Get 'em" that were eventually lost to empty space. I knocked down a street vendor without meaning to. His baskets rolled around, littering the street with little green balls. A child shouted with anger, "miserable nigger," and his shout followed me for a half block.

I stopped when my breath could no longer sustain the unrestrained desire to flee. I had cut my hand in the fight, which then brought me to a pharmacy. Now I had to wait until the man at the counter finished helping a girl who came in after me. I didn't know if that was because of her privilege of being a woman or if it was because of the color of her skin.

"And you, darkie, what do you want?"

The streets must have changed color as well. I didn't have the slightest idea of where I was. It didn't occur to me to ask either. I simply started walking. I was walking as the hours accumulated beneath my feet. As the hours accumulated beneath my feet? Damn, for as much as I try I can't get over being cliché. One always ends up being cliché. And the best thing I can do when I notice it is to just shut up.

II

He heard a voice from the other side of the pasture. The call was persistent, almost unbearable. And Charles, little by little, was giving in. He didn't want to respond at first. His eyes were full of salt, his blood carried the intense steam of hour upon hour of hard labor in the cacao groves. The sun sank into his bones, as if it had formed a pact with the Devil himself. Damn, so many days of sun and water that thicken into an infinite number of faded dawns. Yes, faded dawns because the day finds them still weary. Ahuuu….ahuuuuuuuu…ahuuuuuuuu…

He picked up the shovel and the machete before answering. He sensed danger. And that's what's absurd about intuition, you feel danger, but you can't figure out why. Ahuuuu…ahuuu… Charles… Charles… Tall grass and pasture. He steps through the weeds, flowers, cacao trees, dammit, everything so that he could study and then come back home carrying a canteen as a trophy alongside his degree and go back to swinging a machete?

At least this year's harvest was plentiful just as it had been in earlier times when the price for cacao was good. But Charles McForbes no longer lived on dreams. The sweat, the salt in his eyes, the mud on his boots, the wasp in his hair were real. And he despised all of it, dammit. Ahuuuu… ahuuuu… ahuuuu…. Charles….

The gully was also real. The sludge from the last flood that covered it was real. Feet covered in grime. The black Estrada topsoil, covered by a slippery khaki-colored layer of mud.

"Ahuuuu… ahuuuuuuuu… Charles!"

"Ahuuu…!"

"Charles…! It's your wife, come!"

Damn, the worst injury struck him. He started to run.

"Your wife fell ill!" The disgusting softness of the mud no longer mattered. He also forgot the hatred he had been gathering. He just had the awareness of twenty-three years of a fierce battle against everything. His labor wasted on other peoples' land—callousness, emptiness, and undefinable suffering. A slow and frugal life like the dry cacao, crushing forgotten skulls; struggling with the spirits of a race that occupied these lowlands before them, until the moment European Christians savagely assassinated them.

A sad twenty-three years. When Pete was in his eighties, those were the best years because the old man died without seeing the gradual arrival of wealthy white folks and the banana companies that sucked up the remaining land. Nor did he see the selfish egoists who arrived quietly and without getting stained by the mud. They arrived invulnerable to nature's complicity, which gave them just enough shrewdness to edit legal papers in Spanish that only they could understand and was just enough to impress a peasant.

That's how he marked the twenty-three years. Years that opened his path.

Years that opened like a futile, but enormous groan. He went through the fence with a self-loathing that matched the violence of sun of the lowlands. The round features of Guillermo Brown appeared in front of his dull eyes.

"What's going on?"

"Come, Pastor. Lorena… it's Lorena."

"What's happened to Lorena?"

"Come…"

Guillermo saw him turn around and then start to back away. His feet crushed the fragrant herbs. His intrepid feet. His head inclined beneath the wry smile of the sun.

"My God, Guillermo, what happened?"

"Cho, you pastors ain't easy."

"But, for God's sake and for…," he wanted to say, "for the sake of the rotten whore who gave birth one afternoon to a talking piece of shit," but a pastor mustn't say such things.

Guillermo didn't hear him nor did he seem willing to listen. They gave him a very specific task, go to the farm and call the pastor. Tell him that his wife, Lorena, is ill. Perhaps he didn't even have the slightest idea about the cause of her illness, nor was he aware of her symptoms. In any case, he fulfilled his duty—dryly and with a peanut shell between his lips.

His attitude was like millions of others. His humanity was limited by the mechanization of his actions. The evolutionary process unexpectedly stopped because of the absurd and irrational stratification of a world altered by an illusion—the belief that one group is superior to another for the simple fact of being more powerful. Absurd because first, it reduced one race to the condition of subhuman and then, as a logical outcome of its own development, produced Hitler and then later apartheid. The definitive separation of the races was justified by theology and science. Absurd because it had defined one group as the landowners and all the others as parasites. And still even more painful, Charles is presented with the absurdity of his own race. Because in the final analysis, the damned urgent need of black people was, in his way of seeing things, the greatest obstacle to their progress. Because that talk about "they're oppressed," is only a part of the issue and it was also clear to Charles that black people oppressed themselves.

Of course, Charles recognized that there had been hundreds of years of slavery. Adding up those years of labor by all of those who came before him, plus those worked by Pete, including his own twenty-three years in the struggle. This black man comes and without taking all of this into account, proceeds to tell him that his wife is ill and refuses to say anything more. "May he be consumed by flames, just like all the other devils."

Maybe Guillermo noticed Charles' silent indignation. Maybe he sensed the violence with which the pastor condemned him. Suddenly, Guillermo turned to him and said that he didn't know what happened. "Ruth told me, 'Go tell Charles that Lorena is sick.' She didn't say anything more to me. And that's what I came to do, to let you know and that's all."

Charles remembered an incident that would've gone by unnoticed in any other circumstance. Moments before he heard Guillermo's call, he heard the sound of the train whistle and a train suddenly braking. The memory of another afternoon assailed him—the train coming dangerously close to a little girl with a disagreeable look who was crossing the tracks. The train braking and the desperate blow of the whistle, the attempt to flee in the midst of panic, the machine impotent before the forty train cars of bananas. Already defeated, he saw her fall out of the way, her life miraculously extended, her leg forever crushed.

"Damnit, Guillermo! Did the train get her?"

But before Brown could respond, Charles realized his blunder. If the train had hit Lorena, Brown would have taken much longer to come and tell him.

"Don't answer, Guillermo, you already told me that she fell ill."

"She got sick and Ruth told me to go and let you know. That's all."

Holding back the urge to attack Guillermo Brown, he crossed the cacao grove in silence. They crossed the creek and the crystalline bubbles of the current and they continued up the steep hill in even more silence.

The McForbes house was as unusual from the back as it was from the front. The mud from the last flood still covered the veranda with its rancid odor. There were plants growing up out of the mud that were once unknown in the lowlands, the remains of the indestructible Mount Chirripó being reborn in a new place.

A lime tree adorned one end of the house. Next to it, a gigantic tree with an unknown name, where once many years ago during a cricket game, Clifton—his neighbor, Clif Duke's father—buried a ball somewhere in the tree. The fence (when you open it lets out a distant whine) and a bit beyond the house are some yucca plantings, which are a symbol of the unbreakable will of the small town's inhabitants. Because one had to have an unbreakable will or an innate stubbornness to withstand it all. Or perchance a quality inherent to the culture of a group of people who after every flood, continue to rebuild season after season, year after year. It wasn't easy to cultivate the land with so much determination for eight months of the year and then see all of the hard work destroyed a month before the harvest because of a brutal flood that would wash through, rebellious like the nature of the lowlands, refusing to allow anything to define its path. Today the river crossed through the front of the farm. The next year, it could pass through any other part, maybe even under the house of one of Estrada's residents. Only rural stubbornness, the desperate holding on to the land makes them stay and endure, while they attribute to the justice of God, the unjust reward for their labor.

But Charles was obstinate. Sure, he had studied in high school, took some courses on theology, built one of the best farms in the town, all of this did absolutely nothing for him now. The dehumanizing daily routine was always the same, always. Damn, the same as always.

A staircase rose up from the hallway. The house hung its wooden structure on svelte posts. Charles let his tools fall on the patio and paid no attention to the dog, who would come to greet him every afternoon in his own happy way. The house shook under his weight as he climbed up step by step, as if afraid to lift his foot, as if somehow walking depended on his sense of balance. Step by step to the hallway, where at least a dozen people had gathered in a disorderly get-together. With anger in his eyes—Charles always easily angered—he crossed to the center of the small room where compassionate and mocking looks bubbled; gasping, tense, he slowly walked to his wife's bed. … Ruth, an old friend, looked at him without being moved. Her almond-shaped eyes, mature in the distressing calm which suddenly entered into the room with Charles.

He saw in the half-light, Ruth's able hands massaging the infirm woman's temples with oil and camphor. Another woman, whose identity didn't matter during those terrible moments, rubbed rue on her wrists. Terrible moments because to Charles they were terrible. His gaze lowered to Ruth's chest, her dress was stained and smelled of herbal remedies. He looked down at the floor and there his gaze remained without focus. After a while, fatigue led him to raise his gaze to the cot's cold feet and the coldness penetrated his eyes—and he saw Lorena's pallid face—"Lorena, what happened…Lorena…Lorena…Ruth, my God, what happened?" His wife was there, stretched out on the bed, defenseless and indifferent to the rapid passage of time.

Silence had become a concrete, detectable thing. He passed his gaze from eye to eye, discovering the silent terror in each one. It was as if a traumatic event—like Lazarus's resurrection—had marked them forever into eternity. Finally, Ruth spoke.

"Lorena was turning the cacao. You know what that's like, you have to keep turning the cacao during the day…"

"Ruth, Jesus Christ! I want to know what happened!"

"Then, let her tell you," someone interjected, "Give her a chance!"

"Chance, my ass!" Charles exclaimed. "I want to know what happened."

Someone let the name of Jesus escape from their lips. Such language was inconceivable coming from the mouth of a pastor. Charles felt his blood boiling because for so many years he's worked the land so that now when anguish was shortening his breath, someone comes to tell him that it's necessary to turn the cacao so that it dries. It was more than an ordinary man could bear, pastor or not. Too much. Yes, it's important to consider the weight that a man like Charles is carrying while facing the terrible situation of someone he loves. And to make matters worse, they said it. The voice was loud enough for him to hear, but not enough for him to be able to distinguish the voice from the rest. "A pastor saying that."

A clash of images unleashed a continuous chain of reactions in him. Ice burning in the sky, wind, and drought. And that's why he hated them. He hated all of them, all of the damn, wretched black people of the world, and he cursed, he cursed them all.

"But Charles, they don't even have a lick of compassion for this poor woman who's dying. Whoever said that is just rude and out of order, but you should remember your role at the church and all those years you spent in school. You have no fear of God."

Fear of God. Really. That was exactly what they lacked because it was just cruel to leave a man like that, drowning in despair, without telling him what happened to his wife. Without explaining what terrible event brought her prostrate to her bed, sending her into a trance.

"Ruth, please," he begged, "please."

His rage somehow became a long plea. Dazed eyes, trembling hands, Charles boiled with complete intensity. He got up to confront the people gathered there, "Why don't you all just leave?"

"It's just that we can't say what we've seen, Charles." The afflicted husband gradually became aware of all of the eyes that were on him. They were the ladies of the town, many of them members of his own congregation. They were his flock and they were called to serve.

"Well, why can't anyone tell me what you've seen?"

"We have to wait twenty-four hours…"

"For what? Lorena will be in her grave by then. Tell me, for what?"

Ruth became pale. She saw the effort Charles was making to control himself, it was a conscious, violent effort. Ruth turned toward the women with the authority that comes from ancestry and wisdom. Her eyes gently closed, her lips slightly parted. She said nothing. Not even to change the position of her lips. Her silence filled the house, overpowering the kinky curly heads. The women remained absorbed by the way she looked, imprisoned and ashen.

"I have been Lorena's friend for many years," she said when there was absolute silence. "And I don't really care about what could happen to me. I… I'm going to tell you what happened Charles and I don't want you all to worry."

"Well…in that case, we should let her. She must know what she's doing."

It was a well-known, but veiled that Ruth was an obeah man's daughter.[3] The neighbors were convinced of her knowledge and this belief, little by little, elevated Ruth to a place of privilege in the community as a counselor and as a friend to just about all of the women in the town. Now, she said that she would talk and this encouraged the admiration of the other women in the room. Besides Ruth, at that moment no one else would have dared to say what they saw.

"You know that you have to turn the cacao several times during the day and that's what Lorena was doing," she said looking at Charles.

He stopped looking at her to concentrate on his wife's pallid face. He swallowed several knots that had formed in his throat and he listened to the slow account with the same heroic and decisive attitude. And he learned once again that the cacao needed sun and that it has to be tended to especially this time of the year because it rains a lot. And Lorena must have gone inside the house to take the meat off the stove because when the neighbors arrived the meat was still on. "And look …"

"And look, what?" the phrase escaped his mouth and it was already too late. Once it was formed and said, it was surrounded by the conquered presence of silence.

Interminable vibrations about the opposing votes arose from the kitchen. Boundless sound, tyrannical and cruel like the plagues of Moses. In those echoes, other hopes scarred over him. It was too much. He asked one of the women in the room to go down to the kitchen and smash the radio against the floor. She went and turned down the knob.

---

[3]Obeah, a word derived from the Ashanti meaning 'power.' Obeah man: a powerful man, capable of using the mysterious, supernatural powers for good or bad.

"Ruth, damn you, woman (and that also was beneath the dignity of a pastor, but it was already said). I come to see Lorena here because you sent for me. Brown simply told me to come (Lord, how he hated those damn customs that black people have), and that Lorena was sick, and he gave me no explanation. She's on a cot, looking real bad, and with a panicked look on her face, and you tell me that she was turning the cacao and that you need to turn the cacao and a whole bunch of other foolishness. And no one is telling me what happened to her."

"Lorena was attacked by a duppy."[4]

"By a duppy?" Suddenly the silence returned with intensity, churning through the room.

"A white specter."

"But..."

"And then she went mad, spewing white foam out of her mouth. When we found her, she was stiff."

"Stiff?"

"Yes. Only her mouth was moving and that was only to cuss like a sailor."

The portrait of Pete McForbes, Charles's father, hung above Lorena's bed, looking like he was invoking an eternal Our Father.

It took the distraught husband a quarter of an hour or perhaps more, to begin to understand what Ruth had said. The women started to go home, one by one. It was difficult to accept such a supernatural explanation after so many years of study, although, truthfully they weren't that many. But, he had to face a concrete reality and that was Lorena stretched out on the bed in some type of trance and barely breathing. That was certain.

But the explanation was abstract. A supernatural response to a real fact. They had to accept that one since there were no better explanations available. Everyone was in agreement about the ghost, although only Ruth, as the daughter of an obeah man, could make out its color. A shameless white spirits. It had to be shameless to commit such an act in

---

[4]Duppy is the spirit of a deceased person. In Jamaica, in particular, a duppy is generally considered malevolent.

the presence of so many people and in the light of day. It left by using the front door as if it had been any living being, and then, walking by the railroad tracks, it disappeared into nothingness. "But then I heard Lorena cursing and I said to myself that's not normal." Ruth's face was full of the kind of wrinkles that the passing years leave in their wake in order to hide her personal history behind a veil of mystery. Her eyes, her lips, sometimes vacillating and at other moments moving with assurance. Her vital creed. Her last resort. "I said, 'that's not normal because Lorena struggles to say 'ugly.' And because of that, so many of the neighbors came out and we saw the duppy, and we all looked at each other and we said nothing. But afterward, when Lorena's cursing didn't stop, I had to gather the courage to come and see what was the matter because I wasn't going to leave her like that. I never crossed myself so many times in my life. The other women joined together with me like a stamp on a letter."

The subtle presence of Clarita Duke interrupted the story. She was the McForbes's neighbor and a nurse. The sobs of the women suddenly began to grow until it became completely audible. She looked at them with anger, perhaps denying them every right to believe in what for them were logical and normal principles. Charles understood her attitude very well because their worldview was making contact with science. But then the waters returned to their riverbeds, not to become lost in the supernatural world of their parents, but above all to understand it. But for Clarita, there were no such concessions. They had discussed it several times. Defiant and authoritarian, with just one look she snatched away their cosmogony. The weeping settled into a muted protest.

It was easy to read the intruder's repudiation in the eyes of the village women. It was a rebellious attitude in the face of the dazzling personality of Clarita Duke. Defiant beyond her own control because neither the constant labor of the obeah man, nor the hostility of the majority of the town had been able to break her to change her into one of them, thus wrenching away her foolish arrogance.

For the moment it seemed that Clarita would leave triumphant and that it was going to be easier than Charles initially thought to get rid of the problem. Because they were two irreconcilable worlds, each one with its own logic. But someone started to declare that Lorena was going to die, that there was no longer hope for salvation, that instead of injections, she needed an obeah man. The mortal sentence ran from lip to lip, encircling the sick woman's bed, creating the necessary atmosphere of fatalism in order to accomplish its goal of defying Charles. All of a sudden, he got up and positioned himself next to the outsider. He too was a participant in their strange culture and his pretentious attitude was just as ungrateful as Clarita, who had no reason to come to this town.

Charles was aware of the women's self-defense mechanism. A desperate and irrational defense. That was why he sat next to Mrs. Duke, before those eyes of the other women. The mortal sentence fled and faith was restored in its place. Clarita moved with absolute assurance. She hovered above the infirm woman, opening the syringe that she had wrapped in a white cloth, while Ruth struggled to make one of Lorena's buttocks accessible. Clarita continued looking every so often at the others. She confidently pierced the patient's skin and without losing the rhythm with which she entered the room, squeezed Charles on the shoulder. "Stay strong, my friend. You must be strong."

He couldn't ignore the feeling of nostalgia that arose with her departure. He had wanted to stop her, to drink in her calmness.

"Poor Lorena," said one of the few women remaining in the room, "so young and she's going to die."

"Don't say that, Mary," protested Charles without much conviction. Then he remembered Clarita Duke's calm, the rhythm that infused her entire being, and repeated the phrase with greater determination.

"Don't try to trick me, I know it all too well. Poor thing. She's the only friend I have and she's going to die on me. Poor Lorena…"

"Shut your damned mouth," Charles shouted. He was beside himself. He got up violently and went toward the kitchen. He paused in the entryway, full of regret because it wasn't a good thing for a pastor to say. Aware that they were watching him, he made an enormous effort to calm his nerves. What was happening to him? Without warning, he became impatient and emotional. He looked at Mary, trying to communicate with his eyes that which was too intimate for the lips to even dare to pronounce.

"Mary…Is there any coffee?"

"Yes, Mr. Charles. Would you like some?"

"Two cups, please and please leave me alone here with Ruth."

Burying his hands in his pockets, he allowed himself to fall into the chair. His long sigh revealed bitter fatigue.

"What time did all of this happen?" He still had engraved in his mind the image of the distant afternoon, with all of its dramatic force. Lorena making gestures with her hands from a rock in the middle of the river. He, smiling, refusing to come to her. The moment was prolonged by their joking with each other until she lost her balance and fell into the water.

"I can't go home like this, daddy will kill me. Go look for Ruth and tell her to go to the house and get me a dress."

Charles looked at Ruth, pale, tense, faithfully watching over the sickbed. This was the same Ruth he looked for that afternoon so that they could both evade the jealous obeah man's watchful gaze. Without the jet black hair of their younger days, without the flowery words, but with the same sparkling look as always. Ruth, Ruth Viales. Daughter of his father-in-law's colleague, and inseparable friend of the family for all time. It was impossible to see one without the other. Because Lorena met Ruth at her own house when she went one afternoon in search of Mr. Sam's services and she and Ruth were linked from the very beginning.

It took Ruth and Charles more than an hour to swipe the dress, iron it, and carry it to Lorena. She accused them of flirting and they fought. It was a nasty dispute, as intense as a November rain. A week later, they had another fight for the same reason and Lorena swore never to speak to them again. She kept true to her promise for three weeks. But one day she showed up at the McForbes house and she told Pete that she was pregnant and that Charles was the responsible party. Old man Pete had never seen such boldness and didn't know what to do. He called Ruth to ask her about the nature of the relationship between Charles and Lorena. Ruth defended Charles saying that as a gentleman he'd be incapable of such an irresponsible act. Pete looked for Ruth on another afternoon and in the presence of both Charles and Lorena, invited her to tell him what had happened between Lorena and Charles, but Lorena began laughing maliciously.

The old man threatened to speak with Mr. Sam.

"That's fine because I'm not against it. Just know that Charles had been fooling around with me. And in any case, my daddy doesn't need to know that your son had been fooling around with me. He's your son sir, and you're the one who has to do something. Doesn't it seem like a lack of respect to not only to hurt the daughter, but to also want to injure her father?"

Pete threw Ruth and Charles out of the house and handed Lorena a half-dozen lashes with his belt.

An hour later, Mr. Sam arrived at the McForbes house furiously demanding Pete to account for his audacity and they almost came to blows. The presence of Charles and Ruth forced them to talk. But to avenge Pete's actions toward his daughter, old Mr. Sam viciously slapped Charles.

Old man McForbes would comment later that he had never seen such a spoiled girl in his life and he opposed their engagement for that reason.

Mary brought out the coffee.

"Ruth," Charles said, "I'll be outside in the hammock. If anything happens, call me."

The evening fell across the town. Estrada was consumed by the intense light of the moon. Periodically clearing his throat, Charles let his eyes float toward the depth of the darkness. What had happened to him was bad luck because if he had had luck, he wouldn't be in the midst of tragedy and he'd be able to draw his own conclusions.

He lifted his eyes to look at the time and he saw a horse cross the train tracks with two riders on its back. One of them had his face turned toward the animal's tail.

There was something absurd in that scene. Maybe it was the supernatural beliefs of the neighbors that influenced his thoughts. In any case, he had just had an illogical experience. Was it a real experience or something he had only imagined? At that moment he wasn't capable of making a judgment, but one thing that he was absolutely convinced of, was having seen or imagined that there were two riders astride the same horse. The total certainty that nothing was sure.

He took his gaze away from the darkness and returned to his own ruminations. It was difficult for any husband who loves his wife to see her dying and incapable of doing anything for her. To see her stretched out on the bed and not be able to do anything except feel sorry for himself; maybe cry out in anger and impotence. The feelings of angst that assaulted him deepened his loneliness.

His mind went to Ruth, thinking about the possibility that she could really share his pain. But that thought followed its course with leaving a trace. The night was tenuous in a certain way. He lifted his sight only to again see the two horsemen who were still crossing the railway. The horse hurried without moving from its place. Mother Nature moved fear through the expected channels, and Charles remembered the weathered face of his father Pete, his eyes perfumed by the dense procession of the dawn. He recalled a random morning, while huddled next to the bedsheet, he begged God to receive into his arms the man who had been a joker and blusterer, and even more than a blusterer, a fraud. "Look at me, son: when I'm dead and you're in danger, just make this sign, the one from the lodge."

The riders continued to cross the tracks. Charles made sign his father told him about and the dogs started barking. Seconds later, old man Pete appeared, fleeing from the furious canines. He stopped when he got to the front of his son's house and repeated the solemn sign. Then next to Pete, Charles saw Jake Duke, his neighbor Clif's grandfather. A sort of tenderness passed through his awareness upon seeing them. They were always inseparable friends. Charles remembered his intelligent look, his short stature, his calloused hands, and a book underneath his arm when Jake would come to their house.

"Hi, Pete…"

"Man, the breeze sure is strong here…"

"There's no breeze. I came because I wanted to discuss a chapter in this book."

"Let's see what kind of foolishness you have today."

"Foolishness? You must be making a joke. It's about no less than the …"

It could've been a book about history or religion. Or maybe a news magazine. And then the two old men would immerse themselves into their reading, sending Charles or Clif off to fetch a quart of rum.

And then they spent the rest of the afternoon discussing for as long as the liquor would last. They were grand old men, Charles thought. Grand like their own histories.

The greatness was explained in part because Jake was a descendant of some Ashanti king. And Pete had Scottish grandparents. It was the pride of the family, and that infuriated Jake, who unlike Pete, would proudly boast of his pure African blood.

Meanwhile, the frightened townspeople cursed all the generations of demons and possessed canines. The next day, each one would tell their own version, and the clamor of the dogs would reach the neighboring towns. Many will say, the duppy came back for Lorena but the dogs chased it away. That must've been something Ruth did.

"Damned Bowman," said Charles, when he saw the two riders on the horse vanish, "I'll cut off my ear if Bowman wasn't behind all of this."

He went into the house to check on Lorena. He found her relatively calm and decided to go over to the Dukes to speak with Clarita.

Clarita met him at the door, her voice was kind as always, her gentle smile, her unhurried words simultaneiously carrying toughness and tenderness. It was the usual way of being for people with deeply held convictions.

"Charles. Come in, make yourself at home."

"Thank you."

"Clif is busy right now."

"Well, I'd like to speak with you."

"Oh, in that case, let me get you a drink."

"Yes, thank you, it will do me some good, but not too strong."

"Yes, I know, you've got the 'pastors' complex."

He wanted to have the opinion of someone like her, someone who worked miracles curing the people who lived in the town, but who also still wasn't integrated into the community because she rebelled against their values. That's what he wanted, to hear from those lips some concession, something to help give him a foothold to go from his parents' world to the one he had known since he went to high school, the world of the Dukes. The world that from the outside seemed to be in a total struggle with the one of Lorena and Ruth.

Because it was tough to think about the thousands of old wives tales that didn't have a single notion worth saving. But Clarita Duke was an insurmountable wall. Definitive silence.

She went to look for a pen and paper and wrote a few words and handed it to Charles.

"Lorena needs to see a specialist," she said, "He's a very good doctor."

Charles read the name. Clarita's attitude seemed absurd to him because everything would be fine if the cause of her illness were physical. Conventional medicine would be fine if it were something natural, but the suffering Lorena was experiencing wasn't physical, although the outward symptoms were. Because it was necessary to remember things like that happened. She was attacked by an evil spirit and she fell to the ground yelling and choking. The white specter left her that way and with uncommon brazenness used the front door to leave.

In spite of all of this, Charles had the firm conviction that it wasn't going to be the rue or any of the other herbs that they rubbed onto her body. What saved Lorena from dying right there without even getting the chance to say goodbye to him, were none other than the injections that Clarita gave her. He returned home with the taste of his visit on the tip of his tongue. Sharply in the nape of his neck, he carried the cruel tranquility of Mrs. Duke. He put on his old shoes and rocked himself in the hammock, his eyes began to close.

Clarita Duke didn't want to respond. She couldn't explain the presence of the powder in the flower pot, Pete's revelation, or Nabe's comments. She refused to explain anything. The dream ended with her disquieting thoughts.

The twenty-fourth night at midnight Charles saw on the wall the number twenty-four and his father standing next to it.

"I've come from Panama," he said to Charles, "and I'm bringing you the number. Play it with confidence."

Charles woke up at that time and after turning on the lamp, he stood there watching the Lorena tranquilly sleeping for the rest of the night. At four o'clock in the morning, it occurred to him to write down the number and go back to sleep, but it was already time to get up.

At seven o'clock he was in Gleda Brant's house. There he bought eighty lottery pieces and he could then add them to the 190 pieces he purchased between Rupert and Granados. The Panamanian radio station announced the prize. Charles won 3,420 colones.

The whole village found out. The news about Charles winning the lottery deeply bothered Christian Bowman. That's why the very next morning he started playing 250 colones a week. He had played the number nineteen for eighteen months straight before he was able to bask in the satisfaction that he had won more than his rival. His own glee made the work of the town's run-come-tell-its completely unnecessary. Bowman himself told everyone of his tremendous triumph.

The only people in the town who seemed unimpressed with Bowman's feat were the Dukes. Charles will always remember Clif's unusual comment, "Look, Charles, people are stupid. They make the banks rich, which makes them the true winners. Don't you see that the banks win without investing anything at all, they don't even have to promote themselves."

Charles burned with the desire to explain to Clif that he wasn't like the rest. That he had indeed won with the number twenty-four and that his situation was very different since Pete came from Panama and showed him the number. Only it was just that there was no way to communicate that. Clif wasn't the boy he once knew playing by the river. The friendship had undoubtedly survived, but their understanding of one another had died.

It was a tragic thing to know that, in the final analysis, any man was fundamentally alone. He thought about those adventurous times with Clif. The days when they would go hunting after some squirrel or a bird. The unsuspecting victim sitting atop a guava tree, claiming its right to live. Iguanas, fatigued from leaping; pulling back the rubber, seeing the stone take off on its fatal trajectory through the thick afternoon air, and unremorsefully watching life escaping from the creature's body. And they shared those moments of happiness, it's true, as if it were necessary to affirm their dominion over the other animals. But afterward, the misty silence of the forest remained. The air tinged with violence, the sun, the rain, and the agony of sweat.

The Blue Watering Hole. Display of ability and skill; the physiognomy of his black nakedness in the water, delight, coolness; his still undisputed presence in the lowlands. But later, each one followed his own path. Because when you really get right down to it, every being is left to face the Source of Existence alone. During their years as students, Charles and Clif spent quite a bit of time together. One night in Springfield's they came across two black girls and the memory of that encounter will always remain a topic of conversation. The moment was something the two could share. Remembering the deeply melancholic music that dragged them to the floor; a subtle imperfection that nevertheless returned them for a brief time to the heat of their humanity. Because when a couple dances in Springfield's, they recreate their existence.

He was kissing one of the girls and she smiled jovially. It was then when he felt an enormous illusion about oneness and believed he should share it all. But in that same smile, there was the seed of the tragic human condition, limited because each person is an individual. And he discovered this by himself, just like the ultimate destiny of humanity.

But now, memories of his childhood and youth assaulted him, his communion with Clif, the mutual understanding that seemed to have saved their humanity

No, it had nothing to do with the Dukes. The dream quickly moved away into the distance and brought him back to reality. He got out of the hammock and went to look for his family: one is his wife and the other is his wife's shadow, both kind and attentive, both concerned for him.

"Ruth, you should get some sleep."

"Sleep?"

"Yes. Sleep, even if it's just a little."

"How could you even think of that? Don't you know that Lorena is like my sister, a little sister to me?"

"You should get some sleep in any case."

"I can't. I made you some soup. Have some."

"Thanks. But you should lie down for a little on the couch."

"In a little bit, Charles, in a little bit."

Charles tried the soup. Its flavor was characteristically Ruth's cooking, not as good as Lorena, but you had to know them both really well to see the difference.

"It's good," he said, and she smiled with sadness.

"I'm going to have a little before you get started again."

The night went by silently. Silently, except for the stubborn sound of spoons hitting the sides of the earthenware bowls. Then, unexpectedly Lorena called out to Charles.

"Lorena...," the soup was caught midway down his throat, "Lorena..."

"Charles, where are you?"

"Here...I'm here..."

"Charles. Pete says that there is a white powder under the large potted plant. Did you hear me? Underneath the big..."

"Yes...underneath..."

"Rub lime on your hands and get that powder out right now. You have to do it right now."

"Yes, yes, I'll do it right away. How do you feel?"

"Charles, do it right now."

"Yes, I'm going – just as stubborn as always – I'm going. But, tell me how you feeling?"

But Lorena fell asleep, again she was out of his reach.

He cleared the path to the kitchen, between the condensed air of the house. He was trembling. It wasn't easy to decide to carry out the order because if there were a packet with white powder underneath the pot, and if his wife didn't put it there...And if there were no packet...If he did find the powder, he thought, he would have to call Mrs. Duke. If he didn't find it, he would have to hide this information from her. Period.

He looked for some lime and after cutting it, he rubbed the juice into the palm of his right hand and on the soles of his feet. Then he went to the window slowly, tense, and in a cold sweat. It was a terrible moment. Suddenly his twenty-three years—including his time at school and in seminary—the past and present came together, concentrated at that moment. He lifted the large planter and tossed the powder out the window.

He thought he should call Mrs. Duke for his own benefit. It was true, the powder was there, but only he had seen it. His years in school told him that it was just a suggestion, a strong mental suggestion. At the very least, he thought, that he should call Ruth. But she also would be suffering from the same misfortune and it wouldn't have done very much. Dark forces? That same afternoon he had seen a pair of men on a single horse crossing the tracks. He will never forget the sign of the lodge, the sudden appearance of an ethereal being that looked like his father, the dogs giving chase, the other apparition of Jake Duke. But he also had the paper with the address of the specialist in San José, in the handwriting of the town's most educated woman.

In spite of his consternation, he managed to sleep a little. He then had a conversation with Pete, his father, and Jake, his old neighbor. Both explained to him that with the help of the doctor, Lorena's life would be extended for a while longer, but that the damage was already done and it was too late. A fungus in her stomach was at the root of the harm. And Bowman was the one responsible.

Charles woke up in a sweat. Lorena continued in a deep sleep, indifferent to faithful Ruth's distress who periodically would nap leaning against the bed.

He spent an hour swallowed up by a sort of bitter sweat. And perhaps he would have stayed like that indefinitely if Lorena hadn't called out to him again.

He ran to her side.

"Charles, get me out of this house before they kill me."

"Yes, Lorena … yes … tomorrow …"

"Charles, Bowman hates us and you know it."

"Yes, I thought about that."

"They saw the duppy … it attacked me … They saw it. I was just dreaming … dreaming about your father. He says that there is some white powder in the window."

"I already took it out."

"Nabe did that."

"Nabe, Bowman's wife?"

"You must rub some lime on your hands and get that powder out of here."

"I already took it out."

"It's underneath the big flower pot …"

"I already took it out."

"Oh Charles, Charles …"

The smell of lime filled the room. Ruth grabbed Charles' hands with terror in her eyes. Charles felt an intense tingling along his spine.

III

That afternoon, Christian Bowman saw them cross the yard and approach the McForbes house. He found it difficult to resist that undefinable urge that was overpowering him, a mix of fury and sorrow. It left a miserable taste in his mouth, like that of a friend's betrayal. His tormented eyes were fixed on a pile of manure. But he let them pass. Brown and McForbes continued on their way without seeing him. Closing his eyes for a moment, Christian held his breath. He parted the branches where he stood while he watched from a distance as the men zig-zagged through the pasture.

The weapon trembled in his hands. An iguana that measured the length of two men's steps reposed on a branch with its head raised, muscles tense.

Bowman heard Nabe's voice teaching their children about the Ten Commandments. He watched Brown and McForbes approach the wire fence and then crouch down. He pulled the trigger with rage. The flash of green passed through the tense afternoon air. The iguana fell dead to the ground. A feeling of intense cold emerged from the place where the iguana fell.

Only Brown turned back to see. They crossed the fence, their figures getting smaller and smaller with each step.

Frustrated, Christian headed to his own house.

Nabe was waiting at the door. Her eyes flickered as they always do in critical moments.

"Did you see Brown with that son-of-a-bitch?"

"Yes. How'd you know?"

"They sent for Charles. He went to go get him. Lorena's sick."

"What?"

Nabe went into the house, followed by her anxious husband. Eager for news, Christian repeated the question.

"A duppy got her when she was out turning the cacao."

"What? But, in daylight?"

"In the pure light of the day."

She walked to the bedroom and stretched out across the bed.

"Don't play innocent with me. I know you very well."

Christian walked around the room twice. Then he went to the refrigerator and took out some rum and two glasses.

"Bitch!" Nabe said with satisfaction.

"Are you happy now?"

"Bitch!"

From a distance, the clouds began to gather.

"Close the window."

Obediently, he got up thinking about the long passage of time that had been building up between then and now. Wishing he had been able to control his impulses and that Nabe would've forgiven him for having had a few too many drinks and falling asleep on the night of her birthday.

He walked across the small room, the glass dancing between his thick fingers. He warmed the glass, breathing in the air that was heavy with repressed desires, frustrated dreams, and broken days. Finishing off the last drops, he gathered the pieces together, one after the other, until his body was left at the mercy of his wife's violent caresses. And suddenly the day submerged into moans.

The beginning of the sunset caught him by surprise as he finished off his third drink. It wasn't right to contradict Nabe because she knew very well about Lorena's rape. Ever since that moment, she refused to believe that it was rape, but instead the actions of a brazen woman who willingly gave herself to Christian and for that she hated Lorena. After everything that happened, Nabe said that Christian was a man and equipped by nature to take pleasure in the female sex. Christian, of course, had his hands tied. He had no choice but to leave Nabe with her own conclusions because with God as his witness he wasn't capable of anything else. Just as well, it would hurt that good-for-nothing, son-of-bitch Charles, he would get what he deserves. Charles was always a professional hypocrite. An arrogant man who believed in nothing.

Bowman went into the kitchen to pour himself another drink. Nabe was in a deep sleep, full of sighs. Like burning charcoal, her dark figure glowed in the light that filtered in through a crack.

He poured himself a double. He moved to the front porch thinking that it would be cooler there. The fortunate Nabe could sleep soundly when things had taken such an unexpected turn. The world was like that. Some people react by sleeping or crying in the best of moments. Others merely let out a laugh. But Christian, he was one of the ones who always worried. Because the triumph ends with the goal. And without a challenge, life falls short.

That afternoon Nabe gave herself to him completely. As if persuaded by her hatred of her husband's weaknesses, she wanted to reward him. She realized her great dream: that Christian would hate Lorena. Hate her to the point of wanting her dead. It was a great accomplishment.

But for his part, he was genuinely worried about Lorena's fate. He settled into the rocking chair on the veranda. He saw his enemy come out onto his own front porch and drop into the hammock. "That jackass," he thought, "that's why he wanted Lorena, to make her suffer."

He listened to the first sounds of the night coming from the passionate voice of a yigüiro.[5] He heard Nabe moving in the bed and his thoughts returned to the hours immediately before, the feverish steps, the two men crossing the yard, the green blur of the iguana, its visible trace on the ground; the people gathering at the McForbes house; Nabe, her hand on the back of his neck; the duppy that attacked Lorena in the pure light of day, according to his wife; Nabe's satisfied certainty that he was the one responsible for his hated rival's pain.

"Nabe…"

He heard her moving again in the bed. He got up and went toward the bedroom.

"Nabe, get up!"

"What happened?"

"Get my clothes. I'm going to Limón."

"But … Don't tell me you're getting scared now!"

---

[5]Yigüiro, a bird also known as the Clay-colored Thrush. It is the national bird of Costa Rica and it is known for its unique song that becomes more melodious as the rainy season approaches.

"Getting scared? No, it's not that. I've got to give Charles the final blow now that his defenses are down. Get my clothes ready to catch the pachuco.[6] I just have fifteen minutes."

At five o'clock the pachuco train arrived as expected. He looked for a seat on the side of the McForbes house, completely forgetting Nabe and her waves of goodbye from the veranda. From the window he could see Charles in the hammock, his head barely raised to watch the passing train with its long parade of cars.

The train headed straight and enthusiastically expanded as it made its way through the cacao groves of the lowlands. The hope that he would be able to save Lorena reached gigantic proportions because he could be what the people wanted, but he wasn't capable of causing Lorena harm. Once he tried to do something good for her and it caused considerable damage. Now he would do anything to save her from this unexpected suffering.

Perhaps it had been a mistake. Perhaps instead of grabbing Charles, the spirit made Lorena its victim. Or perhaps it was just by chance. There was only one person who was able to set things straight, the obeah man. The power man. The train got to the port early. The streets were fresh after a recent rain, every so often puddles of water reflected the beauty of the clouds above.

His father and sister lived in Puerto Limón and his first instinct was to call them. Then, he thought about putting aside the idea of meeting with the obeah man, but something stronger than Bowman had made the decision for him.

He lifted the telephone and carefully dialed the number. His sister's shrill voice responded in terrible Spanish on the other side. Christian spoke to her in English.

"Oh, it's you. No, don't come. Boy, don't even think about coming around here or else the old man is going to put a bullet in you. No, don't be stupid." Then she added insulting profane language to her complaints.

---

[6]Pachuco, a train that traveled through the small towns and villages of Limón Province, with the main destinations being Puerto Limón, Turrialba, and San José.

"Daddy says you've betrayed and sold out the family. A disgrace. You've humiliated us in every possible way. You disappointed us, Christian."

For a few moments, he forgot about the divide, the intimate struggle that battled inside to define him. The rusty sound of his sister's voice was everything. He held the mouthpiece in front of his face and then screamed at the indignant woman that he let them know before it all happened. "My sister is hysterical," he said and immediately asked himself if he had used the word correctly.

He went to a nearby bar and ordered a beer. Lorena Sam, beautiful, lovely, the two of them playing in the field with the innocence of children. The two playing, eating guavas in the solitude of the pasture, playing out make-believe scenes that perhaps they always had known; games that came from their genes, games that sprung from other children centuries before them; habits acquired long before Christian would be able to see the gentle flow of the creek for the first time. At the Blue Watering Hole, Lorena Sam and Christian, the two discovered the differences in their nudity. The two of them in the house of the obeah man, which was Ruth's house, and memories of the shouts, screams, and cries of pain when one of them hit their nose against the cot.

"You've betrayed and sold out the family, a traitor. Daddy's right."

He left the bar and walked to the corner. He walked between the red lights of a nightclub and he ordered an "Imperial."[7] From the jukebox, a bolero seeped through the faint haze.

"What can I get you, sir?"

"What?"

"What can I get you?"

"I already ordered an Imperial."

"He ordered it from me," another customer at the bar laughed scandalously, "From me!"

"I always said you have a face of a bartender," said his table companion and the laughter for a few moments overshadowed the rhythm of the bolero.

---

[7]Imperial, a popular Costa Rican beer.

Dreams that hushed his yearning had colored most of his days. But, without a doubt, in Lorena's smile, in her fiery eyes, he found for the first and only time the feeling of tenderness. A tenderness that, as it matures, becomes deceptive. Tenderness that makes you believe that love is a lasting reality and not a simple illusion. A passing storm that a woman or man feels in the presence of the one who leaves them speechless. Like what he used to feel for the burning charcoal that was Nabe. Tenderness was a less vague word than love. That is another thing that happens only once and never again. The bolero. Lorena Sam and Christian Bowman dancing in the half-light of any night. "Lorena, give me a popsicle." "Lorena, let's go for a walk." Lorena, Lorena.

But dreams always end. That's why he hated Charles. He came one day out of the shadows, with his school uniform and his seminary studies and he started to farm the land. He came with his idealistic stupidity and started to work the land that his father had set aside for him. Back then, the elder McForbes was very ill and maybe that was why Charles came back. What was certain is that with so much in his favor, it wasn't hard for Charles to steal Lorena Sam's affection from him. Charles definitely took her from him; along with her refined ways, her wit, her vocabulary, and her light skin color. She was so full of passionate devotion and Charles was a man of the church and a farmer who after a short while struck the path to prosperity. There were enough reports of his success to captivate just about anyone.

Charles put an end to his greatest dream. But dreams always end.

He asked the waiter to give him another. He couldn't leave before ten anyway.

Charles had destroyed his truth, the only thing he had in his world. Since his grandmother's time, his world was a vulgar one. The caustic horsewhip in grandmother's hand, her severity, her punishment for not doing what another had the nerve to do. There was never a lash that scarred so much flesh.

Christian saw or thought he saw Lorena sitting at the bar with her back turned to him. He got up agitated, ready to go toward her. But then he remembered the small town of one thousand five hundred residents where Lorena had been held in defeat by his wife's hatred and among many other disputes. No one could be in two places at once, it wasn't Lorena.

He should forget her and give in to Nabe. Especially now since his own family considers him a traitor. A traitor, a disappointment who sold out his family, just for having voted against their "official" candidate. A ridiculous thing after all—that a Jamaican would tell a native-born Costa Rican who they should vote for. Besides, he told them with plenty of notice, so that they too could choose to be winners. It was a matter of voting to win, and anything else was foolish. Because what did they gain voting for a candidate who vowed to solve the country's problems with a promise to end middlemen? Like that's not an honorable profession? Maybe they don't recognize this in Costa Rica, but a living creature just for the sake of being alive has the right to enjoy the privileges that God or Nature gave him? Wasn't it the common voice that said, "those idiots over there, who wants them?" Maybe in the stories that Mr. Sam used to tell, Brother Anancy didn't always win just because he was the most clever? Nevertheless, now his family called him a traitor as if he had never told them beforehand to vote for the opposition.

Christian never could love Nabe and for him. That set off a chain of regret. Because he remembered her young, open like a flower and that she only could give him her own frustrations.

Miserable old man, accusing him now, after having destroyed everything. Yes, in a certain way, Howard Bowman was guilty of it all. Because he was a stingy and wretched old man. It's all his fault for having lost Lorena and for Nabe's never-ending frustrations. Because he did his part, passing the university entrance exams and Howard didn't want to pay for his overnight stay in San José, simply because his wife had bad feelings toward him. And now the old man talked about "selling out the family," when he sold out his own son so that he wouldn't offend his beloved wife.

The most he could knit together with Nabe were wounds and failures. He was attracted to her body of burning charcoal above all else, but her body wasn't Lorena Sam's body. He gave Nabe his masculine passion, just like he would have given it to any other woman. And he could offer nothing more because it was Howard's fault he wasn't enough to compete with Charles McForbes.

He decided to go ahead with his plan to see the obeah man and he left the bar. He continued on his solitary path, his face exhausted, carrying his last bit of hope on his back.

Clif also managed to leave Estrada. Just imagine! Clif Duke, the poorest of the three. And he had just come back recently with the prestige of an author. Imagine that, an author! And he, Christian Bowman, the son of a wealthy old man, couldn't study because his father's wife decided to close that road.

A light rain bathed his face and dampened the streets of the Port Limón. His childhood came back with the rain; the boy at home crying the afternoon an angry Howard Bowman let him know between beatings that it was wrong to speak disrespectfully to his stepmother. The boy bled copiously, caused by the fury of his own father. "Because I've hardly cracked your skull and come to find out you're trying to sleep with the maid, and your mother tries to get your attention and you ignore her, and you ignore her in such a disrespectful way."

After crossing the Cieneguita River, he recalled the theory his father offered about poverty: those who suffer are lazy and never put in the effort. The smell of the river, always muddy, running from the catch basin to ruin everything. On the bank of the river, the poor have built their houses, paying rent to the landowner. Many of them had been paying for fifty years. The boy who stayed in the house crying when his father, furious, bashed in his face for the second time for giving twenty colones to the maid because he thought she was poor and the idiot maid mentioned it to a neighbor who then said it to his dear father.

Walking down the wide and dusty street in Cieneguita through all of his unpleasant memories was a mistake. But it was better to walk than to suffer. Suffering was a masochistic way of affirming that one is alive.

The boy stayed in the house crying when his father, furious, threw a cup of hot water at his head because he tired of his stepmother's humiliations and he punched her in the stomach. "Evil son-of-a-bitch; you're not my son. Look at yourself in the mirror, you're so black. I don't know how you came out so black. Look at your sister. Your sister is so much lighter. You're not my son, my parents had European blood. You are blacker than a damned African savage."

He said that in front of Charles and Lorena Sam. The three had been in Mr. Sam's house when Clif came to call him: "Your father said that if you don't come immediately that he's going to send you to the reformatory." Christian wanted to run away, but Charles and Lorena insisted that he face his problems. They walked with him to his house where his father was waiting for him with hot water. And he would've thrown a second cup at him if the other children hadn't started to beg him to not be so cruel to his son.

Tired, painful eyes; tears that had been held back for such a long time, without the possibility of escape were trapped in his blood. Just like a flower, the night marched toward the roots of a bulb, as if the budding flower could be held back by returning to its origin.

Tired, painful feet from the rough road.

He stopped again at another cantina and ordered a beer. The foam, instead of stopping, it continued. It wasn't like the sea. The piss colored liquor reached deep inside.

His eyes burned too much. A light drop perforated the crust of time that covered them and began a slow voyage, cell by cell, to some precise place, leaving behind it a perfect trail, easy to trace with a simple glance.

The child's eyes burned when his father, furious, took a bit of bleach water and threw it in his face. "Because no son of mine is going to bring grades lower than a B into this house and get away with it."

Another beer. Another tear followed the same path. He got up to leave and he went to spit into the ditch. The eyes of the frightened bartender widened watching him walk away without paying.

One morning the boy took his suitcases and threatened to scar his stepmother's face if she stood in his way, he left the house in spite of his sister's pleas.

"I'm going to the Lince house. They're my mother's cousins. Clovis said that I could stay at his house. I'm old enough to earn my own living. I'm not a boy anymore."

"What about high school? Are you going to leave school?"

"No, sister, don't worry, I'm not going to leave school."

Christian looked at his watch; it was just a few minutes before ten o'clock. He had to hurry.

He knew the feeling can overtake a devoted client when he gets near the obeah man. A sensation of fear, a sort of somersault that he's never been able to define. Christian dried off his sweat several times: copious sweat that anxiety—but what's that? is it anxiety?—and intense heat caused to flow from the forehead.

He thought about the first time that he had enough courage to see the obeah man. It was July. For four long months, he had put up with the bellicose school principal. But it was already too much. Since they were both delegates for the same political party, there should have been better understanding between them. But that wasn't the case. The principal was petulant and he wasn't putting up with that from anyone.

First, he tried winning her over with charm. Nabe organized a party for her—even though she came at the end of March—they welcomed her into their home, they made things easy for her so that she would feel that the town was her home. But there she was. Rebellious, petulant. Reluctant to accept Nabe's hospitality. First, she didn't want to live in their house. Then she didn't accept the additional salary that the Bowman's gave to all of the previous school principals. He'd never seen anyone so blindly resistant.

Christian decided to get her to fall in love with him. He brought her gifts, treated her with the gallant attention of a sophisticated city professor. And he tried to seduce her, render her powerless, and impose his virile will over her femininity. But the girl rebelled and rejected it all. She didn't even want to leave town for a better job that they offered her. Against all of his polite gestures, she wasn't influenced at all. Against the pressure from Christina, she mobilized a group of parents. And when he wanted to seduce her, she brought him to her house, and disrobed from the waist up and started reading a magazine in bed.

The people of the town, in general, kept quiet. They allowed things to happen. But they didn't forget the girl's courageous denunciation. And that was enough to keep Bowman at bay for a while.

He had no other option but the obeah man. In November the teacher either suddenly fell ill or lost patience with everyone. First, she had problems with her staff and then with the town's political chief, and finally with the parents. That's why one day she took the train without anyone pressuring her and left without saying goodbye to anyone. Nabe spread some gossip around the town—Christian fixed her and he'll keep on doing it to anyone who challenges him from now on. The second time that he went to see the obeah man, he couldn't be helped because the same person who he tried to harm was protected by the obeah man. And it was then when he made a real change, forming a convenient friendship.

Now he walked the streets of Cieneguita, his feet sweating, knees failing him, his throat sore, his hands cold …

IV

Damn, when it rains, it pours. Even when I saw the Centeno family's damn aristocratic air, I still signed on. Doctor Centeno didn't back down, like a cacique.[8] It was as if he were the cacique of San José, and it's not that I'm being cliché or anything. No seriously, I'm not being cliché. The doctor had wall-to-wall carpet in his office and he chewed fine tobacco. The entire room was covered with endless pockets of pedantry. Shit, it's not that I'm being cliché here, no, it's not that at all. It's the God's honest truth.

Engracia was now dead. I remember the morning when I saw the bold headline in the newspaper. She and twelve elderly people dead at the bottom of the Virilla. I knew my father-in-law had given her medical clearance even though she suffered from high blood pressure. He told me himself over a few drinks. "She drove the van for the nursing home and one of the survivors said that all of a sudden she became nauseous and lost control of the vehicle sending everyone plunging down to the bottom of the river."

I imagine my father-in-law behind his elegant desk, asking her medical history with that characteristic indifference he's known for:

"Name?"

"Engracia ..."

"Engracia, what?"

Having known exactly how I knew Engracia, I know his terse question lingered in the air without finding a precise place to land. It danced around without a single ear picking it up, and then to return to the doctor's lips coming back like a boomerang. A word that's not rhetorical. A man's word.

But also, I know my father-in-law and I know the bastard would've yelled at her.

---

[8]Cacique, a Spanish word derived from the language of the Taino tribe, meaning either chief or a local political boss.

Yes, he yelled at her. Engracia herself told me afterward. Of course, she only told me part of the story, the other part she kept to herself. Only if she knew that I couldn't have cared less.

"Engracia Pe… ña."

Engracia's voice was like a soft and sensual melody. Well, I know that is a little….how should I put it? A little grandiloquent. But it's that there are definitely grandiloquent things in the world for true. The doctor had to lift his gaze to forget the patient who was in front of him and began to see the beautiful woman, standing there in high heels, who was nervously looking at him. Unable to contain his primitive impulse, he took off his glasses. He told me himself. The shameless bastard took off his glasses. And he saw her that morning. She was wearing a light green dress. That damned woman was very pretty. The best thing to ever come out of Grecia and I say that with all honesty. I went there to visit and I couldn't find anything or anyone that compared to Engracia. But besides being very pretty, she was unlucky. She was messed up. That's what she was. Messed up as only she could be.

"Age?"

"Forty-five, doctor."

Women that age usually don't look so pretty, but Engracia did. That's what took my father-in-law totally off guard. He asked her to disrobe. When Engracia takes off her clothes, everything is like marble. Polished marble and it's not cliché. It's like seeing a marble statue bathed in light. This would've gotten anyone's blood going. That woman almost killed me. Almost. She had shadows on her skin, blue shadows. Red hair that made me think of my own mother. My mother used to give me watermelon and I didn't like it. But she was convinced that watermelon was the best food for the liver, but her insistence was fanatical. A sweet voice clamoring, "Son, come and eat watermelon." She took old Lucas off guard. Then you throw away the rind. When Engracia's hair falls over her bare shoulders, it highlights the marble which then takes on a rose-colored hue.

He didn't need to beg too much. She just got close to the doctor, well that's what he told me, and confessed to him that her husband was a drunk and she hated drunks.

That was true. He was a drunk who came home night after night smelling of guaro[9] and cheese. Without even bathing he would take off his pants and throw himself on top of her, just pulling up her night-gown as much as he needed. A nasty, flaccid drunk. And she covered her face with a pillow, while he enjoyed his beastly depravity.

One time she fought him off with the anger of a wounded tigress. But in spite of his drunkenness, he was still quite strong and struck her with such violence that it forever took away her urge to rebel.

That day she confessed it all to the doctor. Imagine what it was like for me as a young boy, with red watermelon, fresh, sweet, with black seeds in the middle; and besides a sweet mother who didn't know how to appreciate my preference, begging me. So, that's what happened to the doctor afterward. First, he fell into her clutches. Then, he became the one who was being begged. In reality, she was dying to start over again.

She kept on telling him details of her history. She got mixed up with a guy and she was pregnant.

My father-in-law gave her the medical certificate and continued seeing her. To him, eleven or twelve lives were worth less than her moments of light. Light in the midst of a wretchedly dark world. The poor devil looked for a little bit of peace and found it in Engracia's arms. He gave her the abortion because he didn't want to lose her. My father-in-law is a motherfucker.

I had to be in solid health because to get involved in a family like that is a real mess. I know that sometimes when I'm talking that I can say cliché or snobbish things and other times I can be rather casual. Well, not casual, but at least not like people who are at my same level. It's like what that African poetess once said, "Here I am, trapped between two cultures." Goddammit, and I don't know which one to grab onto.

But I was telling you about my father-in-law. He is from one of those families that go way back. You should see the china, the large table, and the imported tapestries in the house. You have to see the world of portraits hanging on the wall, always there. Dammit, I became cliché

---

[9]Guaro, a distilled alcohol derived from sugar cane from Central America.

again. In their portrait gallery, faces of every stock are joined together. You have to see what it's like to grow up with that and read over each one of their names and what they did. And on top of all of that listen to your mother and other members of the family speak of the glories of their lineage. Glories that are interwoven with the history of the country. Don Ormelindo Gutiérrez Boza, a Spaniard who lived in Orosí Valley. He married doña Felipa González, María Gutiérrez González, their only child, married Féderico Peña Calvo. Oscar Buenaventura Peña Gutiérrez, doña Amalia Soto Himmel … the never-ending succession of names and bronze plaques who filled and affirmed Lucas Centeno's youth. Moras and Granados, Salvatierras, and almost at the end, attorney Oscar Centeno Mora, who married doña Aminga Vidaurre Caramelo, a distinguished Guanacastecan woman and from there—according to Esther—the roots of the family's love of folklore. It was an ancestral lineage of legislators, governors, mayors, bishops and a few nuns. But the greatest of them all was Hugo Centeno Hewit, who studied in Europe in the universities of Poncelea and Cerro Triste and was an ambassador in Washington. Author of the celebrated work, "My Little Coffee Bush," which incorporated a European element into the national literature. He never managed to complete another book because of his political appointments, but during his time he received numerous honors.

My poor father-in-law tried to emulate him. That's why he became the head of the National Hospital, but the thousands of deaths made him leave because each death was added to the one before and it all rested on his shoulders. Every error committed by the doctors and paramedics led to more and more gray hairs. Thousands of employees depended on him. And besides he was a professor at the University and he ran his private practice. And he only earned fifteen thousand colones a month for all of that. Fifteen thousand a month, when he could have made so much more abroad. But he stayed for the love of his country, sacrificing himself. At least that's what he said. And believe me, nothing my father-in-law says is cliché.

Of course, as aristocratic as he was, Engracia's death was a blow. Engracia's skin was much too smooth for him. She often appeared in my father-in-law's office when it was time for him to leave and stayed there with him until tiredness forced them to go to sleep. I'm not saying he killed her on purpose because the truth is that if it weren't for Engracia, my father-in-law would've had to resign himself to stagnate just like his wife. He needed Engracia, but being such a miser, he gave her the medical clearance instead of taking care of her and maintaining her.

I once told him to be careful because he could hurt himself. He told me that he's not a coward like me and that he wouldn't run away. But he had no objection in recognizing that Engracia was too much for a man his age. And also in spite of her age.

He killed her because he was cheap. Shit, I don't think he ever gave her even a piece of candy and she carried on with him just out of fear of losing her job. Or for fear of looking for me. At least according to her, that's what it was. I'm not that stupid to believe that.

Days after Engracia's death, Lucas called me into his office.

It was a sad thing to know that he would have to call me into his office at a moment like that. But my father-in-law had very few friends. Since my mother-in-law's death, he threw himself into his work. He was distancing himself from the real world. Because don't tell me that it's real to live buried inside a hospital, with people dressed in white attending to people dressed in hospital gowns? No, please, that's not real. That's a world of fiction we created to fight against what is truly real: human suffering. The only contact my father-in-law had with the real world was us. It doesn't seem right. Of course, there was Magdalena. But the two of them don't get along very well. Besides, Magdalena isn't the type of person anyone would go to in order to talk about a problem. Especially if it's a sexual issue. And since Lucas Centeno would never go to his adopted daughter to talk about that. Nor to Esther. So that's why he called me. It was impossible for him to call Esther and tell her: "Daughter, Engracia just died, your husband's former lover and until yesterday my lover, has just died."

We couldn't talk in the hospital because I can't stand anything that smells like ether. All hospitals smell of ether. We couldn't talk there, so that's why we went for a drive in Centeno's elegant automobile. He has a beautiful car. Not as large as mine, but similar more or less.

"It's affecting you quite a bit, isn't it?," I asked him after a period of silence.

"I killed her," he said, and damn, at that moment he seemed cliché. "I killed her," would sound ridiculous just about anywhere.

We ended up at the Ojo de Agua Waterpark. Few people were swimming, but Centeno was obsessed with the living image of Engracia. He discovered much too late that she touched him deeply. Too deeply. And it's not that I'm cliché or cruel, but in a certain way, Engracia's death was his own salvation. Because if he got her to stop working, he would've had to marry her. And if he married her, he would have to choose between her and his work. The first option would've quickly reduced her to the sad condition of a vegetable. The second option would imply losing Engracia. Because the intensity of passion is in direct proportion to one's age. And everything that escapes that rule is an aberration. Incongruent in any case. And being on such an emotional level, it would've destroyed them both.

We could've enjoyed Ojo de Agua since as I mentioned before there were few people there. But we just talked about Engracia and more about Engracia and my father-in-law's frustrations. He never measured up. He couldn't measure up because there are things that you learn when you're young and through the years you gradually perfect them. But he didn't learn when he should have. My mother-in-law was a "dreadful prude," as one of the neighbors once described her. Once she asked Centeno for a divorce because according to her some things are reserved for prostitutes. In a certain way, women like her encourage prostitution, since acting like that gives the husband permission to look elsewhere for what he's not getting at home. Then he's to blame. My mother-in-law was like that. A woman with a lot of defects and that was just one of many … But, we weren't talking about my mother-in-law, but rather my father-in-law. Poor guy. If he could've fallen into Engracia's arms thirty years earlier, maybe she could've been saved. But perhaps thirty years ago, Engracia still wasn't Engracia. The things that she and I learned together thanks to an alcoholic husband! That woman would have destroyed me. I learned with Lorena as well. And the things Victoria and I invented. No, Centeno couldn't measure up. Poor devil.

A man like Lucas Centeno Vidaurre grows up in the solitude of his room. A sensitive boy with two brothers overly identified with the family legacy. He had no other choice but to inhabit his world of fairytales. And it's not that I am being cliché, but it's very true. He had to fill his emptiness with fairytales. We could imagine him lost among the fine china, African gold, Peruvian silver, and other things that corrode over time. And through the window his sensitive spirit connected with the distance outside, with the slow fragrance of morning.

Don Oscar, that's what my father-in-law called his own father, don Oscar. So cliché. I think I made a mistake earlier, my father-in-law is cliché sometimes.

Oscar Centeno, in any case, was a wealthy man. Attorney and businessman, he learned how to successfully combine business and the law. That's why they never wanted for anything in Lucas's house because they lacked for nothing. If anything, they had too much—specially prepared foods consumed on imported fine china. And then the oil paintings throughout the house. And lots of abstract art from when don Oscar went to the United States and brought back empty canvasses. Canvasses that said nothing and on the back had a label that said, "Made in the U.S.A."

Then the four unmarried aunts, flowers adorned with ribbons. And a mirror in the living room because one of their ancestors had specified in their will that the mirror must stay in the living room. A grand piano and much empty space. Divan, sofa, three chairs, side table, red rugs, reproduction vase, fireplace—imagine that, a fireplace in a house in the middle of the tropics—and lots of visitors. Hateful visitors.

That's why my father-in-law spent so much time in his own room. At least there he had the inoffensive image of a Nazarene Christ with a feminine face. No peace, but certainly calm. After all, that's what men look for in their home, to be an oasis of calm although they would never have peace. Peace only comes from struggle and not a single tico[10] is up for that.

---

[10]Tico, a term that means Costa Rican.

Well, who knows! I'm not the Pope so I can't get the world to be quiet. I imagine that in any case, Lucas didn't like seeing his mother go off to mass because he said that Esther looked like his mother when she would go to mass. He said that on a day she when was wearing a dress that he didn't like. Those are the sorts of conclusions that one starts making. His mother was very devout. Every day after returning from mass, she would stand in the door and hand out twenty colones worth of provisions to the poor. In exchange, she received the blessings of her regular clientele. My father-in-law also ran away from the honesty of his father, who once evicted a widow with three children from one of his properties and then donated it to the church and then let them decide who could stay there.

He ran away from the shadow of "My Little Coffee Bush" and its distinguished author. And that was very different from his brothers. They defined themselves, he wavered. Sometimes he accompanied his father to the Free Men meetings, to hear them preach about absolute liberty. You have the right to bring into the world the children that you want, earn the salary that the boss freely sets, and pay the prices that the business owners want to set according to supply and demand.

And his father did that in his business. Yes, don Oscar was a bold individual. There was nothing cliché about him. I got to know him. When he entered the Common Market, I saw that he could no longer keep up with the competition. So, he decided to return eighty percent of the capital invested in Europe and with that have his employees sell for a year and a half at prices that were below cost. Since then people just bought from him. Almost all the others went bankrupt. Only one competitor managed to survive and then the two reached an agreement and they raised the prices little by little. Perhaps it sounds a bit cliché but, I liked to hear Lucas Centeno say, "Don Oscar and don Franklin shared their wealth." Afterward, of course, the customers ended up paying more than they ever had before. But that was preferable to limiting his sacrosanct notion of liberty.

My father-in-law's teenage years must have been terrible. I say that knowing he's a sensitive man and as such, susceptible ups and downs. Because of that, he married the first woman who wasn't able to tell him that he wasn't faithfully fulfilling society's expectations. She told him later. She saved it for later. For when she already had the wedding ring and at least one child for him. That's one of those things that women frequently do, they hold things for later and then pounce on the victim when he least expected it. Of course, also some men do it too. But, that's not what we were talking about.

Night and day seemed the same in Lucas Centeno's life. He should thank me. First, my very presence disrupted his routine and second, I brought Engracia.

Centeno grew up and became a doctor. A chance decision to enter into a profitable profession. After bobbing around for a long time like a coconut in the sea, he found in his profession, the pathway that would order his steps.

But he could never free himself from the guilt that the decadence of the Centeno family caused him. Because he carries it in his blood, or at least supposedly he carries it in his genes, all of the courage of his lineage. The audacity of his forebears, those who shaped the country with their virtues and defects, and they gave him a name to leave as a legacy to his descendants.

Lucas's great-grandfather was a brave man. He had the hot blood of the Gutiérrez family line, just like old man don Ormelindo, who brought the furor of Moorish Spain with him and opened the path to Orosí Valley without anyone challenging him. And the fiery blood of the Soto Himmels, who moved the family toward the Central Valley where they cultivated hundreds of acres of tobacco, a hundred acres of vegetables, and a herd of cattle. The Soto Himmels were the ones who consolidated the wealth that don Ormelindo had started to build years earlier and that Felipe Peña nobly increased when he joined the family through his marriage to doña María, don Ormelindo's only child.

It's not that I'm being cliché, but the truth is that the family is worthy of admiration. But to be admired from a distance. So, when "My Little Coffee Bush" arrived in the hands of the President in print, it marked the climax of the family glory. Because in those moments the family was aware of its historical relevance, including the family's very specific mission, to be a model of Costa Rican society. But Centeno seemed to lack the boldness of his illustrious ancestors. The boldness of his grandfather, his father, and above all his great-grandfather, who upon seeing that the Sánchez family (more commonly known as the Sanch family because they changed their name after joining together with an Englishman), cut down their tobacco in order to plant coffee, he asked his neighbor about this sudden insanity. Then he found out that coffee had enormous possibilities for export to Chile and Europe. So, he did exactly as the Sanch family.

The entire family thought he was insane and doña Orlanda Salvatierra de Centeno was so frightened that she called the town priest, who filled her days of worry with holy water, prayer, incense and supplications. But in spite of that, don Oscar Centeno Granados carried on with his destructive act. Then they saw him visit the neighbor's house with too much frequency, and as a result, the priest ruled that it was a contagious epidemic, a consequence of God's anger. Because God gets angry if men don't go to church to adore the Holy Sacrament when it's presented. And the ladies of the town fearing that the epidemic would spread to the entire population, fanatically turned to worship.

Never before had there been so many paid masses in the parish. And an assembly of neighbors was called and after long deliberations, they agreed to call the two who were possessed by the devil to a meeting, with the hope of saving them from hell. The priest started the session with a lengthy retelling of all Satan had done in the history of humanity and ended by exhorting the two supposedly demented men to return to the bosom of the Holy Mother Church.

Old Sanch threw them out of his house by the point of his machete, threatening the priest for such an affront. And he said that as long as the parish had such a fool for a priest, neither he nor his family would return to mass. Because it was the height of stupidity that an idiot would have dared to come and insult him in his own house, in front of his wife and children. And besides that, he swore never again to contribute to the priest's financial upkeep. Centeno stayed true to his friend, united by their common expectation. And when the Englishman came to the town, the coffee was already in production.

The Englishman was in charge of exportation for many years and along with the Sanch family, the Centeno family prospered. They were dedicated to making a profit off of coffee, which produced great dividends. And from that generation, Don Oscar raised up three sons—one became a bishop, one became the governor of the province, and the third became a councilman in the municipal government. But the most famous of don Oscar's sons was don Hugo Centeno Hewit, who was a product of don

Oscar's second marriage after the death of doña Orlanda. Hugo studied in Europe in Poncelea and Cerro Triste. Theology, philosophy, and finally, letters. His return from abroad was indeed a national celebration. Great headlines appeared in the press about this legendary man.

Don Hugo was a professor to presidents and legislators, but the publication of his masterpiece, "My Little Coffee Bush," was the family's greatest moment because for many years his book managed to stave off the undesirable incorporation with the grossly uncouth masses.

Yes, the family was glorious, and Lucas Centeno felt responsible for its decadence because something terrible was now happening. His only daughter, who for so many years he saw growing despising black people, all of a sudden fell in love with a black man.

Maybe it was the Guanacastecan blood of his wife, doña Aminga Vidaurre. Maybe it was precisely that, the black blood that was in her veins.[11] The blood of a Spanish mulata.

And it was nothing personal against me, exactly, because at first, my father-in-law welcomed me into his home. He didn't throw me out before I became a part of their clan. He used to say that he loved black people and that he had many black friends. Black patients would come from Limón to look for him. But my marriage to Esther was an inconvenient matter. She was his only daughter and the one who would pass on the family glory. Since black people were so different—good for sports, dancing, and work—there was nothing to gain by marrying a black man. And Esther, as a Centeno and given her beauty, had no need to marry a black man. Much less a loser who completed secondary school and then went back to the farm. A loser whose faith was such that he gave up being a pastor when his wife died. A loser who returned to the city to study anthropology and received a doctorate in English. A loser, that's what I was to him. In spite of it all, I was never was able to rid myself of my Limonese identity.

---

[11]Guanacastecan blood, Guanacaste is the Costa Rican province located in the Pacific northwest of the country and borders Nicaragua. During the colonial period, enslaved African labor was used in the production of cattle, cotton, and rice. Although official Costa Rican historiography suppressed the African heritage of the province, the Guanacastecan folklore, music, and dances contain a number of Africanisms.

That's why Lucas Centeno felt guilty for having been so good to black people in the past and for having failed genetically, producing a woman instead of a man. Damn, it was so incredible that a physician would take all of that on, but it was true.

According to my father-in-law, his struggle against the witchcraft that killed Lorena showed him that education was necessary to deliver black people from barbarism and destruction. But that's not what I thought, after seeing and suffering the consequences of such practices, I would use them so that Esther and Magdalena, who both had detested black people for so many years, would suddenly fall in love with me.

Damn, and it's not that I have the body of an athlete. But the two fell in love so quickly. And I would've been an idiot not to take advantage, especially Magdalena who was gorgeous, plus she owed me … But, with Esther, it was different. It was more like a long-desired dream that came true. I don't know how to explain it and I'm not being cliché.

As if all of that weren't enough, my father-in-law was resigned to the idea that I was an absolute loser when we couldn't have children. It was fine that Esther would marry a black man, but a sterile one on top of it all was just simply too much. Too much for the old man's gray hairs. But, so you see we became friends over time to such a degree that he would tell me about his adventures with Engracia. We became especially close after my mother-in-law's death. But also his resentment toward me gradually passed. I think he consoled himself by saying that the family's ultimate extinction was better than leaving his spoils in the hands of mulatto grandchildren.

And as a final desperate measure, he started bringing Pérez to the house as if at the peak of his old age and failure, he would try to get Esther to be unfaithful to me. Maybe that way he could've gotten the grandchild he obsessed over. Shit, you can't deny that Centeno was a beast. Good Lord, I don't know. You have to be really obnoxious to do that. Really obnoxious.

V

Lorena was Charles McForbes' wife and it was something that everyone sensed would happen. The signs were there since that blazing afternoon when sun rested on the dome of the mango tree, and the people of the town were in a state of wonder at the strange occurrence, taking it as a sure indication of some important event.

That same afternoon Charles and Lorena discovered that their childhood affection had grown into a burning passion. Since his return from the city, he had barely seen her. It was as if the two of them were afraid of encountering one another. As she lay dying in bed, where for so many nights she had traced so many dreams, she would think about the intensity of that afternoon. Charles' hesitant footsteps approaching the house, the cautious knock on the door, and she watched him from the window and leaped toward the door to let him in.

As she lay dying, he would also think about that encounter, sharing with her what could possibly be their last night, remembering every moment of that distant afternoon that would join them forever.

"Lorena, is your father home?"

"Yes, how may I help you? Would you like to see him?"

"Yes. Just a question."

He smiled. The lines on his face were the opposite of the ones Christian had because his had smoothed out over time. They smoothed out, opening up for her again the incredible harmony that fascinated her so much. Like the coordinated furor of a gigantic wave, the white teeth, perfect, strong hands, long fingers.

"What, you've never seen me?"

"No. It's the first time."

"Uh, huh. I see."

They remembered every single moment of that encounter. She was sleeping deeply, he was positioned by the headboard staying awake to watch her, while Ruth's amusing snores drifted from the sofa and across the room.

Strong feet, big, agile. Youthful steps, a man's presence.

"You know Mr. Sam… I have a problem."

"A problem?"

"Yes, a serious problem."

"Well?"

"Well, you know that two years ago my father gave me that little piece of land and I've come to farm it."

"Yes…since you've been back, yes."

"Yes sir, when I came back, he gave it to me and I've been able to make something out of it. But, now it turns out that Christian bought the farm next to mine."

"Yes, I heard that. And?"

"Well, for the last few days he's put a hex on me."

"What?"

"Yes. The farm just isn't producing like it did before."

"No!"

"No, and the farm is in really good shape."

"Hmmmm. Let me see."

Mr. Sam's subtle hands reached a deep dimension. They reached a place where color originates. Mr. Sam revealed the land's history, its gradual decay, or rather its degeneration, its slow slide, its senseless decline. Just like the way the atmosphere heavy and drowsy with moisture pulled the land along with it to Charles's grandparents' house.

His grandparents' house, suspended on top of ancient wooden posts, sprinkled the city with its early lights. A hostile pain emerged from one of the streets and then stopped in front of him. In the distance, a church, a solitary school, a dreary park. And beyond that the nakedness of Montego Bay and thousands of wounded and naked faces.

"And your grandfather, well, you know how he was. And, what can you do in that case? It's good that your father sent you away to study. But your grandfather left years ago with some idiot woman and I haven't seen him since. Sorry, Charles, but you have to go back to Costa Rica."

That was a terrible frustration. But Charles returned to hear his father's insistence when he said you have to study, Charles. You have to find a way to study. At the very least, if there's no other choice, study Spanish and go to school here.

And all of that, the whole history of his frustrations, his years of struggle, the stormy period of his life; the problems he had adjusting and his personality, his decision to leave behind many of the good customs with nothing to replace them, his proximity to moral death, his rebirth through the work of his theology professor, an intense devotional life (on his knees at the altar, praying the Lord's Prayer, reading a psalm with tears in his eyes), listening to a voice quietly whispering to him, a voice that would roll away his heart of stone and give him one of flesh.

Long years of hope and frustration. Because five years can be long and hard if someone lives in isolation, without even knowing the city, without having broken new ground. A new path.

Two years tossed into the hopper, or hanging beside his diploma on the wall. Years that remain there, like the day he went to speak to Mr. Sam and he found Lorena standing at the door.

While Lorena was dying, she could not forget that part of Charles' history because time had converted them into a single being.

Mr. Sam did not say that Bowman had used obeah on Charles, but nor did he say anything to the contrary. He went to look for an ointment in the chest of drawers and he gave it to his client.

"Each night put a bucket of water on the patio. Then rub this across your body and then go to your bed." Suddenly the conversation became intimate, familiar. As if from that moment their destinies had been bound together. He went on to say, "You have to get up early, early every morning and sprinkle the water around the farm, following the property line next to Christian's land. But you have to be there at the very least two hours before he gets there. And then, in the afternoon, you have to stay there two hours after he leaves. And when you go to the farm, you're going to say 'The Lord is Great and Good' seven times. And you have to do that each and every day until the next harvest."

Lorena took it upon herself to meet Charles again at the door. And she boldly smiled at him; her teeth furiously charged with light. And she smiled at him like that so that he would never forget her. That way she would be sure that he would always remember her smile.

For the months that followed, Charles got up early every day and went to the farm in time to perform the prescribed ceremony. He ate his breakfast in the field and then immediately started his daily chores.

Each morning he got a two-hour head start on his day and two more hours in the afternoon. He kept his farm clean and well taken care of during the ritual; the pruning and the reseeding, clearing the trenches and caring for the roots.

In November, Charles went back to Mr. Sam's house and Lorena smiled again. This time the young man vibrated with her smile. He entered the house beaming, satisfied, and before he could close the door behind him, he said to Mr. Sam, "Success, old man and here's five hundred pesos just so you know that I'm not ungrateful," announcing his triumph.

That year his harvest went beyond his father's and Christian's put together and the town took pleasure in such an achievement.

Lorena wouldn't forget Christmas Eve when Charles came back to the house, well-dressed in a jacket and his eyes shining like a cornered cat.

"Hey, Lorena."

"Hi. Come in. I'll let daddy know you're here."

"No, you don't have to get him. I came to see you."

"Me?"

"Yes. Is your boyfriend coming by today?"

"My boyfriend? I don't have a boyfriend …"

"No? Isn't Christian your boyfriend?"

"No."

"Really, truly?"

"Really."

"So I … May I come by to visit on occasion?"

"I don't know."

"What do you mean, 'I don't know'?"

"I don't know, you know. You're the one who knows if you can come by or not."

"So, it's like that?"

"You're a man and the man is the one who must take the initiative."

"Only you know that, but even so I've already taken it."

"Well, that's what you must do."

"Have you had a boyfriend before?"

"No, why?"

"Should I speak with your father, so he doesn't object?"

"Don't be silly."

"Silly?"

"Yes, silly. You don't have the courage to do it."

"Really? I'll do it right now."

"But … wait … wait, Charles … Christian will be vexed seeing us together," she said.

"And, what right does he have?"

"He doesn't. It's just that … well … since we were kids, we were like brother and sister and I …"

"Like brother and sister."

"Yes, don't you remember? He practically lived in my house."

"Yes, you always were together. That's why I asked you if you were seeing each other."

"No. It never even occurred to me. He's like a brother to me."

"But, he's jealous."

"Jealous? No, he's not jealous just …"

"He doesn't like me?"

"No, it's not that either. I don't see why …"

"Well, it's hard to explain. You remember? There were five of us – Clif, Christian, you, and Ruth."

"And you …"

"Yes, me. Clif and I were able to study, but not Christian. I mean, we were three guys in the group and he was the only one who wasn't able to study."

"But he got his high school diploma. He went to Limón every week."

"Yes, that's true, but Christian is very ambitious. He's not happy having so little. He always tried to be the best one in the group."

"No, I don't think that was it. He must have been resentful because I never said anything about the two of us dating. He would always tell me about his little adventures."

"His little adventures?"

"You know, boyish stuff. That's all. Boyish stuff."

But if they dismissed the topic as trivial, a few days later they suffered the consequences of Christian's uncontrollable jealousy. First, he went to speak with Mr. Sam, asking him for permission to start courting Lorena. The old man called him a fool and told him in passing about her relationship with Charles.

"I have to call you a fool because after all of these years you passed by the house when he wasn't around and you kept your mouth shut 'til you see her with another man."

Lorena would still feel the sting and even the raw fury of the lash against her skin. She would see her father's fist unleash itself on Charles' mouth. Harsh, painful words. The boyfriend's impassivity.

"I'm not going to strike you, Mr. Sam, because you did me a big favor with all of that business with Christian. And besides, you're Lorena's father. But tell me the name of the shameful, lying bastard who told you that so I can go bash his face."

"Who told you that so Charles can go bash his face!" Lorena shouted at him. She screamed at him so he would know. Charles went to look for Howard Bowman and challenged him to either defend his wife or make her take back her words. But the old woman denied being the source of the gossip. Infuriated, Charles went to look for Mr. Sam, demanding that he either confirm what he said in the presence of the woman or take it back.

It was a scandal that held everyone in town captive.

Charles and Christian threw punches at each other because the latter came to defend his father. And perhaps they would have killed each other if some of the neighbors had not intervened. The fight lasted an hour and a half and when they separated neither could walk and were almost blind.

The hatred between the McForbes and the Bowmans festered, but in spite of it all, Charles and Lorena's courtship continued and one afternoon they decided they wanted to live together. Charles wanted to get married. Mr. Sam, red with rage, demanded it, but Lorena violently opposed the idea of marriage.

"It's that, it's that, daddy … If I get married, he's going to think that he owns me and do whatever he wants with me. I don't want to feel tied down by anybody and even so …"

"Even so, what?"

"I'm his woman and that's it."

She will now remember the sudden nausea and her own desire as Lorena McForbes, as it now chewed away at her conscience. Or when the anti-malaria campaign inspector called her Mrs. McForbes. Or when the children called her ma'am.

Christian never stopped pursuing her. "Leave him and marry me," he would constantly say to her. And one day he arrived at the McForbes house playing the fool and claimed that Charles had sent him there to collect a few things.

"But you and Charles don't speak."

"We patched things up."

She didn't want to believe him, but Christian showed him Charles' identification card as proof of his word.

"And he sent you this bottle of wine from Oporto. He says that it's raining in Port Limón and it's going to take him a little bit longer to get back."

While she looked for the papers, she served him a glass of wine, but Christian insisted that they both make a toast to the friendship between he and Charles and she obliged.

She will now remember the sudden nausea and Christian's desire … Christian… or whoever. He carried her off against her will and she couldn't fight him off as he dragged her to the bed to celebrate his lone triumph. He roared like a beast and she could no longer fight him. Defeated and humiliated, she lay hopelessly seething on the blood-stained sheet.

She carried that secret for a long time. But the rumor ran through the town, that the child she was carrying wasn't Charles's, but Christian's. Because Charles never lost his identification card and he and Christian never made amends. And in Limón they sold pills for horses. And the child was born with Howard Bowman's features.

One day Lorena finally told her husband what happened.

The offended husband waited patiently for her to recover from giving birth and he carried the child to an orphanage. Then, he mercilessly beat her for not telling him sooner. After that he fired two shots into Christian's body, wounding him in the abdomen and in the leg. He intended to castrate him.

That's how their hatred continued to grow. Now, on her deathbed, she will recall all the years that followed that event, the irrevocable moments that led to Christian's crushing criminal act and her encounter with the duppy.

Sleep overcame her during the light of day. The years now crudely revealed themselves. Her twenty-three years, five of them married, her unknown child who is living somewhere in the city without a mother.

Laid out on the bed, clinging to Charles, she could remember the night when they told her that Millie, as crippled and stupid as she was, slept with her husband. Millie slept with him in Nabe's bewitched bed. The affair with Millie caused a landslide, bringing their prolonged honeymoon to an end.

Ruth tried consoling Lorena—a husband is like a child. If they're hungry, they'll eat anything. But because she was on her period and because she didn't want to go before the Lord in that state, she didn't make it to church that Sunday.

She made a scene later because that stupid Millie is a bitch.

Always an open wound.

Charles healed the wound. And then came the incident with Christian. But Lorena could never forget the past. And each time that she decided to stay at home for the same reason while he went to church, he got short tempered.

Some Sundays, she would wait for him in skimpy clothes. And she would become enraged if he tried to make love to her because she wasn't like that damn crippled idiot that he had slept with last Sunday.

On Sundays she waited for him, the same way each time, and she tried to provoke him. But fearful that she would say the same thing to him again, he paid her no mind. Then she would complain to him that she was a respectable woman and not like the cripple who he fooled around with without the slightest feeling of disgust, while he preferred to sit and read a fucking book.

One week he didn't come home. Maybe he was at that cripple idiot's house without the slightest sense of repugnance. She had to spend Sunday alone. She got her clothes ready and went over to Ruth's house.

Laid out on the bed, defenseless and defeated, she will think about all of that. And about her love as well. Because love was what got her out of bed morning after morning for so many years to fix his breakfast (bammy, breadfruit, roasted plantain). And it was love that made her wait for him in the afternoons, dinner always ready on the stove, and clean socks and slippers laying out in the sun.

And it was love that made her fall on her knees so many times to ask God to protect him from the poisonous snakes in the bush.

Her love was like that, not extravagant, but love. And she had to love him even if it meant putting up with her own jealousy for so many years.

Clinging to Charles, she fell asleep and dreamed again of old Pete McForbes, her father-in-law. And he will come toward her, without being seen by either Ruth or Charles, to tell her with his melodious voice:

"My daughter, I told you be careful around Bowman."

"But, I was careful Papa."

"Careful? Not so much."

"But, I was careful. You know that."

"Even so, they're getting the best of you. Tell Charles to take out the little bag of powder that's under the big flower pot. Tell him to rub lime on his hands and take it out."

"Yes, I will tell him."

"Right now …"

"Charles …"

"Charles," Ruth shouted (Ah! Ruth the faithful friend), "Lorena is calling for you."

"I told him, Papa."

"Yes, I heard you, my child. Now listen good – you will have to go to San José. That's to say that they're going to carry you to the hospital. They're going to try to get you to go along with them. It's better. Christian doesn't hate you, but Nabe does and she controls him."

And other days and moments will inevitably come to Lorena's memory. The moments that fill her life. The ones that gave her life joy and pain.

Pete McForbes' casket added grief to her pain.

Lorena McForbes and her husband's cold hands and Ruth's blurry face, faithful Ruth.

She clung to those same people over the course of the last few days. Now, with death breathing down her neck, she wanted to deny the duppy's appearance. But she saw it. She saw it and it was white, just as Ruth had said. After all, they were both daughters of obeah men.

It's a pity that Mr. Sam wasn't there.

But life is like that.

But, wouldn't it also be a concern for Millie? Even God tried to stop Millie from causing so much damage and he told the Devil to push her in front of the train that afternoon. But the hussy was lucky and the train just knocked her off the track, leaving her cripple for the rest of her life. At least that way God was able to keep the possibilities of Millie doing whatever she wanted to a minimum.

It was truly a pity that Mr. Sam wasn't there. Her father's miracles went beyond saving Charles' farm. He saved Clovis Lince's marriage. Since he loved Grace Duke, Clif's mother so much, he desperately needed a woman to dampen the negative impact of her rejection. In reality, his only solution was to take up with Mary. At first, they fought a lot. But one day they decided to see Mr. Sam.

From what Lorena could hear, Millie was looking for Clovis like a mad woman, ready to carry him to Nabe's bewitched bed as well. She found out what the cripple woman had that drove everyone crazy. An obeahman, who had been in Nabe's service, told Millie that he would do a little something for her with a "burial." And each time the malevolent force attacked the Lince household, the couple would end up fighting.

Mr. Sam gave them various medicines and some toothpicks for Mary. And when the force of the "burial" overtook Clovis he would have a bad temper and start to insult her, instead of responding to him, she had to chew the toothpicks and say silently to herself, "the Lord Jehovah is Great and Strong."

It was enough. In short order, Clovis was a changed man, to the point of marrying Mary.

"Charles … Charles … the powder. Get rid of the powder."

"I already threw it out, my love. It's already gone."

"Charles … the lime … use the lime on your hands …"

"I already did it … go to sleep … don't worry … go to sleep."

Time was slowly expanding. One year he made it easy for himself, between the Francisco ward of the National Hospital and the room in the city he rented. The hospital smell was now part of his way of life. Occasional visits from friends. At midnight he would always find his way back. Every day her hand was colder, looking for the destiny of things.

Charles couldn't go to the hospital that afternoon because of the checkpoint. He was sure that the doctor would be furious because just a few months ago Charles was pestering him for any reason he could think of, but he wouldn't discharge her. "I know what you have and I can't cure it. Yes, I know very well what you have, *negrita*, but I can't cure it. Then again, maybe that's not what you have …," and he just stood there like he was miles away, looking at nothing at all.

But she wanted to leave, she wanted to overcome her depression.

She spent the entire morning sad, perhaps more like sorrowful. The night before last her hands trembled. Charles arrived at eleven, tired and old-looking.

It was too much for him. His twenty-four years had doubled. He was worn out, weighed down by the responsibility of keeping her alive.

They slept together. Passion overflowed, illuminating them, returning to them like a lightning bolt the hope of coming out unscathed. But when their bodies returned to their natural state, the coldness changed the course of the afternoon, withering it. That had never happened before. For that reason they fell flat on their backs, defeated, frustrated. She cried out of heartache and shame. He got up, and covering himself—he's never done that before—he started to read. They didn't exchange a single word between them. They were tired and both knew it.

They got married on a Monday. In spite of it all, she wore a white dress without the veil. Her father, old Mr. Sam, brimming with happiness spent all of his savings. She was pure light, and the rain failed to dampen her joy. She was finally married, without any sense of fear. She was sure of Charles. Although there is nothing totally certain, but the Charles she knew was a good man. Better than she could have imagined.

The only thing was that God didn't manage to give them a child. The only child she ever gave birth to was ripped from her arms because it was not wanted. In a certain way, it was like the duppy, but the child was innocent. Innocent. Perhaps that's the reason, as some type of punishment, why she was now being abandoned by God.

Now, there were crystal spikes between her eyes.

Before leaving (there's one going at six o'clock and the conductor promised to give me a lift. The harvest is going to waste and we're out of money), Charles tried once again to ignite the lost flame. It was a different experience; a long unnamed ritual.

Her child was snatched away. How many mothers suffered before her, during those shameful four hundred years of criminal inhumanity? They slaughtered the Indian and their own mestizo offspring sang the praises of the conquistador's glory. They snatched away African children to sell them in the town square: "I've got a Negress and her two female pickaninnies for sale." "For the right price, they're yours." "The oldest is two years old." "You can buy them together or separate." How many children like her son, had come into the world just to serve the slave master's will? And, where was God for those four hundred years? His people were crying out. It's just that this son of hers wasn't sired by some slave owner, but rather by a filthy beast just as black as she was. A filthy beast. That's it. But, was he black? Or maybe he had acquired some of the same characteristics as those who sired some of his ancestors long ago. In any case, he's been educating black children in his church-school for four hundred years. Damned screwed-up world. Damned world.

Damned screwed-up world? One of Charles' favorite expressions. She learned so many things from him. Like all that four hundred years business he liked to talk about. And still, in Limón we put on carnival every October, to celebrate Columbus who brought hardship to the lives of Indians under the banner of the Catholic Kings. And we feel proud of our English, the language of criminals. Yes, the language of traitors. Charles read up on the black experience and preached it to those closest to him.

And to think that it was her own black brother who raped her and who now was killing her. And he called that love. Crying, Christian came to the hospital and swore that he loved her. "I'm sending money to the orphanage every month. I haven't abandoned our child." That son-of-a-bitch disturbed her sleep with his stupid talk.

And as she lay in her bed, Lorena regretted a million times over every moment she shared with Bowman. Their interwoven laughter, fiery eyes, walking along the railroad tracks with hands knitted together.

One could understand her nostalgia because, in spite of it all, she loved him like a brother. But he didn't love her at all. That horrific day he clearly showed that he didn't love her at all.

Even so, in the midst of those long years of growing up together, he lived with lurid desire, waiting for the most propitious moment to deliver his blow. Seizing a moment where someone with good intentions, perhaps would've acted very differently. And naively, she would sit around him in any kind of way, as if he were her brother. She had seen him take off his clothes, with little more than curiosity.

But then Charles foiled Christian's plans. And so he avenged himself in the lowest way possible. "Too bad," he thought to himself many times, "Too bad Charles was such a bad shot."

Now she was worried because perhaps they would hospitalize her again. And she would have to go back there, to the same ward and face the nurses again. She will see death prowling the halls, hear the complaints of the old woman who had the gallbladder surgery who died as a result of the careless staff. She will come back to haunt their dreams. Because they prescribed her with a bland diet and the nurse didn't pay attention to the instructions. And the woman who they treated without gloves. And the doctors discussing the size of a very attractive patient's sexual organs. And she saw the tears of the husband whose hopes to have a son were dashed because they confused saline for an abortive. And the doctor who was furious because the man was his cousin, but was hobbled by his own actions, unable to denounce what happened out of fear. Tears clouded her eyes. Each moment of her hospital stay deeply weighed on her. Because to be in a public hospital is to be willing to die of anything that has nothing to do with the suffering that caused the hospitalization in the first place.

The nights were unremittingly hostile, rusty sequences that extend into the long silence of eternity.

After Charles left, Lorena went back to sleep. And she dreamed about the scenes she witnessed in the hospital. A mother walking with the weight of her child in her arms. She screamed and fell to the bed and she cried for a long time.

Memories of the first night came to her. She had arrived gravely ill on the afternoon train. But she had to wait two hours while the hospital workers ticked off their boxes and collected their statistics. Then the piercing scream of the grief-stricken mother who she now heard in her dreams.

The woman had arrived with her sick daughter, popeyed, trembling voice, pleading. Her husband behind her, weighted by fatigue. And she advanced with the weight of the child in her arms toward the nurse … the child on her shoulders. They had to wrest her from death, save her from the unknown, save her for herself, for the world.

"Do you have the forms?"

"Lady, I need someone to see her … she's dying …"

"Do you have the forms?"

"I don't have anything. I left my house and …"

"Well, that's a problem!"

The child wavering between life and death. Panting, convulsing; noticeable paleness.

It's just one plea, just one prayer, just one drop of immense anguish, expanding between her eyes. Saint Gabriel, God, Holy Mother Mary … my child is dying, she's dying …

The nurse pressed the button for the intercom and called for her boss.

"It's just so you can take a look. The lady here is being melodramatic."

"I'm coming."

Lorena, merging with time, could now see the nurse, raising a coffee cup to her lips with absolute indifference.

"So listen and let me tell you …"

"So, what's up?"

"Well, it's nothing really. I guess it's just fine that the doctor is a dog and feels he can talk to people any kind of way, but go figure, he is a doctor."

"Yeah, even you don't agree with him or don't like him, I mean, he has to understand that he can say things in a different way."

"Of course, that's what I'm saying to you. But what's-her-name …" she said making a gesture and the two laughed while drinking coffee.

"Please, miss, let me see the doctor! Please, can't you see she's dying."

"I have to wait for you to be seen by the Head Nurse. But she's busy. You have to wait until she comes."

"But she's dying …"

"Well, yes, right away of course, right? But keep in mind that you didn't bring the forms and you just can't ignore the rules. You understand? It's your fault."

"Oh, miss, why can't you just call the doctor?"

"Mercedes," the nurse insisted on the intercom, "Could you come now?"

"I'm coming."

One of the people in the waiting room raised his voice in protest.

"This is ridiculous. The care in this place gets worse every day. The poor woman is upset because her child is dying and you just sit there like a bunch of lazy good-for-nothings instead of helping her."

"You forget that we're customers who pay your salary."

"Yeah, that's right, sir!" The rumbles spread to the Outpatient Services wing of the hospital.

The nurse felt guilty for the pain of that poor mother. It was true that bureaucracy hindered their work to the point of eclipsing any amount of empathy in the most sensitive souls among them. It was the unfortunate truth.

She got up and went to the Director's Office with a well-formed complaint on her lips and she explained the situation.

"And what did Mercedes say?"

"She was coming, but look, that was a while ago."

"Ok, send her to Dr. Montefrancisco. I'll let him know."

"Thank you, doctor."

The grateful mother expressed with her eyes what she was unable to do with her lips and she entered the examination room. The nurse smiled, understanding the meaning of her expression, feeling the genuine satisfaction that she was able to be of service to another human being.

Inside, the physician gave the child a brief once-over—he had dozens of patients to attend to; so many lives exhausting his own, so much distress draining his eyes—and he proceeded to write a prescription for a suppository for fever and a small bottle of Donnatal.[12]

---

[12]Donnatal is a medication used to treat intestinal cramping.

"Ma'am, don't worry, you can go home now with some peace. With this medicine, your baby girl will be just fine." The relieved mother went out in pursuit of the suppositories and the magic water that was as fresh and green as her hope of saving her little girl. And while her footsteps moving quickly against the tile echoed down the hallway, the Head Nurse finally showed up to give her approval and advised the nurse that what she did was going to cost her dearly, no one authorized her to go over her head.

The patients heard the Head Nurse's threats and remained consumed by a thick silence. Peace and quiet were ruffled and the afternoon's shame also passed into silence.

Crosses appeared painted in the afternoon sky. Birds, flowers, people continued their unceasing pilgrimage through the ether. Thousands of tires, tens of thousands of tires covered the streets. Millions of eyes filled the world.

Lorena felt like escaping, to leave and disappear. She remained in that state for several hours, mechanically going through the day. She couldn't eat. The world crushed her.

Finally, a scream similar to the one Mill let out when the train struck her, wrested her from isolation. She raised her head and the scream took on life in the face of the distressed woman with the little girl in her arms.

A week later the same woman came back to the Francisco Ward. And Lorena remembered the scene that she had witnessed when the woman first arrived, she asked about the little girl. Then she heard the rest of the story.

"Ay, *morena*, my little girl died. That's why I'm here. She died and I brought the papers. She died because of the doctor."

The Matina River suddenly rose in the middle of the waiting room; although no one else could see it. The Matina River was there, overflowing, flooding the entire region and she saw it and no one else did, but it was enough that she and the river recognized each other. She saw the little country house floating downriver ... downriver. Never again would she see her mother's hands ... the scream of horror. The Matina was there although the others couldn't see it, the Matina was there although no one else saw it ... the Matina was there, although no one else saw it.

Burdened by the weight of the tension, she had to keep listening to the voices growing more distant with each passing moment.

"I'm going to take you to court!," the husband threatened, "I'm going to give you lawsuit that you'll never forget. You'll see! I'm going to all the newspapers!"

But before she was consumed by unconsciousness, she heard a voice that came from the air: yes, it's true, he's grief-stricken. He will complain in seven hundred and ninety-seven separate conversations, and there from a place of comfort, from a place of anonymity, they will give him a reason. And he will not know how to follow the road that will take him to a positive state of being, and he, will be absolved, he will visit the "Guitar Bar and Golden Cantina," and with a quart of guaro and pork rinds and another and ceviche and another and garbanzos and still another … he will let his child go in peace. And then, after that, he will do nothing.

Lorena woke up agitated, struggling to breathe. Her blood pressure was high.

"Oh my Lord, I feel so bad …"

It took all of her strength to make it to the small table near the bed, and lifting the bottle, she took two capsules.

"I have to call Charles … what do I do?"

When she was a little girl, the Matina River carried her house away. The image of the small country house being carried away by the current, her mother's hands stretched toward the front door, and her mother's voice raising up an impassioned plea were constantly with her. The Matina River, the house, the pain revealed on her mother's face.

Slowly, slowly, my dear Charles … mine more than ever … if I could just strike at the wall and get them to call Charles for me because … he can, Charles always could.

The Matina glided through the dense vegetation with all of its powerful majesty. The river carrying her parents' house on its shoulders. The neighbors told her father not to build the house there because the earth beneath was loose. That fatal morning, she had gone to buy milk and came back under a forceful rain, then she reached the house to witness the landslide. The earth gave way screaming and the land settled to the bottom of the river, and the little country house on top of the crystalline shadow of the river. Her mother reached the bamboo door, throwing herself into the water and seconds later the figure of her grandmother peering through the window with her palms outstretched to her; and she heard the terrible scream and foresaw her son before he was even conceived as she sunk into the depths.

Tick, tock, tick, tock, the journey of life, blood, echoes of it all, like a slow tango; love gained when young, muttering under her breath the song Charles wrote for her: "You will be bound to me my love, your freedom will be my confinement" … The fatal, inevitable tick-tock congealed on her lips. And she wanted to remain forever on Charles' lips with an immediate kiss. When the neighbor's footsteps still echo against the steps, and the door opens, and she realizes a pair of strong arms grab her and suspend her in the air, tick, perhaps tock, unthinkable…

"Doctor, am I going to die?"

"We will do everything possible to save your life." Sweat runs down Dr. Suárez's face. The question was annoying, "You seem very nervous, why didn't he come today?" The night evaporated. In the distance, the earth revealed lights that rose up blended with the stars. A supreme peace hovered over the night.

Lorena McForbes, in the midst of the intense heaviness, heard footsteps echoing down the hallway, by the balcony where they had been walking for days. She heard the song that Charles once wrote for her, resonating in the echo: "My love, when there are no more summits, let's scale mine. My love, when there are no more valleys, we will descend into mine."

Suddenly she rose up cured and began walking down the hall. As she walked past the corner, she saw Dr. Suárez going down the stairs. She hastened her steps, trying to catch up to him. She saw him suddenly stop in the middle of the room and rub his eyes. He was surprised to see someone approaching him with a pleading look. His heart leapt in his chest then crashed to the floor.

She stopped in front of the doctor who still had the paleness of early morning imprinted on his face. She seemed to then hear Charles' voice, his desperate cry, useless, and she saw tears sliding down the cheeks of an anemic Ruth. The night was broken in two and from her entrails emerged a viscous substance that rose up on one side.

Lorena was born without the fallacious sin that society attributed to her. Because original sin is in the society we're born into, victim of its own wrongdoings. She wasn't to blame for her birth, nor was she the reason for her mother's death. Her mother died because everyone dies. Some during childbirth. Others when they are born. Some get to be old. Such is life, absurd and, nevertheless, full of meaning for those who will discover the art of living it. She was conceived one night along the creek, that whispered, and that wasn't her fault either. And it was very late when a troubled Maria discovered that she didn't want to have the child of a black obeah man. It was an awkward discovery, made when the months of pregnancy made pleasure impossible. She preferred to free herself from it, but Mr. Sam prepared a counter remedy that saved the fetus. And Lorena was born in spite of her mother's criminal attempts, but Maria drowned in front of the wide eyes of the daughter she tried to kill.

Mr. Sam immediately carried Lorena to his house and asked Ruth's mother to look after her. The daughter of the obeah man was an excellent student in the English school run by Mrs. Gretel Duke, Clif's grandmother. And she grew up in the company of the best folk of the town: Millie, Grace, Nabe, and Ruth … It's just that some of them got lost along the way.

In the shadow of her powerful father, the years went by moving between darkness and everyday light. And when the adolescent years came, when a young woman's awareness of her femininity becomes the motivation for everything she does, Lorena became timid and withdrawn.

Finally, one afternoon Charles showed up. And after what happened between them in the brush. And then those years … years … That's it, six years.

She also remembered what happened with Christian. The suffering that came as a result of Nabe's root work. And the night when she woke up with terrible pain and they called Miss Ann, the midwife. And the trip to San José with the child. And then the empty return. And the lie, the child died. The child died. But without knowing why she told Christian the truth.

Lorena had to die remembering that the emerging flower triumphs over the bulb's resistance to see the daybreak. The weight of those nights that she lived. The sun burning her thirsty afternoon face. Her hands holding the tool, the cacao dancing on the grates, the subtle memory of meat burning on the stove. She ran to the kitchen to take the pot off the flame. Then she heard the terrible sound of spirits, and the radio sang out the vote tally, the duppy hitting her and Miss Ann's voice, intermittent, sweaty, the pain drowning the screams of the baby boy, savage, cruel, forceful, cold, Christian's violent hands pressing down on her shoulders and impatiently running down her waist, and she hated him, she hated him in the midst of his insanity but she couldn't push him away, she didn't have the strength to push him off of her, the cold blow against the back of her neck, Miss Ann … "It's a boy." A boy? "Yes, a beautiful baby boy."

She was suddenly rejuvenated as she crossed the waiting room. No one told her, but Lorena knew.

VI

When Esther lovingly reached out her arms that morning, her fingers ran across the pillow in vain. "My love," she tenderly whispered, her mind drowned in exquisite sleep. "My love," she insisted, her lips parted waiting for contact with another pair of thick, live, juicy lips.

"Love?" her eyes opened, suddenly fixed on the ceiling. She thought that he must be in the bathroom, or maybe reading in the living room. Since last night after leaving the lecture, she had noticed something strange about him. Something undefinable, maybe a product of her own imagination. Something, in any case, seemed important to him.

She mentally retraced the scorching speed of his sudden abundance. He wanted it, yes, and last night's speaker could say whatever he felt like saying. At the end of the day, she wasn't from some poor, lower class family and so, no one could say that she was looking for a professional black man to rescue her from poverty.

Nor was it necessary for him to choose her. Magdalena was there, much more beautiful than she, from the same family, surrounded by the same prestige. Because no one talked about "Esther's cousin," it was always the "Centeno sisters."

No, it wasn't that. She loved him as a woman could love a man and it was obvious that he adored her too. It had to be that way. His voice uttering between dreams, almost begging for it to be that way. Because it had to be that way. It was absolutely necessary.

When she woke up several hours later, she couldn't find her husband. His departure was very strange because he left the car in the garage. At first, she thought that he must be somewhere in the neighborhood. Then she worked out in her mind that something must be wrong with the car. But none of her theories explained why he left that morning, without having breakfast, and without saying goodbye.

While she waited for him—for him or his voice on the telephone— she prepared a big breakfast. The housekeeper came in late. Esther was in the bathroom, trying to hide her growing worry. The cold water washed over her, penetrating her pores.

The water accomplished its goal.

Love had something that was frustrating because, in that moment of absolute plenitude when people come together, it inevitably goes by without the lovers being able to penetrate into each other's pores. She left the bathroom startled. Upon seeing her own paleness in the mirror, accentuated by the white wall behind her, she remembered the talk from the night before, "And they look for a white woman, the whitest one possible …"

But that formula didn't apply to them. They truly loved each other; it went beyond hate, they build an intense love from hate, "Oh God, a long life to begin the dream of forgiveness."

The day refused to pause in the same way that she also refused to pause. At eleven o'clock, Dr. Pineres called to find out the results from her husband's visit to the psychoanalyst. That's how Esther learned of her husband's early morning journey.

After noon, she took the initiative and called the specialist to ask for the results. Díaz said that naturally he couldn't give out the results over the phone, but she was welcome to come to his office. And in passing, he asked her out and made some disconnected statements about black people. She pretended that she didn't hear him.

By nightfall, she called Dr. Centeno, her father, who immediately came to her side. He found her melancholic and skin blotched with her chronic paleness.

"Nothing from Charles yet?"

"No, daddy, absolutely nothing."

The old man wanted to call the police, but Esther made him see that calling them would only create problems. Because Charles went to see a psychiatrist, and so maybe something happened to him. Having that in the papers wouldn't be good either for the Centeno family or for Charles.

Dr. Centeno insisted that she was exaggerating and that besides she was being too stubborn in protecting her husband.

"I owe a lot to Charles…"

"Oh really, I think it's the other way around."

"Dad, why do you say that?"

"No reason. It occurred to me that … well … it's not important. Well … Charles probably went back to Limón."

"But … back to Limón? Why would he do such a thing? We didn't have a fight. We didn't have any problems."

Dr. Centeno took off his glasses to clean them with his handkerchief. The lamplight reflected in the glass, in that impossible dimension of things reflected.

"Esther, when you met Charles, who was he?"

She closed her eyes. It wasn't the time for such remembrances. She just wanted to get back *her* Charles, the one who definitively made her give up the single life for good.

But the doctor with his paternal authority was prepared to compel her to think about her relationship with Charles. Esther managed to successfully defy his authority just one time, and that was precisely when she decided to marry Charles. The old man passionately objected when he found out that Esther had said yes to her suitor's proposal. "I like him, but I don't agree with interracial marriage. But, what the hell! If he's a part of the family, I'll have to accept him." And in effect, he closed ranks in a way that her mother never did. She used to say without any reason, "You married a nobody, a black nobody." And for Esther's part, she had to fight Magdalena's rage, "You're a traitor, that's what you are, a dirty, betraying bitch."

And old friends fell away, weakened by the reality of her marriage to Charles as if she had committed a grave sin against them. And finally, the careful and slow rebuilding of her circle of friends.

"Daddy …"

"You remember, right?"

Indeed, she remembered. Charles McForbes entered the house sweating, with deep furrows of pain on his face.

"Charles," Dr. Centeno said, "I want to introduce you to my daughter. Charles' wife passed away recently and the poor man is shattered."

"Pleased to meet you," she said, but in reality, she wanted to say, "Really, daddy, hanging around with niggers."

"We did everything we could to save her," he said, "but we couldn't …"

"You couldn't?"

"In reality, neither Suárez nor I could really get to the root of the problem. If you ask me now, I wouldn't be able to tell you what in the devil that woman had that made her so ill. Lorena, Lorena was her name."

Esther offered them drinks. Charles asked to use the bathroom. His athletic figure relayed a rhythmic gait as he moved across the living room.

"He's a good guy."

"All blacks seem good to you, daddy."

"He's good Esther. You should've seen how devoted he was over the course of the past year. Week after week he would go to the farm and come back. He faithfully cared for her. That's the word Esther, faith. That's why it hurts me so much to know that we failed him, but you know … Now, he's looking for work here. He wants to study."

"What does he know how to do?"

"Farm work, but he went to secondary school and seminary. He came here for that."

"So, what's he going to study?"

"He wants to go to the University, but the poor man is in such a mess."

"Mess?"

"Yes, with women. And besides that, he was in jail. He shot the man who raped his wife."

Charles came out of the bathroom, went over to his chair, and raised a glass to toast to "your daughter's beauty." Esther blushed without knowing why and coughed to hide her distress. Charles smiled, his teeth, a row of marble sparkling with light, called her attention. It was the first time that she had seen a black man who was worth having.

"Daddy, when I met Charles he was a man, just like he is now."

"No, not like now. He was just a nigger from Limón. Now he's somebody. He's a great guy, you can't deny that. The blacks need opportunities."

"But, daddy, he's still a black man from Limón …"

"And that's exactly what worries me."

He said that with a sophisticated air that bothered Esther. Her father couldn't and wasn't ready to understand that she loved Charles precisely because she found in his blackness a deep humanity.

She couldn't help but to love him nor could she have resisted loving him. From that smile, he made her aware for the first time of black people's humanity.

"I love him, daddy. I love him just as he is."

"Really?"

"What are you …"

"He's quite simple-minded – he's dedicated solely and completely to one thing, to be worthy of Esther Centeno."

"All I know is that I love him," Esther indignantly affirmed.

Nevertheless, when she was a child, she never liked black people. From the big picture window of their house, she would watch the days pass by. From behind the spiraling iron gates, the little girl would look out at the accelerated pace of the city, believing she was the owner of it all. The police seemed like toys, put there to entertain her. People, dogs, all invented for her own delight. The dogs copulated on the corners before the astonished children at play. And twice a day, young uniformed men who with time would come to represent the epitome of inanity, marched down the street toward their school.

Her cousin, Magdalena, an orphan taken in by the Centenos, always opened the door each time so that Dr. Centeno could enter and exit. This formed part of Esther's childhood games. And also, Magdalena would open the door for the milkman, who arrived through the service door every day at nine o'clock. No one in the neighborhood bought raw milk, except for her cousin who found special delight in it.

Without fail, the milkman would bring a few bones for the well-trained dogs and he would give Esther a little caress. Then he would close the door to play with Magdalena and then he would quietly leave through the same door.

After lunch, without fail, Esther would take a nap. When she awoke at three, her parents would have already gone back to work—the doctor in the National Hospital and his wife, the head of human resources for one of the government ministries.

Her parents returned home during the early evening. He buried himself in the daily newspaper; she telling him of the latest goings-on at the Lady's Society of which she was a member.

Then her father would put Esther to bed before heading out again and in a bound-up whisper, he concluded his day.

Just a single shadow tarnished her childhood routine, the horrible figure of a black man who took care of the neighborhood yards. It wasn't because he would bring her any harm, but rather because Magdalena and the housekeeper—who from time to time would also shut herself off with Magdalena and the milkman—constantly frighten her with stories about the black man. If you don't do this or that, the nigger is going to carry you away. "Aha, Esther, just you wait, the nigger is coming for you." And they would laugh ecstatically while Esther's heart was devoured by panic.

"Come, Mister Fly, come take this spoiled little girl away," and Esther would flee only to throw herself on the bed and cry uncontrollably. He was a thing to be hated. First, there was no reason for him to choose their neighborhood to do yard work. Then, he shouldn't laugh when the girls called him. And she hated her father when he was full of compassion and said to the black man, "Abrahams, come fix this foolishness. I'll give you a little extra. Would you like some coffee?" And with astonishing calmness, he sat down to have coffee with him, smoking and talking without any sign of fear.

Sometimes her father would go to the extreme of calling her over to greet Abrahams, the black man. Accustomed to doing what she is told, she huddled behind her father, confused by her panic and at the same time in admiration of her father's courage.

"Say hello to the *morenito*," he insisted, "tell him, 'Jau ar yu,'" and then Abrahams, encouraged by the doctor's confidence, smiled and patted Esther on the head.

At the first opportunity, Esther escaped her torment, and then the housekeeper and Magdalena demanded that she wash up and rub herself with alcohol.

"Careful with that nasty pig. Niggers don't bathe or comb their hair. And besides, they come from a place called Africa, where they eat little kids."

Esther had no other choice but to blindly obey the will of her two inseparable friends—the housekeeper and her cousin. She was a submissive, timid, and inhibited girl.

And that's why she became the picture window's faithful friend.

"What are you thinking about now?"

"Nothing, just more of the same. Well, that's not true. I was thinking about Abrahams."

"Oh, that old scoundrel! He's a good nigger. Hard worker, peaceful, always smiling. I like niggers like that, always singing and dancing. I could never figure out why you all hated him so."

"You all?"

"You and Magdalena."

"Well … what do you want me to say? It's just one of those things."

Esther felt like explaining to her father the whole reality of her childhood. Her hours without sleep, her dreams her nightmares, the slow fear that grew inside her thanks to the tireless efforts of Magdalena and the housekeeper. But perhaps such explanations wouldn't result in much except bitterness in the mind of the old man. So, she preferred to remain quiet.

The telephone began to ring. Esther McForbes' world was suddenly turning upside down, giving way to a colossal sense of hope.

The doctor came back to see his daughter. He could sense the depth of her emotional state in these moments. He let the phone ring twice before slowly getting up and going over to it.

"Him or his voice – My God – him or his voice."

The seconds Dr. Centeno took up seemed long to his daughter. More like an eternity, as if with a sadistic vocation he had wanted to enjoy his daughter's intense pain and anxiety. But what was certain was that the doctor had moved like he normally did; Esther wasn't in a state to perceive reality. Her world was at that moment a strange world, drawn on carbon paper.

He raised the earpiece and said, "Hello," with his characteristic calm. The same calm that she would see him exhibit in front of the black man, Abrahams when she was a little girl.

Him or his voice on the other side of the line, she had been waiting for that moment for the entire day. His voice on the other end of the line: my love … my love … And she would have been crying, begging him to come home, to her empty arms.

"It's Pereira; he's asking for Charles."

"Pereira? Tell him to call back later."

Esther was burdened with three significant sorrows on top of her own pain. It was enough to throw oneself onto the bed defeated. So much in one day! Her mentally ill husband, her cousin's cardiac arrest, her father who was totally spent and blaming himself for Engracia's death.

She was taught in the aristocratic prep school of the Esplanade Mata Redonda. Being the daughter of a petit-bourgeois family, inheritor of the blood of distinguished citizens, she had no choice but to enroll in one of the most prestigious schools.

For the first couple of years, she didn't have any significant problems. She was an outstanding student and enjoyed the friendship of her classmates. Nevertheless, she failed the third year, but she didn't have to repeat the grade, thanks to the intervention of her father, after all, she was a Centeno.

Then in her fourth year, she was assigned to partner with a black student. He was a very timid boy, bad-tempered, who pronounced the aspirated "h's" and omitted the "j's."

Trained in the shadow of Magdalena's ideas, she felt a great repulsion toward him: unleashing the hatred she had been building up for most of her childhood. She was the boy's unrelenting enemy. She remembered him being in the classroom, in front of the teacher, while she or someone named Charlemagne, the second cousin of one of the Minister of the Interior, rallied the others to join their campaign. She remembered him standing in front of the teacher, trying in vain to put his ideas together, as he tried desperately to reply to her questions and while the others said a thousand nasty insults in hushed tones.

"Hey Blacky, Blacky don't know nothin'. He don't understand. Blacky only understands cacao and bananas." And he struggled to overcome his heartbreak by concentrating on what the teacher was saying, while Berrumo invited him to sit down.

"Hey, everything is dark! Monkey-head can't see what the teacher is saying." And they started to roar with laughter. The other students, putting his sexual reputation into doubt, liked to call him "the little black faggot." It was the only thing that brought out fierce anger. "You all are a bunch of perverts," he yelled, "Why don't you ask your sisters? They can tell you I'm not a faggot."

One day the teacher heard him say that and she punished him with the general approval of the others. The boy defended himself saying that he was provoked, but the only thing that happened was that his class-mates doubled over in laughter, the same ones who waited at the exit door to "kindly" get a look at his mother.

Pérez was the only classmate who didn't support Esther's campaign. He spent time with the Negro boy, defying the rest and formed a friendship with him. They were both excellent athletes and Pérez was the school's hero. In the end, it was almost impossible to force him to choose between prestige and a friendship that both placidly enjoyed. And on more than one occasion the majority of their classmates refrained from tormenting the black boy so as to not offend Pérez. But the relentless Esther found out about Pérez's humble family. She discovered that he lived in El Cerrito, in a small house and that his father sold vegetables in one of the posh neighborhoods on the east side of the city. One day she stopped by Pérez's house on the pretext of picking him up.

From that moment on, she dedicated herself to chipping away at his reputation. She would see Pérez and the black boy walking together among their classmates, suffering the assault of dirty looks, laughter, and rude comments. "Vegetables and black beans," one of them shouted. "Trash," another answered back.

Nevertheless, as time went by, the black boy grew cynical. His eyes revealed a sardonic smile. Esther doubled-down on her hostility, but she only managed to accelerate the insults. And one day, after seeing her pinch a classmate, he went directly over to them:

"I don't know why you waste your time and take so much delight pinching your poor classmate. Let's go over there and I'll let you pinch me as much as you'd like."

Infuriated, Esther slapped him. He just rubbed his chin and laughed.

"What happened?" Pérez asked as he walked up to them with another boy.

"This woman … Tried to kiss me in front of our classmate here and she got mad because I turned her down … and well, you all saw the rest."

The next day the news spread like wildfire and many of them said, "Well, that explains why she bothered him so much." They paid no attention to Esther's insistent explanations or those of her friend. The lie, for being what it is, spread incredibly fast.

But what Esther felt was hate. She read the reports from the newswire that told of the gross atrocities in the Congo with intense interest. "How could this happen?" she asked her friend. "We're in the 20th century! Yes, I know some whites acted the same way," she said responding to a teacher who challenged her to defend the Congo in the light of history, "I know they were avenging themselves for the very same reasons that Spain sought revenge against the Moors and South America against their oppressors, but those atrocities against the nuns is simply too much."

And she heard the comments of a radical journalist with so much self-satisfaction:

"I was in Watts last week, and the Negroes there live very well."

In that commentator's opinion, life was tolerable for them because of their mediocrity. But Esther, who was the daughter of a well-edu-cated family, knew the sad history of the long years of slavery and she was familiar with what Dr. King was talking about in his book *Why We Can't Wait*, a book her father read to her in the original language; and the freedom to die of hunger, the humiliating discrimination a whole race of people suffered during their pilgrimage through history.

But also, Esther knew another history—the one written by offi-cial voices, distorted in some areas and idealized in others. Emerson's "Fable" remains true for those spirits who always need to live from illusions.

This stayed with her. It was her reality: "The Negro evolved from monkeys; they're in a permanently inferior evolutionary state," period.

So, that afternoon when her father brought Charles to the house, she had to make a great effort to behave in a way that reflected her stand-ing as a respectable woman of a certain class and refinement and not immediately ask him to leave or leave him sitting in the living room enjoying the company of Dr. Centeno, who took so much pleasure with his presence. Naturally, Charles' friendly smile changed her perception from that moment on.

For the next few months, Charles was a frequent visitor to the house. He was studying and needed Dr. Centeno's help. As time passed, Esther started to explain a few things to him and she was surprised by his intelligence.

She witnessed him earn high marks for three years in a row; bringing flowers to the house after each series of exams that he passed. He helped her with her English; staying by her bedside when she was sick; suppressing many of his habits and customs just to please her, changing himself for her, dressing the way she liked, and finally, winning over Magdalena's affection and later her jealousy.

Truthfully, the relationship between Magdalena and Charles didn't last very long. In the beginning, Esther's cousin was just as merciless in the way she treated him.

But perhaps her cousin gave in the same way she did and gradually allowed Charles to carve a space in her heart. One day, according to Magdalena's version of the story, the two of them were in the bathroom. Something had broken, a wall socket, a towel rack, some random item of little importance, and Charles was fixing it and Magdalena walked in and suddenly found him to be very human and most of all, to be very much a man … and it happened right there and then later …

But it didn't last very long. For Charles, it seemed to be an act of revenge for years of suffering and for her, a sincere gesture of repentance. As if her unexpected surrender to him could erase the history that had mounted up over time—Esther's childhood, her years in high school, her first contact with Charles.

And the feelings died inside him, while she clung to him more and more. And meanwhile, Esther was burning with envy. One night she found herself crying and her tears silently ran down her pale cheeks. Because without realizing it, all of those years had been preparing her for him. One night Pérez came to see her. He was her best friend in addition to being her most faithful suitor. And he would have loved for their friendship to become a marriage. But Esther resisted. She refused to give over to him what society considered as the most important thing and in her mind, it was just a membrane that would later be forgotten. And she didn't marry him. Pérez was desperate, so he started cultivating a relationship with the people he hoped would become his in-laws.

Pérez arrived that night, slightly drunk, willing to take his many attempts at persuasion to extreme consequences. He was possibly convinced that he had nothing to lose and he decided to take Esther by force. He took her into his arms, pushed her onto the sofa, and began to kiss her.

He was sure that he would accomplish his goal that way, but he didn't count on Charles being there. Charles was sleeping in the guest bedroom when he was awakened by Esther's protests and he quickly moved toward the agitated light in the living room. Things did not end well for Pérez. He had to be hospitalized at the National Hospital for two days.

That night, Esther was in tears and took comfort in Charles, keeping him close to her out of deep fear and apprehension. That night, Esther was in tears and he kissed her for the first time.

Now, lying alone on her bed, the tears flowed freely down her face and along her ears. She heard in the distance the clock chime at midnight and her tiredness made time feel even longer.

Centeno poured himself a cup of coffee without offering her any.

"You married Charles because he saved you from being raped, isn't that right?"

"Daddy, I married Charles because I loved him. Pérez didn't rape me, he kissed me, that's all."

"But Charles thought that he was trying to rape you and since …"

"Daddy, I'll say it again, I married for love."

"So, you allowed yourself to be convinced about Charles and you came to the conclusion that he was the rightful owner of the very thing he saved, or in any case, believed he had saved."

"Daddy, I'm not going to allow you …"

"You're 'not going to allow me,' Esther? A black man that I found in the hospital one day destroyed and on the brink of killing himself because his wife had died from no apparent cause. Absolutely no apparent cause, but she died anyway. And then he left to return to the bush where he was born, and he left a white woman with a child in her belly; a married woman, much older than him. And then he looks for me, he asks for my help and I give it to him, and I welcome him into my home against my daughters' wishes and I turn him into my adopted son. Damn…and then, he makes one of them his lover and then marries the other one, and one day out of many he grows tired of her, he goes crazy…"

"Daddy, I'm begging you …"

"Don't interrupt me, Esther. He goes crazy and gets up and leaves her. And then both of my daughters have an attack. One between life and death and the other …"

"Between life and death?"

"… And the other, here she is, she hasn't died because she's as thick as a rock, and finally, I collapse, worn out, and then maybe I split my head open on the steps. And now, I am speaking, I want to speak, this mouth is mine, these daughters are mine, and I brought him to our home. And I want to speak. And if your mother were still alive, she would say this to me, 'this is where you've brought us to!' And I want to speak, and my daughter tells me no. She says she is not going to allow me. What in the devil is that! But, don't I have the right to complain, to protest when my two daughters practically don't speak to each other because of that nigger? Damn, as if that's not enough …"

And if her mother were alive. Esther remembered her leaving her house, as usual, heading to the beauty salon. Her alabaster white hands, placed against the black background of the steering wheel. Every weekday morning she would stop by Esther's house to have breakfast and to help her with her hair. (Charles insisted that Esther keep her hair long.) And then she left mid-morning for the beauty salon or to take care of some matter on behalf of the Ladies Society.

And that morning she left in her car as always. At four o'clock in the afternoon, Esther heard the news of the accident on the radio.

"Daddy!" Esther threw herself onto him, "Daddy, you don't understand, daddy. Charles is like a fire. You run away because it burns, but you need the fire, daddy. The flames consume everything, but you need the heat that they give."

"Like fire, huh? Like a piece of coal if you ask me."

"Daddy, try to understand. Charles is a strange man – he's not black, he's not white. He's way beyond those definitions. Maybe he's a little satanic; a strange mixture, in any case, that's what drives me crazy. I'm in love, daddy."

"Yes …," the physician let his heavy sigh fall to the floor like a strong wind. "Yes," he repeated, "Let's go for a walk."

"A walk?"

"Yes, a walk."

"At this time of night? And what if Charles comes back?"

"He's not coming back for now. And if he does come back, he can wait a little while."

"But …"

"You've been waiting for him all day. Come."

"Walking at this time of night."

"Let's go in the car then. Besides, it's a bit chilly outside …"

The park, the La Merced Church, another park, another church, tall buildings, pothole-filled streets, few passersby, miniskirts exposed to the cold nighttime air, the agony of a people that moans, the slow sequence of dying things, the deep footprints of pain through the streets, fliers from the last electoral campaign with photos of the candidates, dust …

Esther glanced up at the expanse of the sky where the moon hung, splatterings of stars in the endless vastness, beyond infinity. The car advanced slowly. Along the highway, the greenness of the plants cast a yellow hue of light and darkness; bringing light to the horizon, as inconceivable as sunrise at midday.

A group of young women, joking with each other on street corners as they waited for their evening customers. They also watched out for red cars, just in case some patrol car wanted to surprise them. And every once in a while, Centeno had to put on the brakes to give way to a speedy getaway that set them out into opposing traffic.

"What depravity," Centeno said, "What depravity these young women find themselves in these days."

"Daddy," Esther responded to him after a long silence, "the young people today are the children of people who were once young themselves. If they take the wrong path in life, it's because we haven't taught them well."

"Please don't go making excuses for Magdalena."

"What is she up to?"

They left the city and took to the open road toward the west.

"Magdalena has been going out with a professor. Sociology or something like that."

"Julio?"

"No, she broke up with Julio a while ago. I think this one is named Martin or something like that. It's just that he's put all kinds of strange ideas in her head."

"Is he a communist?"

"No, maybe it's not that extreme, no, not that far. But … listen, according to him, prostitution is a logical and necessary product in our society."

"That's it?"

"Yes, he says that our society is based on money. There isn't work for everyone, he says, and for that reason, there are so many prostitutes … Magdalena believes in him just as she believes in God. But they both completely forget about the moral problem at hand."

"Daddy sometimes a man can do more than what's moral."

"Esther, let me tell you something, these prostitutes are what they are because their parents are either indecent or ignorant. They're that way because they lack education."

"Go on, daddy."

"What do you mean, 'go on daddy'?"

"And the poor don't have education because …"

Lucas Centeno remained silent. The evening light penetrated the car, illuminating them both.

Part II

VII

I walked around for a bit. I don't know why, dammit, but it never even occurred to me to ask where I was. I honestly just let myself walk around like an idiot, accumulating hours beneath my feet.

Perhaps the fact that I didn't ask was just my fear of returning home. So it was an unconscious pretext that forced me to continue on walking in suspense, while I tried to understand exactly what was happening to me. Because just imagine if I show up at my house, and looking into my wife's joyous face, greeting her.

"What can I get for you, my love?"

And me just standing there like a jackass, without knowing for certain what was the best response. Because, how do you tell your wife that you turned into a black man overnight, just a little before or after making love to her?

And even more ridiculous, expecting to be able to walk right back into the house and claim her as my own. Showing the house keys, wearing the same clothes, having the same voice. No, the truth is that the situation was simply too absurd to be faced. Because you can face big problems and overcome them, but you need to have some type of logical direction. But, what do you do when you're facing something so absurd? (Oh my darling girl, why is he so black?)

The first drink went down easy. The intense heat started to take over my gut. The whole earth started to burn.

(As a young boy, a beautiful little girl with blue eyes and blonde hair sat in the front of the teacher and asked, "Teacher, why is he so black?")

We all anxiously waited for her answer. Because we all played in the river, in the grass, and in the mud without thinking about our differences. No one ever made any distinction. But, damn, it had to be the blonde girl.

Soon after, we found ourselves in different groups. Opposite sides imposed by a strange biological condition that no one had given much attention to before and the teacher's answer was important. For his part,

Walker resigned himself for the first time to the reality of his color as he looked at the others. He was in a white world. I'll never forget his desperate eyes, searching for my eyes, begging in the name of our long friendship that I at least extend a hand.

Walker's eyes burst with panic and in them, they saw the severing of the umbilical cord that had totally connected him with the rest of the group; fear of being labeled, which would isolate him from the others once and for all.

The teacher, for her part, was incapable of pretending. When she spoke, it was already clear to us that something was terribly wrong in the world, since we didn't create our differences, but nevertheless, we found ourselves divided, taking us beyond the bonds of affection that had connected us for so many years.

It was clear that the teacher also didn't want to label Walker and with a high-pitched tone of apology she said, "We are all equal before God." And we discovered with absolute certainty that we were all different and one way or another that difference affected us.

"Walker has dark skin," the teacher said, "People with dark skin are just the same as us. The only difference is skin color."

One of the children let out a nervous laugh. Without wanting to, I grabbed him by the hair and spit in his face. That got me kicked out of school for the week.

The second drink wasn't as pleasant as the first. The color of the ground was definitely changing before my eyes. Something was clouding it over. Something was burning.

"Hey, darkie," said an old man as he approached me, "this world has gone to the dogs."

I invited him to have a drink with me. The old man gave me a look of appreciation and sat down without complaint. "Well since you insist," he said to me, "I'm going to keep you company for a while, darkie."

(Darkie? Walter had dark skin. He wasn't black, but rather had dark skin.)

My table companion was a short man, well-dressed, with small round eyes. I tried to imagine him with another three drinks: his chubby face would start to turn red. In the violent desert of the Peruvian coast, the sun descends until it becomes a red ball before it disappears behind the western sky. The intense dust tossed around every so often by the evening breeze, so much the opposite of the stunning bright green forests of my beloved land. My short-statured table companion suddenly seemed Peruvian. His round face, his strong features, just like the race of men who once populated the continent long ago. But he didn't sound Peruvian.

"Something to eat, darkie? To go with our drinks?"

"Yes, sure, whatever you'd like," if he were Peruvian, he would have called me *zambo* or maybe even black.[13]

"Hey, pretty lady! How about bringing us two chorizos and a couple of raspas."

"Raspas?"

"Yes, thinly sliced fried plantains, it's their specialty."

An inexplicable calm started to penetrate into my bones. I bit the sausages with the green plantain and ordered a few more.

The waitress tried to complain, but my short companion's timely intervention reminded her that we were paying. After a while, the short man decided that the locale was far too gloomy for me and we decided to go to the Wet Skeleton. It was a place that was drenched in red. We sat at a small table near the platform where a girl dressed in all black sang an old bolero.

"Gentlemen, rum?"

The light rippled across the singer's face and voice. It was a provocative song, her voice matched the rhythm and aroused the intense interest of the audience.

At the bar, a group of young women watched a gringo who had just entered. The waiter served us the rum and gave us a pack of cigarettes on the house. From what we gathered it was the club's anniversary.

After the song, a so-called illusionist took to the platform. I drank down what was left in the glass, slowly savoring it.

---

[13]Zambo, a Spanish term used to describe a person of mixed African and Amerindian ancestry.

My table companion went to the bathroom. The illusionist had just performed an old trick and the crowd hissed at him. It took him a while to regain their attention, but then he showed off some of his more original tricks and the audience rewarded his efforts with exuberant applause.

The short-statured man returned to the table accompanied by two women.

"They want to get to know you, darkie."

"I saw him first," said the whiter of the two, "I get first choice, isn't that right, papito?"

The young woman leaned on my arm. A beautiful black woman stepped up to the platform and started to dance the conga. The movement of her body stirred up among those present a tremendous expectation that exploded into enthusiastic shouts. Even my table companion, who up to that point had been indifferent, seemed suddenly drawn in by the surprising ecstasy of those rhythmical movements. The music gradually died down and the club returned to normal.

The young woman who was leaning on my arm, asked me to buy her a drink. Her skin, rather shrunken, was marked by the pallor of long cold nights without a coat, which left the most attractive parts of her body exposed to the coldness of the street. She kissed me on the cheek.

"These darkies have the advantage of being able to be smothered with kisses and go home and their wives don't notice a thing."

The laughter of those around me was contagious. What she said was really cliché, but it made us laugh. Well, to put it another way, it made the people around me laugh, I just ended up laughing because it was contagious.

She sat much too close and started telling jokes and making movements that encouraged love. Love? It's that no one has invented a more appropriate word as yet. A blonde woman who was introduced as "Flor from Brazil" went onto the stage and started stripping off her clothes to the swinging rhythm. The little old man all of a sudden vibrated with vitality.

"Are you a good dancer?," the young woman at the table asked me.

"More or less."

"Now it's my turn."

"Really?"

"Yes, I'm up next."

Married and divorced in Nicaragua. She didn't seem Costa Rican. I thought about Walker again. We ran into each other one afternoon at the baseball field. "Hey, man!" He also had traveled the continent. "It's a drag, but at the same time an advantage," he said to me. "Listen, in Argentina I'm a gringo or Brazilian. In Peru, I'm from Lima or from the coast, if anything. In Chile, I'm gringo or Brazilian. In Nicaragua, from Bluefields. Shit, and they either speak to me in English or Portuguese. Never in Spanish."

"That's okay," I told him, "but don't tell me that they thought you were a gringo. Tell me they thought you were from the United States."

The young woman got up and kissed me on the cheek and headed to the stage, soon the room filled with music. I now noticed that she was very pretty.

"Fucking society," I exclaimed without meaning to.

"What's going on, darkie?"

"Nothing."

"Do you like the little lady?," the old man asked.

"That's not the problem."

"So, what's the problem?"

"These women have to do these things just to survive."

"Don't get all moralistic."

"No, it's not even a moral question. It's a question of fairness. It's not right."

"Yes, but they fulfill a role and besides, they don't do it for free."

"Yes, they have a role. They help us deal with all of this."

The young woman was finishing up her act. She was really quite beautiful and she would have been even more beautiful if the cold nighttime air hadn't taken its toll on her skin.

"She's beautiful," I mentioned to set my table companion at ease. The other young woman smiled.

The murmur of voices, suffocated by the orchestra stirred up a sad torpor that overwhelmed us. The young woman was naked before the audience and then pretending to be embarrassed, returned dressed to the table. I stood up to receive her.

"Congratulations," I told her, "Besides being quite beautiful, you have so much grace." But inside, I was shouting, "Fucking society, damn, damn, damn."

Tired from the inertia, we walked across the room toward the dance floor. The young woman seemed to really enjoy herself, as if she saw me as something more than just a customer. Well, at least a special customer. "Blacks are passionate," I thought, emulating the words of the lecturer, and it made me laugh.

You are the kiss that sets me on fire,
the hand that takes me higher,
and my destiny …

Pulling her closer, shamelessly brushing against the delicate fabric between us, I could see her face in the mirror that decorated the dance floor. She closed her eyes, a profound expression of hope rested on her face.

And I want your sadness
Inside my night to rest
And together we awaken.

Without warning, she whispered a phrase into my ear. (Just like this, papito, just like this.)

It was already past midnight when I left the club. As I was leaving, the image of the dancer pursued me: her sighs, her passionate suffering, her fiery complaints. A moment of light, perhaps, in the midst of a string of tedious nights.

Her words reverberated in my ears as I walked again, with no particular direction in the middle of the cold early morning hours. "In Masaya, I met a black man. We became friends. He was from Bluefields. Blacks are very passionate and dance a lot." I thought about my condition as a black man: a condition that either was discovered or imposed, something I didn't ask for and something I didn't share with anyone. All of a sudden I woke up one morning trapped in this skin, as if I had been born with it. Black people are good dancers, they carry the rhythm in their blood. And besides being passionate, they're intelligent too. As if every single one of them was cut from the same mold, one by one, same physique, same moral attributes, same defects.

I looked at my blackened hands. I lifted up the hem of my trousers to get a good look at the dark skin that covered my ankles. Black, as if it were a punishment.

The words of the dancer were like a shovel that kept digging. She had a sister. A sister as evil as Satan himself, with a black heart. I thought, black like my skin. As evil as my skin. And she said it twice: she was darker on the inside than Oscar was on the outside. Because Oscar was smart and good. And passionate too. Then all blacks are smart and good. And passionate too.

But her sister didn't think highly of black people at all and that must have been an experience. When she was a little girl a mean black woman pinched her. You can't deny that the dancer was a little cliché. She said, "a mean black woman pinched my sister," and I wanted to say, you have to be really cliché to say such a thing in a place like this.

It was a black woman who made vigorón and her sister stole a piece of meat.[14] That's why she pinched her. And her sister had mentioned that the black woman was darker on the inside than she was on the outside.

Black like my skin. Even so, black people are divine like dolls. And it made me think that toys are there to be played with, just to play with. Perhaps the little girl grew to love her little doll. Maybe she grew to love it just like a person. But the doll will always be an object. Much loved, but always an inanimate plaything.

I remembered her lukewarm hands drawing me into her, inviting me to a lukewarm night. In the best case scenario, a fiery night, so hot that neither one of us would remember our names. And we would always be, that handsome Negro from Costa Rica and that beautiful woman from Nicaragua who met at the Wet Skeleton. The passionate and sweet dancer. That night. And an emptiness. A deep emptiness that would nevertheless remain.

Fucking society!

I found myself walking the streets of the Hills of Ocloro when the police spotted me.

---

[14]Vigorón, a typical Nicaraguan dish of marinated cabbage, yuca, and fried pork (chicharrón) wrapped in a banana leaf.

"Darkie, where are you going at this hour?" Another man, a Latino, passed by without any notice, something I kept in the forefront of my mind.

"Listen, darkie," one of the officers said to me, "this isn't Limón, so watch it."

Without intending to, I went back and stood in front of the house that we once rented and spent many sleepless nights. The neighbor with her extravagant moans and how that little shack trembled every so often with her lover's labored words and the neighbor's nervous laughter. We had to wait for the neighbor's lover to satisfy his desire and leave to start to turn off the lights one by one and get some sleep, all of us prisoners in that tiny structure of wood and zinc. And have wet dreams about women's bodies, only to be startled by a barking dog and the cry of a cat in heat celebrating the beginning of a new cycle and looking to take refuge in a male.

And at night it was very, very cold. A cold much deeper than the cold I feel now. It was a cold that dug into your navel. Then I started to think about how good it would be to go back home at this hour and just end all of this. Why? Why?

I imagined arriving quietly at my house, my hands cold from the harsh early morning air, my frozen fingers gripping the key, and maybe later I could just rest on the sofa and wait to hear Manuela, the house-keeper, scream when she got up.

("Oscar is a filthy nigger." "Don't say that about him, he's black, but he has a heart that is much whiter than yours.")

Fucking lecture. Yesterday I was a free man, but we went to that damn lecture.

Just imagine, good morning, Esther. I'm sorry, but I don't remember you. I'm your husband. What? And the certain laughter that would fill the neighborhood. But then she would take notice and the laughter would stop.

I knew her before I met her. What I'm trying to say is that my father-in-law had described her to me with such detail before bringing me to his house. But the physical descriptions were short. The first night that I saw her, tall, cheerful, I fell captive to the exquisite way she carried herself. Her voice above all would melt mountain peaks and sensually drift down its slopes.

A few days later after our first meeting, I managed to open the first small hole in the shield she had erected to protect herself from black people. Magdalena denounced the unexpected friendship as a "breach of trust." But nothing could stop the slow, but steady feelings of love that grew between us. I admired her—watching her design her own dresses with such good taste. See her laugh, buzzing with life and enthusiasm.

So, why not go back home and talk to Esther? End once and for all this terrible sensation of a slow death that was weighing on me. I had all I needed to prove my identity—the keys to the house, the wallet that she gave me for my birthday, my identity card, everything I needed to easily prove my identity. And then I would hear her scream, "Manuela, call the cops. A murderer, a criminal murder! What have you done with my husband?!"

The path was very clear. The alternative was to either face the consequences of a completely absurd situation or run away. Run away and at least carry with me pleasant memories. Or return home and face Esther's eyes, hear her screams of horror.

Without knowing why I started to think about my mother and brother. Rafael is the one with fine features. Ah, yes. I thought he was like the other one. Not at all, he's too ugly. Too ugly? His white, white teeth make his skin look really black. Yes, he's black, black. He looks African. Jesus! Rafael came out looking just like his father—he has good hair. Spanish hair. You know? He's like that, even though he has dark skin, he's got that good Spanish hair.

Where was I? I stopped to look at the street number. It was Fourteenth Street. I suddenly decided to go to the psychoanalyst's house. That was the best thing I could do, go to his house and ask him to put me in the hospital. Díaz is a perfect idiot. Without a doubt he would call the police and have them carry me off to the asylum—he's capable of doing that. "That nigger is crazy, I think he probably killed someone," Díaz would say. They already know, it's not the same to be black as to be a man. Because men are white.

That was the best thing to do, after all, I had nothing to lose. The worst has already happened to me. In any case, I just wanted to end this absurd state of existence of mine once and for all.

But after walking for an hour, I ended up back at Fourteenth Street. Shit, there was nothing more I could do. I went into the Las Cantarranas bar and ordered a half quart of aged rum. I don't know what motivated me, but I asked the waiter what time the first train leaves for Limón. Damn, I think I was already going crazy.

VIII

Damn, it wasn't easy to go back and travel by train after so many years. It wasn't easy to forget Lorena Sam. Following old Pete and Clarita Duke's instructions, we stopped the morning train in front of the house to carry Lorena to the hospital. She cried. The symphony of the train on the rails, her dilated eyes forever remained part of my memory. No one could tell me that her uncontrollable weeping wasn't anything but a sad farewell. A final cry from a turbulent life. Damn, I'm always contradicting myself. Because I often said that it wasn't so much a turbulent life, but rather a routine one. Now all of a sudden I say that she had a turbulent life. Who would understand me? It's that, damn, it's not cliché, but it takes so much out of me to explain certain things. Because, believe me, Lorena was like that—routine and turbulent at the same time.

Many times I went back to work, the rain seeping through my boots, the mud causing chaos with my quivering, unsteady footsteps, only to find Lorena upset, cursing the day we began our relationship because she had a quarrel with Nabe or with Millie over some rude statement or some side comment that they mumbled as she walked by.

Such scenes played out over and over again with indescribable crudeness, while my skin absorbed the humid air with the same tendency as the air and the cold and the water passed through my flesh and into the bone.

So, that morning when we said our farewells to the people in town, it was, in reality, Lorena's last goodbye because she never returned to Estrada. I got up early and with Ruth's help, the always faithful Ruth, we got Lorena ready. Her eyes were extremely sorrowful that morning, but she appeared to be getting better. I looked at her, sitting against the back of the train's seat, I worried about some type of absurd resignation that I sensed from her. It was as if she had given up on life to accept her fate.

And I'm telling you, damn, it's not easy to accept that in anyone. And it wasn't easy for me to accept that resignation in someone I had seen fight with all of her strength for so long, facing the merciless beatings from Mother Nature. Her indomitable spirit brought together vast sectors of the community who revolved around our house. Suddenly, Lorena was vanquished, conquered, without hope and it was hope that had kept her alive. So, when a black person loses hope, death is inevitable.

I watched her fade away like a wounded flower—her thin figure, light complexion, kinky hair, her drab dress in my memory, her wrinkled forehead, her eyes fixed on me. The dreadful noise in the train station, the anonymous faces that back then like now were part of the world, of my world, the same fatal world to which I was now returning.

"You going to Limón?" asked an old man who fumbled his way to the seat next to me.

I said yes just to respond to him with something.

"You wanna smoke?" the old man asked.

"Alright," I didn't want to offend him.

I reached for the cigarette to put it between my lips. As he gave me a light, I looked at the faces of some of the young people who were a few rows ahead in a heated discussion about the soccer match. A white lab coat balanced on the hook, dancing to the rhythm of the train's noisy beat. Outside, you could barely make out the unsteady greenness of the pastures and farms that serenely bordered the railroad tracks.

The cigarette was made of good tobacco. Suddenly the old man grew on me. But in any case, I didn't strike up a conversation. Suddenly the train let loose a long whistle. Well, it wasn't the train exactly, but rather the locomotive. And it's not that I'm being cliché, but you have to say exactly what things are. The fact is that the whistle reminded me of Lorena. And this related to nothing in particular because since she died, I spent more time thinking about her until Esther filled, at least in part, the deep emptiness that she left.

Her voice came back to my memory with such cruelty:

"Go away …"

"But, Lorena …"

"Go along, go on. The sooner, the better. When do you want the divorce? I didn't want to get married for that very reason. You see? A man can't get married unless he let's all this business about power and control get to his head."

"But, Lorena …"

"But, Lorena, nothing. I am not like that filthy pig Millie. You hear me?"

The train continued on its way, indifferent to my suffering. It felt like a journey through all of my years. Behind me, Lorena's voice constantly there like a giant burden, the expression of scorn on her face, her eyes, those eyes that had held me captive for so many years, ever since that fortunate afternoon when I went in search of Mr. Sam's advice. I managed to light another cigarette with some difficulty. A powerful ray of lightning illuminated the sky and the reflection briefly distracted me. But the moment escaped, elusive, leaving me again facing Lorena, absorbing her indefinite and indefinable glare that she used to bind me to a fixed point within her grasp.

"Alright," I said with a force that was equally cruel, "I'm gone."

For an instant, Lorena didn't know what to do. She didn't expect that reaction.

"I'm tired of this, this foolishness. Dammit, I admitted what I did and it wasn't worth a damn. I corrected my mistake, nothing else has happened ever again and you keep accusing me."

Then she looked at me with an expression that children sometimes have when their parents separate. Only they know that look, it wasn't a look of pain or contempt, but rather shock. Everything that they formed a part of is now shattered in two. The two-dimensional way that they had loved, suddenly becomes two separate and distant beings. Children whose parents separate stand there just like Lorena did, trapped by time in between two opposite poles.

Many nights, I remembered her in that way, her face withdrawn, preoccupied, perplexed, with no guilt other than that of her own voice. I don't know how to explain it: she was the cause and the effect at the same time, the seed and the tree, and I hurriedly moved away, trying to contain the sobbing.

The old man was saying something to me and I didn't hear him.

"Sir?"

"If you want any."

"What is it?"

"Yucca with beef lung."

"I haven't eaten that in years. Sure, I'll have the biggest piece you can find. How much?"

"Three colones."

"Here."

"Thank you, papito …"

The old man stuffed the meat into his mouth and voraciously chewed it. For my part, it disgusted me at first and then made me nauseated. I stuck my head out the window pretending to take interest in the passing landscape and let the last mouthful fall to the ground. The engine went back to filling the air with its long whistle, the smell of burnt oil contaminated the breeze.

The old man wiped his mouth with a large handkerchief. He was satisfied. He was like the mango tree that adorned old man Pete's house, always content with the soil, water, and sun.

"Now, here come the colas," he said, "after eating, there's nothing like a nice cold cola."

"This time I'm treating you."

"Alright, alright. Two bottles please, the young man is buying."

I fixed my gaze on the back of the seat in front of me and to my astonishment, it felt like I was looking at the very seat that Lorena sat in during her last ride on the train. The bottle was quite cold. The soda gave me a good excuse to not think about anything in particular. I could follow it, running down my throat, refreshing my innards.

"You from Limón?"

"Yes, well, I'm really from Estrada."

"From Estrada? What a coincidence. What's your name?"

"McForbes, Charles McForbes."

"You don't say!"

"Yes, time has gone by so quickly. And you … the truth is that I don't recognize your face."

"Clovis."

"Clovis Lince!"

"How about that! Give me your hand, man! Let me shake your hand!"

We shook hands.

"You going to Estrada?"

"Yes, I think so. But …"

"I don't live in Estrada no more. I went over to Matina. It's better there."

"Really?"

"Yes, my harvest is much better there. In Estrada, the plantains just rotted away."

The young men filled the train car with their thick laughter. Two ladies who traveled in the seat in front of us turned back to glare at them with a mixture of surprise and reproach. The young men let loose in spite of them and then, went back to their emotional equilibrium as they continued their discussion.

Clovis Lince mentioned Lorena's death. Her death was unfair because she didn't die of natural causes. She died, plainly and simply a victim of the destructive powers that ravaged her body.

Lorena died unfairly. She experienced this condemnation because of a wicked man who raped her and then his wife, happily made his victim pay for her husband's sin. That's why Lorena knew that she was going to die before she left Estrada—because it was a supernatural thing, revealed to us by supernatural means. But what happened is that in reality I never accepted Pete's explanation. I preferred to hold onto Clarita Duke's scientific aspirations. And they weren't wild guesses—Lorena told Ruth to come see her in San José because she wouldn't be coming back to the town alive.

Nobody paid her any mind. Just like they didn't pay old Jake any mind when he went through the town, from house to house, to say his goodbyes to everyone. Nor did they pay much attention to the many who did the very same thing before him.

"That Devil," Clovis said, "that shameless bastard hasn't changed one bit."

"Who? Christian?"

"Uh, huh. Christian, that filthy dog. But now he has so much debt and one of these days he's going to have to pay."

"He's still up to his dirty tricks?"

"Not too long ago he grabbed the daughter of the Spanish man who owns the shop."

"Really?"

"Yes, but of course she was a bit … a bit loose, but Christian should be careful. What he does drags the rest of us through the mud."

"Us?"

"All of us black people."

"Us black people?"

My journey through the city in the hours just before I got on the train, immediately seemed absurd. And the speaker we heard at the National Theater, suddenly revealed its true meaning to me. At precisely what point did I lose my identity? What constellation of dreams put me in conflict with the culture that I nursed from my mother's dark bosom and sucking each and every drop as I sat at Pete McForbes feet?

You all can see my skin, dammit, it's not black. I mean to say, if it weren't for my hair and my features, I could pass as Latino just about anywhere.

But I was raised in a black town and I nursed my first taste of life from a black woman. Dammit, the truth is that I can't understand it and it's not that I'm trying to be cliché. No, it's not that at all. I really don't know what has happened to me.

A chill left an imprint on my veins. And I remembered the lowlands in all of its dimensions—where I rode my first horse, going up on one side and down the other without stopping. Clif and I killed our first bird, which we prepared in a stew with so much pride. And the traps that we set in the forest, and fishing, and working the land.

Now I return to the black soil that pierces and penetrates into the pores. The black soil that suddenly clings to your gums and cleans the varnish. Timeless soil, formless soil that gets onto your tongue.

Dammit, when we got to Matina I was sweating like the Devil himself. The earth has burning embers in its entrails.

My family didn't have the same pretensions as the Centeno family. We simply didn't have them. Some Scotsman landed in Barbados and married a daughter of one of those noble English families who was kicked out of the country after the great civil war and was reduced to slavery. He immigrated to Jamaica a few years later where he set up a large sugar mill. Damn, in that type of labor, so many blacks spilled their sweat and blood. So that Scotsman didn't have any objection to having intimate relations with one of his slaves and from that clandestine relationship, the

McForbes family was formed. We are McForbes from the paternal side, the maternal family line was lost in the cane fields of slavery in Jamaica.

But, it was Saltiman McForbes who changed the direction of things. He built a lumber mill on the ruins of the great plantation he inherited from the Scotsman. It was a major occurrence for Jamaica and there, all eight of the McForbes children grew up before they migrated to different parts of the American continent. But above all, they were subjects of Her Majesty, the Queen. They didn't have the same pretensions as the Centeno family because in their past flowed the blood of freed slaves. But they had their own sense of aristocracy. They were mulattos, and along with other mulattos, they formed part of a special caste.

They never ceased to emphasize their Scottish heritage. It was a note of distinction that gave them a lighter skin color, their inheritance, and the necessary prestige to be placed among the best families of their social class.

Saltiman McForbes made sure that all of his children attended high school. It was an exclusive high school where only mulattos could attend. There they learned to dream about their future glory and Saltiman wanted to ensure that the McForbes clan would have space just for them in the broad and complex spectrum of Jamaican society.

The great plantation that the McForbes family erected over the course of twenty years caused a stir among all social circles. No one could understand how it was possible for a former slave to succeed at such a feat unless it was explained away by the prevalence of Scottish blood in his veins. They decided that must have been the case and with that conclusion were able to make peace with it as part of the normal and natural order of human beings.

He married Miss Milady Brubanck, a mulatta from West Indian high society who was so white that it was only out of tradition that they continued to identify her as mulatta. He tied his natural instinct for business with the Brubanck fortune. Saltiman created "McForbes Lumber and Service, Ltd.," monopolizing a large part of the lumber industry on the island and later he started importing and exporting lumber.

At night he would convene his sons to remind them of who they were. He would tell them, "You are not black, nor are you white. You are brown, you are people of color, don't ever forget that. And understand that the blacks are incapable of joining together with other blacks, but we as people of color, are capable of doing what they can't and I've shown you the way. Now, get this into your heads, you are the future of this island. You and other people of color are that future. You cannot expect much from the blacks. On the other hand, the Englishman is a sly character and this will make things complicated for you, but he will eventually move on. The English have a lot of territory in Africa. When the English leave, all of this will be in your hands. If you don't want the blacks to overtake us and turn this island into some sort of savage Congo, you need to understand this lesson. I don't want any of my sons married to a black girl. Look for a mulatta or an English woman. You must improve the race and escape this foulness we're living in. The black man since the time of Noah was condemned by God to suffer. He's going to always suffer, so stay away from them as much as possible. You must whiten the race, that is the solution. You must whiten the race."

With that philosophy, Saltiman created his own financial empire. But soon after his death, the family quarrels started. The eight brothers decided to divide their inheritance into eight equal parts, and then two of those brothers started buying out their siblings' rights to the property. In the end, two of them were face-to-face and neither one of them was willing to sell their portion to the other. So, that's how it all ended. Both sold their property to third-parties, which seemed to them a much more logical thing to do rather than give in to McForbes family pride.

Pete was one of those brothers who in a short amount of time became just as poor as any black man. And was forced to live among black people and learn how to act like them to survive. He immigrated first to Panama in search of a way to restore the glory of the inheritance his father had passed on to him and his brothers, who because of their lack of financial knowledge and lack of an identity, couldn't manage their share of the inheritance, not even for a couple of years. In eighteen months, they destroyed what Saltiman had built over the course of twenty years and squandered the profits that had sustained the family for another thirty years under Saltiman. Pete's mother died greatly distressed by the near total ruin that pulled her away from Saltiman Junior, her favorite son.

But in Panama, Pete never found the fortune he was seeking and then he decided to try his luck in Limón. And he died in Limón, still trying his luck.

He was a failed black man, but Pete learned how to wake up the great dreams I had inside of me. Damn, I don't know if this was good or if it was cruel. It would have been good at the end of my years of studying to finish with some kind of profession at the end. But I guess I did in a way because when he died, I was able to give him a Christian burial thanks to my studies in seminary. It wasn't much for an old man who lived off of dreams. For a man who first sent me to Jamaica to study where his family didn't want to help me. For a man who sold the lottery, worked on other people's farms while also working on his own, and who also worked on the docks during the worse possible moments just so that his son could go to school in the capital.

It wasn't much, but what Pete McForbes did for me was enough. He had been able to give his son enough education so that he could educate his own children with better skill. He gave him roots so that he could adapt to this new land, master its national language.

My father died peacefully and joined old man Jake and all of those who like them who courageously one day decided to leave Montego Bay in search of their fortunes.

Dammit, one has to recognize all of this to live. And it's not that I'm making excuses, but you have to think about those long hours with sweat pouring down your neck and the prices that go up and down, and the insect bites, and all of that. Shit, and all of that.

Pete lived and died among the daily and cruel silt and rust. Assimilating, drop by drop, the bitterness that had been served to him from the time he could reach his father's knee. Suffering molecule by molecule the agony that he sucked from his mother's mulatta bosom—between rebellion and conformism, things were becoming distorted for him. It was all marching by, picking up bird droppings from among the people. Dammit, and his vision of the world was contagious for me until his dreams dug deep into my bones. It was impossible to continue studying. I had to reject a scale of values that for me was much too significant. Because history is in some way was already preconceived in the minds of thousands of men, and you needed more than pure willpower to change the river's direction.

And death had to come calling. Many more deaths than those of Pete and Jake to make a difference.

Dammit, one has to understand that. That's all.

The lowlands are a coiled serpent with its head tucked away in some part. At the slightest movement, it strikes. You have to be alert, find the head in time, and cut it off. People who live in the lowlands don't understand that this is death. Damn, the Devil will carry you away if you don't understand that.

My family didn't have pretensions, but it held onto dreams. All of the dreams except for one, the denial of our blackness. Damn, Pete drilled that into my head: look at stubborn old Jake Duke. He was a pretentious old man who didn't fit into the mold of other black men. That's to say, the black folks who are around here. Jake kept his African pride. I think they must have castrated one of his early ancestors when they ripped him from the African forests. He was opinionated and headstrong, but I envied him. He would say, "Charles, you are black. Your father Saltiman is an old fool."

So, where did I lose my identity to the point of rediscovering it with so much horror?

Without a doubt, something happened over the last few years. Something left me between the never-ending tracks of the railroad and processions to the cemetery—between lukewarm and timid lips, songs of faith and fits of rage. Because through the years I had come up against indifference many times, but the indifference came from friendly hands. Damn, could that be? Friendly hands?

Bowman destroyed Lorena. Bowman was black. Could that be? And maybe that's why I fell in love with Esther's white skin, her vivid blue eyes, her youthful spirit.

I began to measuredly walk toward Estrada, with the slowness of time pressed in my voice. White were the hands that lulled me to sleep. Black were the hands that tried to destroy me. But…but…neither Lorena nor Ruth were white. Damn, neither was Victoria. Shit, nor Clarita Duke, nor her know-it-all husband, Clif, nor Jake …

Victoria? My God, I completely forgot all about her.

IX

Daybreak.

Damn, a man gets bored with nothing to do.

Honestly, it's nice to think about the fresh flow of the creek's current moving to its own rhythm. And that's not being cliché. It's just simply nice to watch it flow.

But now, when you have nothing to do and besides, being in a place like this where you've collected so much time beneath your feet, you get bored.

Here, next to the same creek that the people here call San José Creek, I spent so many hours, so many footsteps. A type of shell has covered our mind and swallowing us up into everyday mediocrity. Yes, a man has to get bored if like me he's had to work the land to feed himself and still remains hungry, destiny driving him to no particular place. Getting up in the mornings like I once did, like a damned idiot. Continue on the next day with his intestines being eaten away by parasites and spend another day between silence and fatigue and sweat and come home to an empty house, without illusions and then, without Lorena Sam's sweet voice that back then was the only consolation I had.

I remember her vivacious as if in a dream, ardent, always busy. And I adored her just as she was.

Damn, this business of dipping your feet in the water isn't worth it. But, at least I'm not dipping them in the mud. My God, how I detest the mud that time shovels under your feet.

After working on the farm, I would come here sometimes to lose myself in the filth of the lake. Lake?! No, it wasn't a lake. It's not a lake, but why do people call it a lake? In the end, it's all the same. Lose myself in the filth, naked, just to dramatize a bit, there in the solitude of the forest and the deep reality of my being. A man, a being in transition.

And then, trembling from the cold—a curious thing, the lake's water was very cold at daybreak and at dusk—all that was left for me to do was to get dressed to seek out either Lorena's warm arms or, like now, the burning heat of the sun from the top of a guava tree.

It didn't take much effort to climb the tree because when you have really mastered something, like some kind of art or a profession, it stays with you forever. The fruit tastes like sand and the nectar reminds me of poison. A seed got caught between my teeth, bringing back memories of my childhood. Under the direction of Gordiflón, who was half-man, half-beast, the children would happily sing in a chorus,

> *Teeth, teeth, teeth of the saw*
> *Eyes, eyes, eyes of the macaw.*

And my eyes and teeth denounced in their own way the terrible suppression of fear and rage. I learned to hate, thanks to Gordiflón. It was as if he were the instrument of a violent nature, an enemy of human beings. Nature reduced us to the passive condition of a worm. In the lowlands, we became tigers or worms—there is no in between.

Years later we discovered the weakness of hate, watching my efforts die in the mud and silt of the annual flood.

Damn world, without a doubt. And that bastard Christian is probably laughing now. It's worth killing him for. But, who knows if he's really laughing. It's likely that he knows I'm here even though I'm not sure how. The train got in late and I got off in Matina and walked to the town.

A man has to fight against this land, a place where an ant can start a fire with his backside and when climbing a tree you can fall into the dormilona plants that open and close their leaves and violently extend their thorns. It's normal to feel the way I feel today, in a bad mood.

When you feel this way, it's worth it to go out and crush some plants or whatever insect happens to be around. It's a way of affirming that you're human.

Human beings can be cruel, as cruel and relentless as Mother Nature.

And believe me, there's nothing cliché about that. It's the absolute truth.

I think that it was good to go back to the river and put my feet in the water. It's peaceful there. The fish don't bother me very much, but they do tickle.

A nice assortment of guavas will keep me occupied for a long while. One morning, some time ago, I remember having done the same. With the naked blade of a leaf, I freed the seeds that had gotten caught between my saw-like teeth. I ate guava seeds for two weeks because I thought they would weaken my appendix. A friend of Lorena's had told me that guava seeds would do just that. I wanted to get appendicitis or anything to change the wearisome daily routine and that damned life that I had been living since Lorena died, for any other damned life I could have. Shit, those were the casualties. That morning Guillermo passed by there.

"What's going on Charles?" he said, "How are you doing?"

"Well, you can see."

"And Ruth?"

"She's alright."

"Looks like she kicked you out this morning."

"Naw, nothing like that. Just from time to time I like to get up early, you know?"

I shouldn't have said anything to him. Or maybe at least I should have cursed at him.

I lifted my gaze to look at Guillermo Brown's violent face. A face that in my memory would always signify the death of someone or something. A sturdy face, like the heat of the indomitable coastal slope that we live on. A million wounds and injuries are reflected in his face. Timeless imprints of his entire race.

"I get up early just to take it easy every so often."

"Hmmmm, cho[15] ... I'm not swallowing that pill. Seems to me that you had to leave in a hurry."

The laughter sent various explosions across his sturdy face. I thought about the mute laughter of his mule, while the two, man and beast, faded back into the nothingness from where they had emerged.

"Cho," I said spitting into the water, "That bastard still riles me up."

A small flower traveled on the shoulders of the river. I imagined it wilting by sunset. But the flower was luckier than Guillermo and his mule because by late afternoon they would fulfill their destiny. They were quite a pair, one was a caricature of God, and the other was a caricature of its owner. Nevertheless, I thought now they were better off than me, with my hurrying through Mondays, Tuesdays, and ...

---

[15]Cho, an expression of annoyance in Costa Rican Limonese Creole English and Jamaican Creole English.

Victoria. That same day I saw her for the next to last time. But as I ate guavas and cursed Guillermo Brown, I didn't think that the next day I would be so far away. Far, far away. I had gone to see her on a Monday and she told me that I couldn't come into her house. I couldn't come in. Imagine what that feels like. I couldn't come in.

"Why?"

"Papa doesn't want you to come by to see me."

"But … well, that's his problem. Besides, he's not at home right now."

"It doesn't matter. He doesn't want you to come see me whether he's home or not."

"But …," I leaped inside the entryway anyway, "we like each other. That's all that matters my love. That's all that matters."

We went inside the house and I closed the door.

"It smells good, what are you cooking?"

My hands instinctively searched her shoulders. And uncontrollably glided slowly down toward her waist, wanting to arrive without being noticed like a thief at midnight.

"Victoria, tell me what happened?"

"What happened with what?"

"With your father."

"He was speaking with the pastor. The pastor came to see him."

"The pastor?"

"Yes, Pastor George. The one who took your place."

"Oh, Alfred George. He's an animal."

"Don't say that."

"In spite of everything, you still defend him?"

My hands arrived at her waist, she let out a light sigh. I stopped myself, breathing with difficulty, avoiding falling into total distress.

"They talked," she forcefully freed herself from my embrace, "they talked about all the ways you've been up to no good."

I drew myself close to her again and rested my body onto hers, I searched for her support and I thought then that Victoria was an exemplary woman. But I had crossed out the idea of marriage. I want to say that with Lorena it was different.

Once was enough. I didn't want to dismiss all of those years we spent together, but … once was enough. In the next room, my son's sleep was restless like the wind only to become a soft snore. The boy was the child of a really good mother. But neither the monogamy that her father insisted on nor the idea of marriage seemed like a good deal to me. Neither was something men could do unless they were castrated by other men. It's that love shouldn't be constrained. Although the truth is that I had my limits during the time I lived with Lorena. And then on top of it all, having to put myself in that ridiculous suit and suffer two hours of abusive talk.

"They were talking about us…"

For reasons that I didn't quite understand at that moment, Victoria almost couldn't speak. It wasn't my touch, nor the intimate memories that my caresses evoked.

"Just stop right there," I said to her, indignant.

"The reverend made him see that we were living in sin."

"Oh, really? Of course, he would think that."

"And besides," she suddenly recovered her composure and was free again, "he told him about all the ways that you've been up to no good."

"No good?"

"Yes, all of the things you've been doing Charles. You think it's a small thing? You were a pastor once and now …"

"And now what?"

"You're with three women."

"With three what?" but in reality, the question came out needlessly. We both understood that because Victoria just stood there in silence. Then, as I swallowed my saliva, she looked at me again with her kind eyes.

"Charles, you were a good husband to Lorena. We all saw that. I like you, not the man in front of me now, but the one I've known since I was a little. But since she died, you've let yourself go to ruin."

"Lorena is dead. You know that."

"Dead? Dead, yes, but you still think about her. That's what bothers me. It's not George's story, although …"

"Although?"

Dammit, that just completely killed me. I just couldn't take anymore. It's that, look, you just don't get a woman like her and that's that. Damn, that just took me completely off guard. Really.

Heading to the kitchen with a look of disdain, she told me that it was best not to talk any more about it. She wiped away her tears, dammit, even that—she started to cry. It wasn't that idiotic sobbing that some people have, but a real cry that came out of her even though she tried to avoid it. And finding the strength from her sadness, or at least from her already prolonged resignation over her lover's unjust role.

Well, I don't know where she found the strength, but she served me a plate of food. I felt guilty for the first time since Lorena's death. Victoria was the mother of my only child. And she was the mother, not because she was indecent, but because she loved me. She gave herself to me, without limits to the dream that had been growing even before Lorena fell ill. She had seen the dream she had as a girl and it became reality. And I needed a woman like that, a woman who would heal the deep wound that Lorena left when she died.

That afternoon I watched Victoria overcome her jealousy, move the vase of flowers, set the table, and serve me a plate of food.

I couldn't get the food down my throat. And never before had we sought each other out with such intensity, and never before that afternoon had I heard a woman give herself totally to love, and never before did I feel so human.

Later she got up to walk to the window and singing softly the same melody that Miriam Makeba sang from the Chinese shop owner's jukebox.

A man who has nothing to do has to be bored. Absolutely nothing to do. First, when they buried Lorena, I decided not to return to the farm. Damn, and I managed to do that. Once a man decides to do something and he must do it.

I spent all of my savings during Lorena's illness. When she died, I was almost bankrupt. And I could've lifted myself out of the ashes with a lot of determination. But I didn't have that drive and nor did I have the desire to do it.

So, when all of that happened with Victoria—what I just told you about—I just continued without any strength and very tired. I lost that night in the shadows and the dim light of the country to hide my weeping. Only God, and perhaps the flickering fireflies that populated that Monday night were seen surrounding my pride. Well, in reality, the fireflies didn't do that. That's a bit cliché.

That Tuesday I went to Engracia's house. She was an exotic woman from Grecia. Her white skin burned by the lowlands, still held onto the fresh spray of the sugarcane of her home.

The week following Lorena's death, I fled into Engracia's arms, to the refuge of the night and from her husband's drunkenness. I simply met her downtown, she asked me to walk her home and then to open the door to carry in her husband, who we had found drunk in a cantina. The next day we made a date and I arrived at the dark refuge to softly touch the wooden blinds and wait for the response, push the door and come inside. Penetrating the darkness gave the sensation of plunging into a vat of sugarcane foam and drinking it to the point of intoxication. In some ways, it was a new way to live. Engracia didn't have the firm muscle tone that Lorena had, nor did she have the same strength when she grabbed my back. No, but dammit, going to Engracia was always penetrating into the mystery of life, to feel that I was a man with her feminine maturity; hear her whisper about tamales and tortillas in the gentle early morning hours of her vital nostalgia. To see Engracia's years sketched on her skin was to master the world and reaching the ends of her corn-colored hair, to be consumed by that way of loving that she invented, changing the noun in every possible way.

But Engracia needed me and I needed her. She needed my blackness to soften her pale skin. She needed my youth to hold back the passage of time. I took revenge on life. I took revenge on those who had dominated me for so many years, those who had robbed my father of his very humanity, and those who robbed his parents and grandparents before him, while at the same time planted my own maturity in her.

She needed to turn me into a brute, return me to a wild animal, to her irrational spontaneity, to return me to the far-reaching dimension where only emotions exist and forget the drunken husband who ruined her, while I forgot for a few moments about Lorena. I forgot about the indecent drunk who came to her stinking and just threw himself on top of her with his horrible grunts and snores. I forgot about a mulatta who was such a strong woman and the now useless passion for the man who was her husband.

But she didn't manage to erase my regret. That's why I was on the edge of the creek, or river, or lake, as the folks around here call it. It's all the same.

I returned home. Ruth was waiting with breakfast ready.

"It took you a long time …"

"It's that …"

"Man, it took you a long time …"

"Yes, I know, forgive me."

I inhaled the boiled green banana, still thinking about Guillermo's caricatured face and his ridiculous mule. The always faithful Ruth, as if she owed Lorena some kind of debt, or as if she had inherited the responsibilities Lorena once had and cared for me after her friend's death. She came to the house on her own, washed clothes, made up the bed, and prepared food for me.

I left the house in search of work. It was a daily exercise, I would go through the town looking for something to do. A man gets bored when he's got nothing to do.

I ran into old man Mr. Clarence. He was a stingy old man, one of those who would rather watch a coconut rot rather than share it with others. Anyway, I asked him for work.

"Well, there's work, Pastor," in spite of my protests, he would always call me pastor, "well, what I don't have is money to pay you. Frankly, I would like to help you, but things have gone from bad to worse."

"That's alright," and I left murmuring something about all the years I had known that cheap old man and always listened to him complain about the same thing. And I knew that his situation, in reality, was really quite good, since the bank auditor, the Coolie woman, was one of his friends and she told his mother in confidence who then confided in Fat Stella, and then what Stella knows, the whole town knows, in confidence of course.

"Don Gunar, good morning."

"Hey, how's it going? What are you up to these days?"

"I'm looking for something to do," the story of each of my days collected in my anguish and grew, I now understood my sense of defeat.

But that morning Don Gunar offered to buy my farm.

"You will buy my farm?"

"Yes, I'll give you five hundred …"

"Five hundred pesos a hectare? But, my God Don Gunar!"

"It's a fair price."

"A fair price? At an exchange of forty … No way, fifty and so many years of work."

"You all have lived off of that with no problem. In any case, it's not really up for discussion. How much do you want?"

"A thousand pesos."

"A thousand pesos?"

He stood there looking at the clouds floating by, pushed by the morning breeze as they sought out the highlands to the west.

"Nine hundred," he said, "and then it's a deal."

"Nine hundred. Alright."

I returned home late, tired of walking through pastures, burning in the fading rays of the afternoon sun. Ruth had left dinner for me on top of the stove. I changed clothes and went to look for Victoria.

"Papa's inside," she told me, "and he's ready to put a bullet in you. The neighbor told him that you had been here …"

"I've come to give you this money …"

"Money?"

"Yes, eight thousand colones."

"Eight thousand colones!"

"Yes, well I took out around two hundred for me, but this is for you and my son."

"But, where in the world did you get this from? …Charles … Charles …come back, don't go …"

Damn, it was terrible to hear her calling after me and I couldn't turn around. But shit, the night before when I was drunk from Engracia's vitality, she told me that she was pregnant and according to her the child was mine because "the drunken bastard is sterile." And that same night, after returning home Ruth was waiting for me with her gentle way of giving herself over to the peaceful wave and her long rhythm like the water's wake, and the abundant sweat that flowed from her skin and the ardent steam clouding our eyes.

It was too much. And finally the sale of the farm. I was untying myself from the remains of a withered life.

That night, I could hardly sleep. I dreamed about a song that survived the hardships of the desert; a bongo that brought joy and a flock of birds that were migrating for the summer. And I woke up upset, burning on Ruth's hot embers, thinking about the light that was traveling toward the west.

"Ruth …"

"What happened, Charles? What's going on?"

"I'm leaving …"

"What?"

"I'm leaving …"

"Where you going to?" she asked, rubbing her eyes while her nude cinnamon colored breasts still burned. Engracia was a volcano and at that very moment I realized Ruth was a mountain. Victoria? She was my son's mother and a great woman.

"Where you going to at this time of morning? You're crazy as hell."

"Yes, perhaps …"

"But where are you going at this hour? But if you're thinking of moving away and all…"

"I'm serious, Ruth, I'm gone. I'll leave you the house. It's better than the one you have now. Come live here and rent yours out."

"Dear Lord, Charles, where are you going? Where, Charles?"

Ruth seemed like she was in despair. Ever since Lorena died, she had become more than a friend. She clung to me and consoled me during my crises. She supported me during my struggle to just survive, to resist the temptation to kill Christian. Now I was going. I was going, leaving her alone for good. Without a reason to keep living, I just calmly told her, "I'm leaving you the house."

"Charles," she told me almost sobbing, "don't do anything foolish. Where are you going?"

"I don't know where the hell I'm going, Ruth, just that I'm gone."

Now, leaving the flowing brook, I decided to go look for Victoria. I arrived the night before, got off in the neighboring town, and walked to my old home under the shelter of darkness. The strategy seemed to work. I don't think anyone saw me.

I slowly walked toward Victoria's house, trying not to be seen by the people who would be starting their early morning chores. I greeted a dozen people or so along the road, who glanced at me for a long time, possibly asking themselves, where had I seen that face before.

I see Victoria on the porch of her house, her head raised toward the wind as I approach. Her eyes were deep as they always had been, her hair shining, her hands stroking the child's head. My heart leapt, damn, and I'm just standing here like a splattered tomato.

A man abandoned his world and now he has returned.

She sees me and stands up. Her face was suddenly captive with an anxious expression. Her fingers gripped the comb that she was using to fix the boy's hair.

"Charles …," she managed to faintly whisper my name.

I didn't say anything. I approached, looking at her, looking at the girl who I had left on this same porch many years ago, calling after me, or that afternoon I had seen her showing off her shapely figure as she sang a Miriam Makeba song.

"Charles, where have you been?"

"Over there so."

"What a way to leave."

Her reproach was as if it all happened yesterday.

"Yes," I respond to her tenderly, "you're right. And the boy, how is he?"

"Ah, yes, the boy, of course. Thomas, look at him. Thomas, say hello to Uncle Charles."

"Uncle?"

"Yes, Uncle Charles!" she responded, putting the stress on the word "uncle."

"So…"

"Tommy, go call your papa and tell him that your uncle is here."

I couldn't let him go in at that moment. I picked him up to hold him against my chest for a long while and kiss him until my eyes began to well up with tears.

"Go on," she said several times, "Go tell your papa that your uncle is here."

He's … he's my son. This is my town, my people. They're mine.

Alfred George comes out of the little house and stands there looking at me. I purposefully looked at Victoria's svelte body, her sweaty forehead, her red lips, her athletic figure, her waist above all, in a distinct place from other women. Esther's waist wouldn't be positioned there.

I continue holding the boy. Dammit, what an awkward moment for poor Alfred. For my part, I felt like saying to him, "You bastard," but I resisted. I resisted because the truth is I abandoned Victoria without fully comprehending that this was my place. Without understanding that these were my people.

"Pastor ... May God bless you ..."

"And also you ... Charles ..."

"My nephew is beautiful," I say to him slowly, looking at Victoria.

"He's a healthy boy," he hastily responds.

"Thank you," I turn my gaze slowly to look at him.

"You're welcome. Thomas is our boy."

"Thank you anyway," sometimes it's necessary to insist.

We go into the house following behind Victoria. Damn, that isn't easy. I tell you, a man leaves his world and comes back looking for it only to discover that the past is past, trampling on deeply held yearnings.

"Alfred and I got married in June, the year before last."

"Hmmmm ... I'm late for the wedding toast." She captures the double meaning and looks at me out of the corner of her eye.

"My papa died," she added nervously.

"Poor old man. In spite of everything, I really appreciated him. Thank you for taking care of Thomas so well," I gave the pastor a pat on the back.

"Don't mention it ..."

"I'll say, one has a ... a nephew, right? One has a nephew and one morning decides to leave him. One leaves because he's bored and fed up ..."

"Bored and fed up?"

"Bored and fed up with being a nobody. Tired of seeing everything frustrated. So, one just picks up and leaves, runs away."

"You don't run away from God," Alfred responds with a ceremonious attitude.

"I'm not sure about that Alfred. I'm not making a big deal of this, I just don't know. But what I do know for true is that you can run away from yourself. That's for certain."

Victoria perhaps fearing an upsetting outcome carries the boy to the kitchen. The kitchen where once we passionately thirsted after one another and perhaps a little bit of that deep passion remains.

The bushes in the pasture were green once again and a few well cared for animals grazed the fresh herbs adorned with tiny drops of dew.

"Charles … you left Victoria and I …"

"I don't want to discuss that, Alfred. You liked her ever since you got to town. That's why you did everything possible to separate us …"

"You were living with Engracia and everyone here knew that. And also you were with Ruth Viales. Two women who were older than you. Victoria was a girl and you were unfaithful to her."

"Keep it formal, Pastor, I don't want us to have any problems."

He tried to take it to a familiar place and I wasn't going to allow it. I let my gaze drift into space for a brief moment.

"Charles, in the name of God …"

"In the name of God? I'm a fool. I ran away. I was scared of facing life."

"Alright, now what?"

And now my eyes are recovering to the definite present. I look at the pastor and I notice he's nervous, sweating, and continually shifting back and forth in his chair.

"Why have you come back?"

In the end, I got what I wanted, that he treats me with respect.

"Not to worry, I'm not going to take her from you."

"Not going to take her from me! What a thing!"

"I'm not going to try, Alfred, so you can rest easy. I'm not going to ruin another pastor. I'm not sure why I came back – maybe to say hello to Ruth. How is she doing?"

"Ruth has a husband now."

"Pastor, I asked you, 'how is she doing.'"

But I, dammit, know good and well that I have run away again. I'm thinking that yes, it wasn't a question of trying to take to Victoria right now. It was absolutely ridiculous to propose to her the idea of living together. But if I got a divorce, who knows …

At least I could make this bastard suffer for a little while. But they are my people, they are mine.

"I'm going to go see how things are going with Ruth. What time does the train pass by? No, the one that goes to Limón."

I meet up with Ruth, damn, she seems old. She had become old little by little, perhaps because she didn't know how to hold onto someone else's youth like Engracia. But her eyes radiated tenderness as always.

"I'm doing well. I got married again."

"I haven't gotten married, but I'm living with a friend. Charles McForbes, why don't you at least have a seat?"

The house was in order. Through the open door, I could see the room that in earlier times witnessed the nights of my first marriage. Ruth has respected its arrangement.

"Your room is there, just as you left it," she tells me after seeing my curiosity and immediately caressed my hair. "I owe so much to Lorena, Charles, so much."

I look her in the eyes. Ruth wasn't beautiful, she never was. But she had a type of grace that was pleasing.

"And your man friend, who is he?," I ask.

"Charles," she says with a certain malice, "they tell me your wife is white and I haven't even asked you if that's true or not and much less her name."

"Yes, she's white, from a good family."

"From a good family. And Lorena, was she from a bad family?"

"I mean to say from a bourgeois family."

"Bour … what?"

"Bourgeois. A wealthy family."

"Oh, that's what they call it? A Turkish family?"

It didn't make sense to correct her. She looks at me with such tenderness that dammit, I will have to kiss her. An old kiss that springs up out of memory and erases the ugly words that I uttered when I left. I didn't kiss the Ruth that I see now in front of me, but rather I am kissing the

Ruth who kept vigil at Lorena's bedside. And she's kissing Lorena Sam's widower. A friend who needed from her more than words to survive.

"My wife's name is Esther," I say to her just to say something, "And your friend?"

"Guillermo."

"Guillermo?"

"Yes, Guillermo Brown."

Ruth seemed to hold on to some irrational need to stay connected to Lorena's life and death. It was as if she tried to keep her alive through her own existence.

"Ruth, what time does the train pass by?"

"Which train?"

"For Limón …"

"You're leaving?"

"Yes, I came to see you Ruth. I saw you, and now I'm going. I happened to see Pastor George's wife and Thomas McForbes."

"Thomas McForbes? Thomas George. In any case, you leave just so. This might be the last time I see you in this life and you leave just so."

"Ruth, what are you saying?"

"Charles, just suppose that you come back, I won't be able …"

I watch her cut off the sentence and lower her gaze.

"And you leave just so …," she says with a profound sadness. The chair falls over and we go down to the floor. It's a gentle fall, almost without force. It's like swimming in San José creek, in the part that people call the lake in the middle of the morning. But the copious amounts of sweat release burning steam that rejuvenates the skin.

X

Any man in these circumstances would be nervous.

Limón seemed gigantic to me. It had grown in its old age, like the cactus in deserts of full of sand.

The airplane lifted off on the breeze and the sea appeared suddenly out of the window. I looked out the other side toward the depths that extended into space, wavering between blue and white. The plane gradually leveled itself. In front of me, a young girl looked at me, as if she had a tremendous urge to be kissed. To be kissed by anyone, to feel that the world exists. That the world exists and that she is still a vital part of its existence.

I took a book out of the small bag that I had with me, my only luggage, and I started to read. It was written by a black man. "It's boiling," it read, "the water buried in the veins of the earth, the porous and humid earth … and the wind is boiling."[16]

In reality, I wasn't reading. My eyes were looking between the lines to find the courage that I needed to face Esther and ask her for a divorce. Dammit, that wasn't an easy thing to do.

"Once there was a man from Cartago and a Jamaican who were friends …"[17]

Once there was love between two people. Because I loved her. I loved her a lot. A type of love that betrays the one who is loved as much as the lover, but that's the way I loved her. "Love," according to the book I was reading, "is a dawn song."[18]

So much optimism! Imagine that, a song at that hour of the day.

The truth is that the book seemed like something that romantic women and their compliant husbands would enjoy.

---

[16]Reference to Duncan's story, "La carta"/"The Letter" from the collection *Canción en la madrugada*.

[17]Reference to Duncan's story, "Dos amigos"/"Two Friends" from ibid.

[18]Reference to Duncan's story, "Cancion en la madrugada/Dawn Song" from ibid.

For me, I was looking for another sense of peace. And in that sense, the man who died on the edge of the ocean with his feet buried in the sand seemed more real now.

That dream still causes me to shake with fear. Really what I needed was the courage to avoid screaming. Although somehow I know that I screamed, but it remained trapped in my throat.

The dream was really something awful. I want to say, not to be cliché, but to see yourself sleeping is frightening. Shit, I don't even have to tell you, you can already imagine it for yourselves.

Now, the truth is that traveling in an airplane doesn't seem like the appropriate time to bring up those types of memories. A man gets nervous in these types of circumstances. But, anyway, dammit…

The world is full of stupid people. According to the book's author, there are things like the Watchman's Light[19] that have no logical explanation. I was a boy when that happened. When the brakeman fell from the train and the light appeared seven nights later. That was true, but the world is full of black folk who …

Until today, my life had gone on without much meaning. A never-ending routine. That was my life with Lorena Sam.

We made love at night. We ate together in the afternoons. Then I spent my time doing what she called "man's work," while she washed the dishes. And we would go to bed early. We would go to bed and I would caress her and she responded with more caresses until our angst would explode into sighs.

Sundays we would go to church, except on the days when she was menstruating and when that happened, I would go by myself. Two Sundays a month, I was in charge of the worship service and for the other two, the pastor from Limón would come. So, I preached two Sundays, and then when I got home, I argued with Lorena over any little thing.

---

[19]Reference to Duncan's story, "La luz del vigia/Watchman's Light," which is based on Limonese lore about a mysterious light from ibid.

She never found a way to forgive me for the affair with Millie. That damned Millie. She used to look for me every Sunday when Lorena didn't attend service to make me see her in her new frocks, among other things. She was a seamstress and she loved to design her clothing.

That particular Sunday, she was more attractive than ever. She was really quite pretty and she would've been the most beautiful woman in Estrada if it weren't for her foot. She told me she had a problem with her sewing machine and begged me to accompany her to Nabe's house to start it up, which aroused in me old feelings of sympathy for her that were born the day I witnessed her accident. I agreed without suspecting her clever plan. But when we arrived, she told me to wait for her while she changed. The Bowmans weren't home and I was a bit nervous thinking that Lorena may have seen me go into the house of her archenemies.

Millie came out wearing a silk dress. Her cottony hair was loose, her hips were rhythmical…the world blinds you sometimes, and damn, with that dress that was almost see-through you lose all sense of reason and most of all with soft hands and warm caresses. The truth is that … shit, I'm a man, you know?

The thing is that I stayed until nightfall. Then Millie told Nabe about our little adventure. For her it was just another conquest. Another outfit she could show off to Nabe. And I don't know how, but Lorena found out about what had happened and I had to confess. Even though I am being a bit cliché when I say "I don't know how," because the truth is that in Costa Rica, gossip is a national sport. The favorite sport.

The plane started its descent and the girl in the seat in front of me fixed her gaze on me once again. I smiled and I appreciated her expression of gratitude. She kept looking at me as if that was enough to calm her nerves.

I fought with Lorena on Sundays because she was set on making me see that it wasn't the stupid idiot Millie who was the problem and that I couldn't take the same liberties with her that I could take with another woman and who was going to believe me after everything that had happened. Because she said the days of slavery ended a long time ago.

We didn't make love on Sunday because it was the Lord's Day. Instead, Sunday was our favorite day for fighting with each other. Sundays, I was the asshole who thought that Millie was the whore who sat in the front pew of the church and got her hooks into the pastor. That damned cripple whore.

And when we dreamed about Pete, we had to buy the lottery. She used to buy the clandestine Panamanian lottery a lot. And she almost never won.

Dammit, it was a damned desperate routine that I don't want to remember. A routine that left me sick after her death to the point of looking for something in other women and that became a weakness. But the truth is that life with Lorena was convenient for me. It had to be because at that time I was as at my best.

But, damn, thinking about it now, it was a routine and it's not that I'm being cliché.

The plane touched down just as the heart of the passenger in front of me was about to give out. The color began to come back to her face. We left the heat of the plane and walked into the December coolness of the Central Valley. The young woman nonchalantly walked next to me.

"You were nervous, weren't you?"

"Yes, a little."

"Me too."

"I don't believe you. You looked so calm."

"I wasn't. It's just that in reality, it's not a matter of nerves, but rather how much we try to triumph over them."

"Really?"

"Yes, that's it. And when you discover that, everything else becomes much easier."

She had a naive smile on her face that invited the discovery of those things in other people's lives that weren't that interesting to most folks. For example to know that I used to live in Limón, that I studied, and that I came to get some paperwork in order. Those simple things that are more than skin, and that reveal the humanity in all of us. Things that in the end, unite us in the image of God.

We went downtown in a taxi that I paid for. Lorena and I took this route once while she was dying a slow, routine, unspectacular death. She just died, stubbornly until it conquered her.

Along the way, the air took me back to the coolness of my past in Estrada. Maybe it had to do with Bowman or Nabe. Centeno never could offer a convincing diagnosis and he confessed this to me when he tried to use it as an argument against my relationship with his daughter. Dr. Suárez couldn't even give me a concrete diagnosis, nor the dozens of doctors who helplessly watched Lorena's slow and ordinary death.

Then I felt tired, bored with the routine, and I fled into Engracia's arms…and…

I ended up imprisoned between worlds, trapped between two cultures, between cottony black hair and hair the color of corn; between the heat and the cold. My terrible and unrealizable desire to possess both worlds without having to make a choice between the two.

Or could it be that I had wrongly chosen a scale of values that went against the essence of my being? Or could it be that I will always be split? And if that's the case, then it would explain my aspiration as a manifestation of myself, of my true personality.

And while I traveled with the young woman in silence, I was transported again to that terrible moment when I decided to leave everything behind and change my life. Victoria demanding that I give Thomas my last name; the brothers of the church accusing me of being a sinner; Ruth sleeping in my bed, giving her entire self to me; Engracia, pregnant, tired of her double life between a younger man and a useless, alcoholic husband; a man has to get fed up, dammit.

I left the girl at her hotel with the promise of coming back in the afternoon if I could. I went straight to a cheap hotel and after getting dressed, I thought about going to look for my wife. Damn, a man has to get fed up with so much on his nerves. A man, in the end, is just flesh and bone. But instead of going home as I had initially thought, I went back to the places I used to go to before I graduated. The places of the poor, the streets that you always carry with you. I walked along the Paseo de los Estudiantes and I stopped on the corner of the La Nave bar. Because that corner is something of a legend. Then to the Italian ice cream shop, the Botica Primavera, cars lining up like ants; the eyes of the people, white faces, teeth with the scent of ivory shining in the late-afternoon chill. And I couldn't explain how it was possible to walk the streets just like my neighbor Elber, who offered to show me the city. The streets were full of wind, the cold wreaked havoc on my body in spite of the sweater I wore. In those times, the sun in San José would shine without bringing heat. Those were the times when the severe face of La Soledad Church and the empty rotunda, the lottery sellers, the bread shop, Frescosal, the tax office, La Geisha, the Quesada furniture store, and a vacant lot. Traffic lights, thousands of traffic lights, signs that say "keys made here," Chelles Cantina and stores. I walked along those streets once again with explicit images engraved in my mind; walking along Central Avenue, the inexplicable presence of so many people walking. Nothing was rational back in those days. It was a magical world with thousands of toy cars. Clothing stores, mopeds, and motorcycles and car exhaust; Artillery Plaza, the Bank of Costa Rica, and more and more stores, La Gloria, El Ibis, La Constancia, the Central Market …

After everything, damn, it's not that I'm being cliché, but none of that was worth it. I knew it, that's for sure, before marrying Lorena and during those incredibly unreal years of secondary school. I knew it back then. But then after Lorena's death and having experienced profound hunger, the street got stuck in my veins. A sudden gust of wind pulled me out of the past and lifted up a young woman's skirt. A motorcyclist hit the bumper of the car in front of him. My feet devoured block after block of concrete sidewalk, while the sun faded in the distance. The lights of the city began to emerge. Was there at one time a Botica Estrada? San José wasn't Limón—that salt encrusted lung between the railroad and the sea. San José took on gigantic proportions at night, much more than Limón. The lights became ash and salt and earth and I continued along weightless, my strength without support in the growing solitude.

Then I came back, full circle to the Paseo de los Estudiantes. The empty lot was no longer there and in its place a cement building that made the city even uglier. The furniture store was forgotten. An elegant office building replaced the old Geisha. The church is still there and a leafy Guanacaste tree gathers light in the rotunda. The stupor has passed. I was now regaining the sharp clarity of things.

The night was intense and cold.

XI

Manuela opened the door.

"Don Charles," she shouted, hugging me, "Come in, come in … Your wife is very worried."

The house was the same. The furniture was in order, as always, the cassette player worked. The smell of bread and cheese wafted from the kitchen.

"My wife?"

"She's taking care of something with the Puma."

"Something with the Puma?"

"Yes sir, Puma called here asking for help with something."

"But how, Manuela, asking for help? Help with what?"

"But, don Charles, you don't know anything about this family … What's wrong?"

"It's precisely that Manuela, I don't know anything about them. Tell me."

"Well … I didn't know what happened either, but something going on between Magdalena and The Puma …"

"Between Magdalena and Puma!"

"Something having to do with drugs … I really don't understand any of it, but now Puma said that if they don't help him, he's going to sing like a bird and tell everything he knows about Magdalena and your wife is dealing with all of that."

The Puma. A long tragedy started with him. He was one of those people who knows how to take control of your will. He said no one who was part of the gang would want for anything as long as all of us were alive and traveling through life's great ups and downs. I started to follow him almost really without realizing it. First to a cantina of ill-repute. Then, as if my stepping down from the pastorate and into nothingness weren't enough, we started frequenting the Redhead.

I can't tell you all the things we did together. Then, one night he brought me to the gang to put me through their initiation.

First, they stripped me. Then, tying my feet and hands, four big guys reduced me to a state of helplessness. All I could do was call out for my mother, for her caresses perfumed with milk and bread. A terrible pain rose through my intestines and a ball in my throat choked me. I think I shit on myself just before blacking out.

Damn, The Puma is an animal.

"Manuela, did Esther say where she was going to meet Puma?"

"No, she didn't say anything. She never tells me anything, but I listen."

I left the house in desperation. I was familiar with some of the places where Puma generally met people. Wherever he was, I had to get there in time and save Esther as much as Magdalena. The night they "initiated" me, I ended up vomiting, while four sons-of-bitches breathed and grunted like animals. When I was a boy, sitting on my mother's knee, I would dare ask her, "Mommy, how could the Lord sweat blood?" She looked at me with that intense look that fighting cocks have when they've been beaten by their challenger.

"Son," she said, her eyes clouded, "you will understand in time."

I ran from place to place, without finding a trace of my wife. My thoughts went back once again to the night of my initiation into the gang. Blood poured from my mouth and my pores and onto the floor, without muffling the shame. Above my head, I heard all of the things I believed as a child escape. I was betrayed, humiliated, and my humiliation was merely savage rage.

Some police officers found me and picked me up from a vacant house.

A vacant house!

I told the already suspicious taxi driver the address of the empty house. It didn't make sense that Puma would ask Esther to come to a house the police have already raided, but he was always skilled at meeting in the most illogical places.

I didn't clearly remember all the exact details the way I wanted to. But I know that when they picked me up from that vacant house, they took me to the hospital and then to general detention. There I was put through intense interrogation. Damn, partly out of fear, partly out of a desire for revenge, I decided not to reveal the identity of the animals who brutalized me.

"Who was it, darkie?" the officer repeated over and over again. And each time he repeated the question, he did it with more vehemence. It was never-ending torture that increased my West Indian stubbornness.

"Darkie, you should speak for your own good. How many were there? Tell us how many."

Sometimes they would ask me how in the hell did they find me. Then I found out that it was Luxe's doing. The same one who told me later, "I couldn't save you. They messed you up because you resisted. They say that four guys almost got you. I couldn't do anything for you, so that's why I said let's leave you there and I was the one who called the police."

"Listen, darkie," the interrogation continued, "I'm new to this case. I came to clean up this whole business, you understand? Clean it up. Tell me, how many of them were there. Tell me who the devil they are!"

"And what if I don't feel like it?"

"We'll arrest you."

"I haven't done anything."

"Of course, we'll accuse you of complicity and for contempt for not following police orders."

"Are you even capable of doing that?"

"Don't you get fresh with me, darkie. Be careful."

"Of who? The ones who fucked me or you? Which is worse?"

The officer couldn't resist the temptation to hit me.

"I'm not going to beg you either," he said, because maybe you liked it, you faggot."

Furious, I took a step toward him, but his men grabbed me.

"I'm sending you to the holding cell right now, darkie," said one of his officers, "You fucked yourself over with all of this trouble you're causing."

"I haven't done anything," I said to him, trying to calm myself down.

"We'll see about that, we're in control here. You got me? You can't come here and start mess."

I was in solitary confinement for several days without speaking to a single soul. The darkness was continuous because you can barely call the weak rays that peeked through every so often between the bars light. I just knew that at a certain time they opened the little window and a hateful hand would shove three bowls and pick them up a few hours later.

The smell of death covered the cell at all hours. Damn, if you're not a delinquent going in, you'll be one coming out of our jails. I don't know what the hell they're for.

I withstood as much as my West Indian pride would let me. It was painful having done nothing and on top of it all be punished. First I got into Puma's gang and I ended up paying the price. Then, without getting any of the benefits that according to Puma, that son-of-a-bitch, I was supposed to have by joining them. The police forced me to betray him.

When my pride reached its limits, I called the officer.

"Is the captain in?"

"Yeah, and what?"

"Tell him I want to talk."

"Hmmm….it's about time, darkie. That's the way I like it."

A half hour later I was in his office. The light completely blinded me. They gave me a cup of hot chocolate and bread with butter.

On the other side of the office, I could barely see the Captain, who I could tell was looking at me with great satisfaction. I ate like a desperate man as if not doing so would be a great offense that I didn't want to commit.

The captain waited for me to finish eating and then he cautiously approached me.

"Colonel Sibere has a personal interest in the matter. Like I said, darkie, we're new and we want to clean all of this up. It's good for you to collaborate with us. If responsible citizens don't collaborate, how are we ever going to put an end to crime and delinquency?"

He remained quiet, waiting for the response.

But I didn't dare open my mouth.

"The Colonel will be here in about an hour. You have to wait until he comes. In the meantime, why don't you have a cigarette," he said as he offered me one.

Colonel Sibere arrived at the appointed time. He was a man with a vicious appearance, but with a gentle smile. Damn. There are people like that. You really can't define them. In short, you don't really know what they are in reality. The Colonel, for example, who was he? The old vicious-looking man with the stern face or the mild-mannered old man with the smile?

"Who was he?"

"The Puma."

"The Puma? Who the hell … oh, yes, the Puma."

"He and four others I don't know."

"Describe them."

I gave them a made-up description. The Colonel looked at me with a sense of doubt, as if he could sense that it was a ruse.

"Darkie, don't you have anyone here who can vouch for you? Where are you from? Limón?"

"No," I lied, "I'm from Heredia."

He took it as a joke and went back to displaying his gentle smile.

"Could you ask Dr. Lucas Centeno to vouch for me?" I told him.

It was evident that the name took him off guard—Dr. Lucas Centeno Vidaurre. For a few moments, he didn't know what to do.

"But, how? Is Dr. Centeno a friend of yours?"

"Yes," I told him, "he's been my friend for a couple of years."

"But… Look, darkie, don't yank my chain."

"Colonel, I'm not yanking your chain. When are you going to let me go?"

"If someone comes to sign for you … That means a lawyer …"

"Dr. Centeno will do it. Why don't you let him know? Tell him that Charles McForbes is in jail. Tell him that and nothing more, he'll take care of the rest."

"Are you sure?"

"Absolutely, Colonel."

"Alright." He turned around and started to leave.

"Colonel," I called to him when he had gone through the curtains that separated the office where we were from the hallway.

"What do you want, darkie?"

"Are you going to call the doctor?"

"No, it's not necessary. I'm going to let you go."

"But, the charges…"

"We detained you for public intoxication."

"Public intoxication!"

"Yes, public intoxication."

Damn, I felt such rage. It had been just a matter of saying the Centeno name. The name alone was enough. He didn't even dare to check to see if I was lying.

"Colonel," I insisted, "are you going to clean all of this up?"

"No doubt about it, darkie."

"Well then, you better start somewhere else."

"What?"

"Start where the real guilty ones are."

The Colonel turned around, suddenly interested in my foolish talk.

"The real guilty ones? Are you hiding something?"

"We all know who the real guilty ones are," I said angrily.

Honestly, anyone would've been angry if they had been pent up like a pig for so many days and then let go so easily after everything.

But the Colonel smiled. I think that he took a liking to me. Maybe he admired how I acted so rebelliously since I landed in jail. Maybe he could see himself in me, before society contaminated him, making him complicit and forcing him to console himself with the illusion of "cleaning things up." Perhaps I reminded him of how he was, before frustration after frustration descended upon the powerful and then able to attain cushy jobs, thanks to the intervention of some friendly Centeno or an Archbishop or a politician.

"It was the Puma, for certain, but it's not Puma's fault. The ones who are guilty are the upstanding, respectable ones. The ones who raised The Puma to be an ignorant fool."

"His parents?"

"No, the ones who raised his parents … the politicians or businessmen from the Avenue."

"Look, darkie, you're partly a communist," he said, "The Puma is an ignorant lowlife, a first-class scoundrel."

"Just like how some smugglers go to mass," I told him.

"Be careful, darkie. Sign the declaration and move on. Keep calm."

It took some doing to contain myself. I felt like punching him, to return the blow that semiliterate officer had given me earlier.

Damn, and it's not that I blame him for being an ignorant fool himself. I don't blame anybody, it's just that…

"Esther," I said aloud, and the taxi driver looked at me in the mirror. His face reflected justified anxiety because of the way I was acting. He was sweating profusely. Damn, I don't know if I'm suffering for Esther or if it's that the thought of what that animal Puma could be doing to her enraged me. That son-of-a-bitch Puma.

The Colonel ended up arresting him, but let him go the next day. He went looking for me, claiming that I testified against him. It took a lot for me to make him understand that I had put up with five days of torture before I said anything and that the only thing that came out was his name.

They didn't kick me out of the gang, but from then on every so often they demanded that I contribute money to get someone out of jail or give something so that the family of one of the members could eat.

We got to the vacant house. The taxi driver drove away as fast as he could, still trying to figure out my mental state. I tapped on the door with the secret knock and they let me in. Towards the back, you could see a faint light, which let me know that Puma was on the other side. Suddenly I remembered, too late, that I didn't have a gun. I could make out his head in the shadows.

"What do you want?"

"Nothing," I told him, "What do you think? I don't want anything."

"You came for Esther, didn't you? How the hell did you find me?"

"There are snitches everywhere."

"Goddammit."

"Charles!" Esther yelled after hearing my voice.

Just as she was about to reach out to me, she stopped, perhaps paralyzed by overwhelming fear.

"Esther, what are you doing here?"

"It's … it's Magdalena. Puma wants to destroy her."

"I don't want to destroy her," Puma protested, "I need ten thousand pesos."

"Ten thousand pesos? Go look somewhere else."

"Charles, her father's got it. Stay in your lane."

"Stay in my lane?"

"I want my ten thousand," Puma said defiantly.

"Puma," I said, "I'm just getting back from Limón. I haven't seen Esther for three days. We haven't even had a chance to talk. I came to the house looking for her and the housekeeper told me Esther left the house and was looking for you. Nobody knew where you were, but I found you. And, not only that, but in the midst of all of these jackasses who according to you are watching your back. Be quiet Puma, this isn't a negotiation."

"I'm going to crush you, you son-of-a-bitch."

"I wouldn't do it, Puma," I quickly moved toward him pretending I was armed. "Just remember Puma," I told him, "I found you. There's no deal here."

We cautiously left.

Esther's eyes were suddenly hard and silent. I turned to look at her. Her legs were as white as her sighs and her kisses. Damn, she was really white.

"If you've come for a divorce," she said, "you can forget it."

"Is that a threat?"

"No. I don't want you to leave me. Charles, it's difficult for me to say that."

"Yes, it's hard. But, do you realize that by binding myself to you, you are binding yourself as well?"

"Charles," she said, her eyes lost in the depth of the night, "we are all chained together. They're God's chains."

After we arrived at the house, I went straight to the bathroom to look at my face in the mirror. A broad smile illuminated my skin.

CPSIA information can be obtained
at www.ICGtesting.com
Printed in the USA
BVHW040207080119
537301BV00006B/16/P